CHESAPEAKE CRIMES

FUR, FEATHERS, AND FELONIES

IN THE SAME SERIES

Chesapeake Crimes
Chesapeake Crimes 2
Chesapeake Crimes 3
Chesapeake Crimes: They Had It Comin'
Chesapeake Crimes: This Job Is Murder
Chesapeake Crimes: Homicidal Holidays
Chesapeake Crimes: Storm Warning

CHESAPEAKE CRIMES

FUR, FEATHERS, AND FELONIES

Thirteen Tales of Critters and Criminals

Edited by Donna Andrews, Barb Goffman, and Marcia Talley

Introduction by Chris Grabenstein

WILDSIDE PRESS

Chesapeake Crimes: Fur, Feathers, and Felonies

Coordinating Editors
Donna Andrews
Barb Goffman
Marcia Talley

Editorial Panel
Brendan DuBois
Mary Jane Maffini
Leigh Perry

This edition is published in 2018 by Wildside Press, LLC.
www.wildsidepresss.com

CONTENTS

INTRODUCTION

BY CHRIS GRABENSTEIN

I remember, years ago, a mystery writer friend of mine was informed by his publisher that there would be a cat appearing on the cover of his new book.

My friend was perplexed.

There was no cat mentioned anywhere in his mystery. Not even a beatnik hep cat or the guy who sang about being followed by a moon shadow. But his cover was given a cat because cats and cozy mysteries go together. In books and in readers' laps.

How wonderful, then, to discover this anthology created by the Chesapeake Chapter of Sisters in Crime, home to so many amazing and award-winning mystery writers. In this volume, you'll discover that cats aren't the only animals that mix well with mysteries, cozy and otherwise. In these pages, you will find short stories featuring a menagerie of cats (of course), dogs, crows, angel fish, rabbits, exploding cows, an octopus, crickets, Chihuahuas, and rats.

Face it—you can't really have a good mystery without a few rats. And yes, having been a dog person for over two dozen years, I do consider Chihuahuas a separate species.

What's fun about this thirteen-story anthology is seeing how each of the very talented writers took a few common notes (critters and criminals) and, like the masterful jazz word musicians that they are, concocted such different and delightful tales. It reminds me of my days doing improvisational comedy. You take a few suggestions and spin them into something wonderful.

Animal. Mystery. Go!

In "Pet," Shari Randall introduces us to Katya, a pet groomer entangled with a wealthy family where the dog might just be the nicest person.

"As The Crow Flies" by Carla Coupe is a wonderful trek to the English countryside where we meet Hermes, a crow that out-bloodhounds the hound of the Baskervilles. (Is it any wonder that a group of crows is called "a murder"?)

In "Rasputin," KM Rockwood creates the unforgettable Rasputin, a dog who has a quite an adventure between meals.

Alan Orloff's funny bone is on full display in "Bark Simpson and the Scent of Death." Or maybe it's his funny Milk-Bone.

"A Snowball's Chance" by Eleanor Cawood Jones weaves a wonderfully twisty cold-case tale where we meet Gabriel the angel fish and Snowball the bunny.

In "Hunter's Moon," Robin Templeton unleashes a wonderful Irish setter named Rupert and a character who likes animals more than humans (especially the ones who act like animals).

Barb Goffman's extremely clever police procedural "Till Murder Do Us Part" gives us some exploding cattle and a sheriff called out of church on a Sunday morning—not to mention a glimpse of the rustic "farm-to-wedding-table" movement.

"Your Cheatin' Heart" by Marianne Wilski Strong is a wonderful trip back in time to Scranton, Pennsylvania, and a Halloween night death in a saloon. Maybe because I spend most of my time these days writing mysteries for the eight-to-twelve-year-old crowd, I particularly enjoyed this story about a kid sleuth and her dog.

Linda Lombardi jumps into the tank with my first encounter with an octopus mystery in "The Octopus Game." (I wonder what *that* would look like on the cover of a cozy?) There are also crickets involved.

"The Supreme Art of War" by Josh Pachter is everything a mystery short story should be, with a clever twist and surprise ending that would've made O. Henry proud.

Joanna Campbell Slan gives us the Chihuahua named Jonathan—a caregiver's best friend in an otherwise miserable situation.

"Curiosity Killed the Cat Lady" by Cathy Wiley is an apartment-building mystery with (at least) eight cats and several rats—some of whom are the deceased's fellow tenants.

Karen Cantwell closes out the anthology with a 1930s Hollywood noir bowl of hard-boiled kibble called "Sunset Beauregard" that introduces us to a colorful cast of characters and one movie-star dog.

I hope you enjoy these thirteen tales (tails?) of critters and criminals as much as I did. Read them with a cat in your lap, a dog at your feet, or an octopus in your aquarium.

Chris Grabenstein is the #1 *New York Times* bestselling author of the Lemoncello Library series, the Welcome to Wonderland series, and *The Island of Dr. Libris*. He is also the coauthor of several fun and funny page-turners with James Patterson, including *I Funny*, *Treasure Hunters*, *House of Robots*, *Jacky Ha Ha*, and *Word of Mouse*. www.ChrisGrabenstein.com

PET

BY SHARI RANDALL

Katya left her Redondo Beach apartment, hurrying along the cracked pavement past nail salons, empty storefronts, and a crowd of cat-calling men outside a car wash. She tried her best to ignore them, the way her boyfriend, Lev, always instructed as she headed to the pet shop. Black-and-white letters affixed to pink lattice spelled Rosie's Pet Spa.

Despite being located in an area dominated by surf shops and fast-food restaurants, the pet spa had a reputation that lured the well-heeled. Katya pressed her face to the window, the tension in her body ebbing as she admired dogs that cost more than everything she and Lev owned. When she and Lev left Russia two years earlier, he promised that they'd live in a mansion. That they'd be free. That every day the skies would be the same color as her eyes. Most days the skies were blue, but she felt trapped in the tiny apartment they shared with four other young Russians.

Katya turned as a pink van lumbered to the curb. A Chihuahua poked its little head out the window and yapped.

The driver got out, followed by the dog.

"Reaper, stop!" the driver shouted. The Chihuahua barked and raced around the van to Katya. Katya laughed and bent to stroke it.

"*Nyet*, *nyet*," Katya said. When the driver approached, she switched to the English she'd learned from the video games played by the guys who lived with her and Lev. "Chill little man, chill." The Chihuahua vibrated madly, licking her toes and worn rubber flip-flops.

The driver, a stocky woman with pink streaks in her hair, set a carrier on the sidewalk with a grunt. "I liked the Russian better." She scooped up the Chihuahua. "And you should chill, Reaper." The woman held out her hand. "I'm Rosie."

Katya hesitated, then shook the woman's hand. "Katya."

"Reaper sure likes you. You like dogs." It wasn't a question. "I've seen you here before."

Katya nodded slightly, unsure if watching the dogs was allowed.

"I'm looking for someone to give baths. One of my shampoo girls took off with some asshat surfer."

"Asshat surfer?" Katya said.

Rosie laughed, a short bark. "Sounds better with a Russian accent. You looking for work? A job?"

Katya thought of the boys who shared her apartment, the way they looked at her when they thought Lev didn't notice. Of Anya, the other girl she lived with, how she only left the apartment to buy cigarettes, how her eyes looked dead. "Yes. A job. Please."

"You're what, eighteen?"

Katya nodded. That's what the papers Lev had bought said.

"I've got dogs out the wazoo needing baths. Come on in." A bell chimed as she pushed open the door into a bright pink storefront that smelled like peppermint and dog. "Let's talk."

* * * *

Three months later on a Saturday afternoon, Katya helped Rosie ready the shop to close.

"You need to get a life, Katya." Rosie flicked off the lights in the bath area. "I'm your boss, and I think you work too much."

"It's not work. I like it." Katya nuzzled a Pomeranian that now sported one of Rosie's trademark pink bows.

"That dog hates everyone, but she likes you. Whatever you've got, it works on Cujo. Sorry." She bent toward the fluffy ball in Katya's arms. "Caro. She belongs to Mrs. Ashburn. Richer than God. Can you believe it? The old bag gets to name a dog and what does she name it? Her. Own. Fricking. Name. Sure she changed one whole letter—from Carol to Caro. But still. Gotta get her ready for the chauffeur, right, Cujo?" Rosie called all the biting dogs Cujo.

"She's just nervous because she's so small," Katya said.

"You have to make sure Caro's ready outside. Her mama's time's worth billions. Don't forget the carrier."

"I'll take you out for some fresh air, Caro." Katya picked up the carrier. "Come." Caro followed on her heels, tail wagging.

"Fresh air in LA. You *keel* me, Katya. See you Monday."

Katya sat on the neon-pink bench outside the door and lifted Caro onto her lap.

Lev turned the corner, strutting in slim designer jeans and sunglasses. Katya froze. Lev rarely left the apartment during the day and he had never come to Rosie's.

The Pomeranian yipped and jumped off her lap, leaping at Lev's legs, scratching at his tight jeans, and latching her tiny pointed teeth onto his ankle.

"Caro!" Katya jumped up.

"Overfed rat dog," Lev sneered. He kicked out, his boot catching the Pomeranian under the ribs.

Caro yelped and skittered across the sidewalk.

Katya winced. She'd felt the impact of Lev's pointed leather boot as if he'd kicked her and not Caro. She scooped up the trembling dog.

"How could you?" she whispered, her heart thudding as she cradled the tiny body. She whirled toward the door, but Rosie was nowhere to be seen. Cars flowed by; nobody stopped.

"You want me fired?"

"Katya, they're stupid, spoiled dogs!" Lev straightened the collar of his shirt and checked his jeans for tears where Caro had tried to scratch him. "What a joke."

"This joke pays the rent." She pressed Caro to her shoulder, the dog's fluttering heartbeat matching her own.

Lev snorted and looked away, the reflection of a passing Lexus sliding across his Ray-Bans. "Katya, Katya, we didn't come here to wash dogs."

A black limousine pulled to the curb. A chauffeur heaved himself out, tugging on his too-tight jacket. He stepped slowly around the car, his glance moving from the top of Katya's head to her rubber flip-flops. He frowned. Katya felt her cheeks burn.

"Madame would like to speak with you."

As Katya pressed Caro to her hammering heart, Lev put his hand on her lower back and pushed until she moved forward. *Had they seen Lev kick Caro?* she thought wildly.

The chauffeur breathed heavily as he opened the rear door. A smiling blond woman reached out her arms from the rear seat.

"Caro, come to Mommy!" Katya mutely handed the dog to her then stepped backward, bumping into Lev's chest.

Mrs. Ashburn, the "richer than God" lady who owned Caro, had a deep voice, smooth as honey. Katya was dazzled. The woman's wide white smile and silver-blond hair reminded Katya of a woman she'd seen in a movie once, a woman in a pink dress draped with diamonds, dancing with dozens of sleek men in tuxedos.

"Caro, my baby!" She held Caro to her shoulder, just as Katya had. "You're Katya." Mrs. Ashburn smiled even wider and waved Katya closer. "It's okay, pet, I don't bite." Diamonds glittered like fairy dust on her every finger. "My baby is so pretty and happy when she comes home. I thought, who is the girl who makes Caro so happy? I've got to meet her."

Relief flooded Katya. Mrs. Ashburn hadn't seen the kick. She felt Lev's hand on her lower back, again pushing her toward the open door. "I'm, I'm Katya."

"So nice to meet you, Katya. Call me Carol." Katya watched Mrs. Ashburn's eyes slide past her to Lev. "And who is your handsome friend?"

* * * *

If Lev hadn't pushed her into the limousine, Katya would have said *no thank you* and gone back to the little apartment that reeked of stale beer and cigarette smoke. But Lev always had a nose for money.

"What do you say?" Carol had enthused on the drive to her home, The Manse. "I need someone to live in and take care of Caro. You can have the little pink bedroom. It will look so pretty with your blond hair."

And that was it. Katya moved in to care for Caro full-time. The little pink bedroom was one of twelve bedrooms at Carol's home. The Manse was a half-mile away from Golden Oaks. Carol had grown up at Golden Oaks, a mansion so stuffed with artwork, antiques, and artifacts that she had turned it into a museum and moved down the road to the smaller house.

Just days after Katya began working at The Manse, Carol's chauffeur, Morton, retired to Florida.

Carol asked Katya, "Why doesn't your boyfriend take Morton's job and move into Morton's old quarters over the garage?"

Why not? Carol was a good boss, and the grounds were beautiful and safe.

Lev sneered at the offer. "You're a nanny for a dog, and I should drive the old broad around?" But he took the job anyway, as Katya knew he would, and he behaved properly around the other employees. Carol's staff was old and well-paid enough to be loyal.

* * * *

Several months later, Katya and Carol sat on the floor of Carol's dressing room, a room larger than Katya and Lev's entire apartment had been. An engraved silver tray with porcelain cups of tea and Oreo cookies gleamed under the mellow light of an eighteenth-century chandelier. The women laughed as Caro chased a small rubber ball across the Aubusson carpet.

Faces on three oil paintings watched from the wall. One was Carol's deceased husband, an amiable investment banker who had the good manners to leave Carol even wealthier after his early death. One was five-year-old Carol with Caro number one, wearing matching emerald-green ribbons. The last, a slightly smaller painting, was of Carol holding her son, Max.

From the time she was a little girl, Carol always had a Pomeranian, always named Caro. This particular dog was the latest in a long line of Caros, all female, all purebred, all spoiled. When this Caro died, she, too, would have her portrait hung in the gallery outside the music room. She, too, would have her small remains interred at the feet of the statue of Diana in the garden with the other Caros. Carol would buy another Pomeranian to replace her.

Carol pulled open drawer after velvet-lined drawer, putting bracelets that had graced the wrists of murdered princesses around her dog's neck. Carol's grandfather had swept through Europe in the days after World War II, buying art and jewels. It was a time when a ruby bracelet was a small price to pay for a loaf of bread.

The dog regarded herself seriously in a floor-length gold-framed mirror. Carol and Katya laughed, and Katya snapped photos with her phone.

Carol set aside her teacup and reached into a cupboard. "This is where I keep my special things."

The cabinet was stuffed with leather jewelry boxes, but also, on the bottom shelf, a green satin-covered photo album, a teddy bear, and a roughly carved wooden box.

Carol touched the box and shuddered. "When Max was little he and his friends used to get into my grandfather's stuff from the Amazon. They shot blowdarts with curare at Caro!"

Katya blanked for a moment, then remembered the oil paintings of the different Caros outside the music room.

"Curare?" Katya asked.

"The tribes used it to hunt. It paralyzes the animal, makes it easy to catch and kill." Carol patted the box. "Safely tucked away. Actually, I wanted to throw it away, but my husband said,"—Carol pulled herself up and lowered her voice—"'Doll, those professors at UCLA would give their eye-teeth for that stuff. You can't just throw away priceless artifacts from the Amazon.'"

Carol giggled and Katya laughed. Caro barked and turned in a circle, tail wagging.

Carol opened a blue velvet ring box and pressed the ring into Katya's hand.

"It's the Star Mountain diamond. Bigger than the one Onassis gave Jackie O," Carol crowed. The little dog cocked her head and watched as Katya slipped the ring onto her slim finger. The diamond burned with a cold fire that made her think of ice coating the iron gates at the orphanage back in Russia. Katya reached out to stroke Caro.

"It's so heavy," she said, pulling it off. "I think it would catch in Caro's fur."

Carol slowly took the ring back, then nodded. Her wide movie-star smile flashed.

She slid open a different velvet-lined drawer and took out a pearl choker, three strings of glowing ivory pearls linked with a diamond-and-emerald clasp. She put it around Katya's neck.

"This belonged to an Austrian princess. I want you to have it. Don't say no, pet."

Katya felt the pearls tighten around her neck as Carol fastened the clasp. Like Caro's collar, she thought, but pushed the idea away when she saw her reflection in the mirror.

"Lovely." Carol sighed.

Katya noticed that Carol was looking at herself in the mirror, not Katya.

"Thank you," Katya whispered. Caro climbed onto Katya's lap.

* * * *

A week later, Max's silver Porsche Spyder skidded into the drive twenty minutes before his mother's seventy-fifth birthday party—the same day Lev discovered the pearl necklace, which Katya had left in her underwear drawer. Lev whistled, then put it back among the faded cotton panties. "Finally, you're doing something right," he said.

Katya met Max at the party that night.

"You're the Russian girl," Max slurred. Max was tall and broad, his graying hair shaggy and long. A diamond winked on his earlobe. He waved his drink, spattering the bodice of Katya's dress. "We'll have to drink some serious vodka together."

Katya yearned to escape as he stood too close to her and talked about his collection of cars, but she was trapped in a circle of glittering women, all smooth hair and white smiles, all intent on Max's words, his easy charm, his expensive watch.

"So what about you?" Max asked.

"Me?" Katya whispered.

"What do you do for fun?"

Katya felt Lev watching from the bar where he helped serve drinks. "Caro. I play with Caro."

"You are single-minded, Katya. I'll give you that." His laughter boomed, and the circle laughed and pulled tighter, the impossibly beautiful women squeezing her out, but not before Max took her hand and whispered, "So am I, Katya."

* * * *

Max spent more and more time at The Manse. Katya often saw him with Lev in the garage, Max's broad shoulders dwarfing Lev's slim frame as they bent over whatever sports car Max had driven from his apartment in West Hollywood. Whenever she felt Max's eyes on her as she walked Caro or sunned by the pool, Katya remembered Babushka's stories of clever foxes and hungry wolves. She began making sure that whenever Max arrived, she was busy with Caro or in the kitchen with Mrs. Floris. Both growled when Max appeared.

At first Lev had been wary, too, but he warmed to Max.

"Katya, he's a cool guy. The old lady won't live forever. He will inherit and be our boss. Be nice to him."

Soon Max began showing up at times Katya couldn't anticipate. So Katya started avoiding the main house and took Caro to a pool in a garden by Carol's private wing. The marble-lined Arbor Pool was for staff only, but one Tuesday afternoon Max walked to the pool's edge, holding two glasses. He lifted his eyebrows and set the glasses on a table.

"If you get thirsty." His words were only a little slurred. Mrs. Floris joked that there were three taps in Max's bathroom suite: one for hot water, one for cold water, and one for vodka.

Caro worked herself into a frenzy at Max's approach. Her tiny body shook with an intensity that made Katya fearful, especially because Caro was fifteen—old for a Pomeranian.

"You'd think she'd like me by now." Max laughed. "No love for old Max from that pooch. Actually, I don't think any of the Caros ever liked me."

Katya pulled Caro into the pool, away from Max.

"So Katya, you've made a lot of friends here. The hound from Hell sure likes you."

Caro, Katya thought, but she said nothing. When Max looked at her like this she often blushed and slipped back into speaking Russian, which she knew Max enjoyed. He slid a terry-cloth robe from his shoulders. The chaise creaked under his muscular frame as he stretched out in the sun.

Caro growled and lunged over Katya's shoulder at Max. Katya tried to soothe her, walking across the shallow end of the pool, farther away from Max. She leaned on the wall opposite, turning Caro away.

Lev hurried down the marble steps to the pool. "Max, Mrs. Ashburn sent me to ask you to join her in the library."

Max groaned as he sat up. "She who must be obeyed." He winked at Katya, knocked back his drink, and then rose.

Caro broke from Katya's arms onto the deck and ran around the pool at Max, leaping at his right leg.

"Ow! Little beast scratched me." He grabbed his robe and hurried toward the house. He turned and waved at Katya. "Don't worry, just a flesh wound!"

Lev looked from Katya to Max but said nothing. A flash of green in the window overlooking the pool made Katya glance up just in time to see Carol turn away.

* * * *

"Mrs. Ashburn's going to change her will," Mrs. Floris said later that afternoon as she and Katya watched Max slam the door of the Spyder and roar down the gravel drive. "He'll still get everything in the trust—The Manse, Golden Oaks, and all the companies—but not his mother's money. That's separate. And that bad boy needs money bad. He was supposed to get half of it, with the rest going to Caro."

Katya turned from the window in the breakfast nook of the staff kitchen. She wasn't exactly sure what a trust was, but she had seen the phrase "The Ashburn Family Trust" on all the museum exhibit signs throughout Golden Oaks and on the programs at the Opera Hall when Carol took her to see *The Queen of Spades*.

"Caro? A dog gets money in a will?"

"Yes, the money goes to Caro. And the staff all get bequests, too. Don't you worry." Mrs. Floris patted Katya's hand. "But Mrs. Ashburn's sick of the way he's throwing money around and who he's spending it on."

Mrs. Floris leaned toward Katya.

"His first two marriages went kaput. Didn't even give Mrs. Ashburn any grandchildren."

Mrs. Floris sipped tea from a heavy ceramic mug, leaving a deep red lipstick stain on the rim.

"And now he's dating one of those awful *television* people. You know the show. The one with the kids of those famous *actors*. The ones who lived with the *monkeys* from their dad's movie. Max is going to propose to the oldest girl and told reporters he promised to give her the Star Mountain diamond. He didn't ask his mother first. Oh, was she steamed! The girl's twenty years younger than he is. Her name's *Trinket*."

The thought of living with monkeys intrigued Katya. "Still, there are monkeys?"

"There might as well be," Mrs. Floris said dryly. "One of the housekeepers heard Mrs. Ashburn say to Max, 'You're out of the will. Now, you're the monkey.'"

* * * *

Three days later, Carol stopped Katya as she walked past the music room.

"Katya, you work so hard." She stroked Katya's hair, then patted her shoulder. Katya felt the strength of Carol's grip through her thin cotton blouse, the heaviness of her hand, which had two jeweled rings on each finger. "You must take a vacation."

"But Caro—"

Carol waved a finger. "Now I won't take no for an answer. Off to my little beach house. You and," she hesitated, "your friend Lev."

Katya's cheeks burned. She tried to keep her overnight visits to the chauffeur's quarters secret, but the garage was just beyond the Arbor Pool and gardens outside Carol's suite of rooms. It was hard to keep secrets at The Manse.

Carol smiled. "You must take a week. Relax. Then come back next Friday night so you'll be here for Max's engagement party on Saturday."

Carol scooped up Caro and hurried down the hallway. When Katya turned back to the staircase, she was surprised to see Lev exit Carol's suite with an armful of boxes. She hurried after him.

"Isn't she wonderful, Lev?" Katya said as Lev put the boxes in a closet down the hall. "Did she tell you about our vacation?"

As Lev closed the door, his lips twisted into something that was not quite a smile. "*Da.* Let's go."

Carol insisted they take the Bentley. Once at Carol's "little beach house"—another mansion fronting the Pacific with a staff of three—Katya forgot about Carol. But not Caro.

"I hope she's okay," Katya fretted shortly after they arrived. "She must go to Rosie's for her grooming appointment."

"Who's crazier, you or the old lady?" Lev handed her a glass of Champagne. A heavy gold watch encircled his wrist.

Katya brushed it with her fingertips. "Is that a gift from Carol?"

Lev nodded, then turned her to face the view. The Pacific headlands rose over marble goddesses that stood sentry over an infinity swimming pool perched on the edge of the ocean.

He kissed her ear and slipped his finger under the strap of her bikini top. "Now, let's forget those crazy people."

* * * *

The Manse was dark when they returned late Friday night, but their headlights illuminated the silver Spyder when they pulled into the drive. Katya sighed. "I'll stay in your room tonight."

Lev looked from Katya to the Spyder, then nodded. "*Da*."

When she woke several hours later, troubled by a dream about Caro, the sheets beside her were cool. Katya noted the light under the bathroom door before she drifted back to sleep.

* * * *

As sunlight warmed her face, Katya felt the bed give slightly under her. She rolled over.

"Caro!"

Caro yipped and licked Katya's face.

"I missed you! How did you get inside?"

Katya stroked the little dog and smiled as she remembered the week with Lev. He had never been so attentive. Perhaps this was a sign that their relationship was changing. Perhaps he was becoming softer toward her. Usually he wouldn't allow Caro to visit his room, no matter how much Katya pleaded.

Caro's tail wagged as she circled on the bed, her nails pulling at the sheet and leaving brown smears. Katya lifted Caro's paw and exclaimed in dismay. A sticky brown substance smeared her fingertips, and Caro's nails were much too long. "What have you been into? I'll give you a bath and trim your nails and make you pretty again."

Lev exited the bathroom, tossing a towel to the floor. He lit a cigarette.

"Good idea. Make her pretty again, but be careful of those nails." His words were joking, but his body was taut as he blew a stream of smoke.

Katya carried Caro into the bathroom, kicking aside a pile of Lev's clothing. She held Caro to her shoulder as she ran the bath water.

"Did you go for a run?" She cuddled Caro and stood by the bathroom door. "Where did you find Caro?"

Lev stripped the sheets from the bed and put them in the hamper. "Mrs. Ashburn asked that we keep her here." He drew on the cigarette and looked out the window. "There's been an accident at the house. Max got drunk and drowned in the Arbor Pool."

* * * *

After bathing Caro and trimming her nails, Katya reluctantly closed the door of Lev's apartment. Lev insisted that Carol wanted Caro to stay in his apartment while the police were at The Manse. She could hear Caro whine as she and Lev hurried down the stairs.

"Mrs. Ashburn said that many of the other staff were away this week also," Lev muttered. "We didn't hear anything last night. We were asleep. Max got drunk and went for a swim alone. He must've been drunk enough to hit his head and drown."

"Why are you talking like a robot? Is that what Carol said? It's terrible." Katya hunched forward in the cool breeze as they skirted police cars crowded into the circular drive of The Manse. They hurried around the house, past the vast patio already set with tables for the engagement party.

"I saw Mrs. Ashburn early this morning when I couldn't sleep and went for a run," Lev said.

"She found Max dead?" Katya shuddered.

Mrs. Floris opened the door to let them in. She rubbed her eyes as she poured cups of coffee. "What a mess. What a *scandal*." She nodded her gray head toward the television. "Reporters will be at the gates soon, sniffing around. Mark my words."

The intercom buzzed. Carol's honeyed voice called down that the police wanted to talk to Lev.

"I was with Mrs. Ashburn after she found the body," Lev explained in answer to Mrs. Floris's surprised expression.

"She's lucky to have you to rely on," Mrs. Floris said.

Katya and Lev hurried up the narrow servants' stairs and then across the gallery, their footsteps soft across the Oriental carpets.

Lev pulled her along, but she stopped at the windows that overlooked the Arbor Pool.

"Wait." Below on the patio by the pool, several uniformed police officers conferred with others in white coveralls. How strange they looked from above, their heads and shoulders making shapes like a computer game. Max's body, still solid and vital-looking, lay sprawled full-length by the pool, a large bottle by his head. She leaned forward and caught her breath. She could just barely see scratches that ran along the front of both his calves.

Caro, she thought, remembering the scene by the pool. *Caro must have scratched him again.* Her heart beat faster as she thought of the brown substance under Caro's untrimmed nails. Katya shook her head. The brown stuff didn't look like blood.

"Do you think Caro scratched him? That she chased him into the pool?" she whispered.

Lev spun on her, his face red. "Shh, Katya." He embraced her with such force she was breathless, then he smiled, a smile that struggled then surrendered. His green eyes bore into hers and for a moment she was afraid. "You're being crazy. That little dog? Couldn't hurt a flea. Ha!" Now his smile was genuine.

Katya sighed. Yes, the thought was really silly. Max was a big man. How could a little dog hurt such a big man?

* * * *

Two men in dark suits and sunglasses were waiting in Carol's suite when Katya and Lev entered a minute later. Police officers, she was sure. The men tried to act cool as they walked past a French king's clock on the marble mantelpiece, the Picasso over the desk, the little cross studded with dusky gems by the doorway to the dressing room.

"Oh, good." Carol stood at the dressing room door, wearing a jade-green tunic over white leggings, heavy gold bracelets on her wrists. "Lev, before you talk with these nice gentlemen, could you help me with the picture over the safe?" She stepped into the dressing room. Lev and the police officers followed.

"Of course, Mrs. Ashburn." Lev went to the second portrait, the one of Carol and Caro, took it down, and set it next to the wall. Then he went into Carol's bedroom and brought back a little embroidered footstool and set it in place for Carol. He helped her step onto it. Carol smiled her thanks.

When, Katya wondered, had Lev gotten so familiar with Carol's bedroom. And with the safe.

"The officers had heard the report of the engagement and the Star Mountain engagement ring. They want me to make sure there was no theft." Carol reached into the safe and pulled out a box. All the men raised their hands to support Carol's arms as she stepped off the footstool, like footmen helping Cinderella step from her pumpkin coach.

"I know you must investigate every angle." Carol's voice dipped on the last two words, expressing the skepticism she was, of course, too polite to put into words. "But my son had a drinking problem." She shook her head. "I tried to help him. A mother tries. And as you can see, gentlemen, the ring wasn't stolen." Carol held out the blue velvet box. Katya could feel the excitement of the men next to her. Carol's charm turned everyone into a child in a cave full of treasure.

The men bent their heads close as Carol opened the ring box. Katya lifted her eyes to the safe and caught sight of the carved wooden box she'd seen Lev move from the dressing room to the storage closet down the hall. She looked at Lev, but he was watching Carol.

"Bigger than the one Jackie O got from Onassis. Max was going to"—Carol bit her lip and closed her eyes—"going to propose to his girlfriend." She took a deep breath and then leaned heavily on Lev's arm. "Dearest Trinket."

Katya's heart beat faster as she wondered about the wooden box, now in the safe. The sticky substance under Caro's nails. The scratches on Max's legs. But she lowered her eyes and stayed with Carol as the men left the room.

* * * *

Two weeks later, Katya walked with the other servants along the path from the private chapel at Golden Oaks to the private cemetery just outside the walls of the parterre garden. Black fabric swathed the grand doorways of the mansion. Tours were canceled.

Trinket and her family walked ahead, also swathed in black. Trinket wore a black pillbox hat with a full veil, the fragile lace brushing the deep V neckline of her bandage dress. Katya watched in wonder as Trinket tottered on stiletto heels down the gravel path.

Katya took a seat between Carol and Mrs. Floris. She held Caro on her lap. Lev had stayed behind to help manage the valet parking for the funeral.

Mrs. Floris pressed a crumpled tissue to her dry eyes. With a dreamy expression, Carol gazed at the carved cherubs on the Ashburn family crypt. She stroked Caro's head in time to Trinket's wails. Katya looked at the other household staff, all somber, respectful, and dry-eyed. Her hand flew to her necklace as she realized that Mrs. Floris and every female servant at the funeral also wore a pearl choker.

The sky was blue, so bright it hurt to look at it. At least Lev hadn't lied about that.

Shari Randall is the author of *Curses, Boiled Again!*, the first in the new Lobster Shack Mystery series from St. Martin's Press. She's had two other short stories published in the Chesapeake Crimes anthology series: "Disco Donna" in *Chesapeake Crimes: Homicidal Holidays* and "Keep It Simple" in *Chesapeake Crimes: This Job Is Murder*. You can see what's new with her at www.sharirandallauthor.com.

AS THE CROW FLIES

BY CARLA COUPE

"You're frightened to walk through a *field*? Don't be ridiculous. It's a right of way." Beryl Mayhew hoisted her skirts and clambered over the wooden stile. "Young Tom Perkins may want to close the footpath, but everyone still uses it."

Her brother George stared over the fence, then shrugged off his tweed Norfolk jacket, slung it over his shoulder, and followed. "Come on, Leighton. It's the fastest way to Heatherington."

Grumbling, Nigel Leighton joined them, and they set out across the field, following the well-trod path. Once they reached the lane, a short walk would take them to the bridge that crossed the small river and then on into the village. A copse of trees ahead marked their goal.

"I don't see why we couldn't ride there in the dogcart," Leighton panted. "I'll be exhausted by the time we return."

Beryl glanced at him. Leighton was almost twenty and had obviously spent his time at Cambridge indoors, engaged in sedentary pursuits. Wisps of flaxen hair poked from the sides of his cap, and his skin was pale, in contrast to Beryl and George's dark hair and freckled faces. Beryl sighed. Why had George brought such a whining weedy specimen back for the summer? Surely he was not playing matchmaker.

They were only a few yards from the end of the path and the fence when a voice bellowed.

"Get out, you damned trespassers!" Young Tom Perkins charged down the hill toward them.

With a glance over his shoulder, George hurried his steps.

"Is that a *pitchfork*?" Leighton broke into a run.

"Young Tom!" Beryl turned and faced him. "You know this is a public footpath, and if you don't stop this nonsense, I'll tell Constable Wright that you're pestering us."

Pitchfork in hand, Perkins strode up to Beryl, glowering. Although almost thirty, he would be "Young Tom" to the locals until his father died, and possibly beyond. "That's as may be, Miss Mayhew, but some of those village young'uns chase my cows 'til they won't give milk. How am I to grow my dairy with no milk? My customers depend on my deliveries."

"I'm sorry to hear that," Beryl said. "But this field is a right-of-way. Did you tell Constable Wright about the children?"

"Yes'm. And he did have a word with them." He picked a blade of grass and chewed it thoughtfully. "'Twould be a grand field for my bull."

Beryl laughed. "Don't even think of moving your bull into this field. Why, Sir Denys would have you up before the bench in a heartbeat. Now," she continued, lowering her voice, "a few goats would be another matter, and I doubt the local lads would get much satisfaction from chasing them."

Perkins grinned and touched his cap. "There's an idea."

Her grin mirrored his. "And one that won't cause more trouble. Good day." She made her way to where the young men waited just outside the fence.

As she climbed over the stile, George murmured a comment, something about "bearding the lion," and Leighton snickered. Beryl shot them both a hard glance and bit back a remark about running from the field of battle; she had promised her aunt not to antagonize her brother during his stay. Not often, at least. She headed down the path. It was short walk to the lane, which was bordered by high banks and hedgerows.

Shade dappled the dusty, rutted road. The still, warm air smelled of honeysuckle.

"Race you to the bridge!" George called suddenly, already three steps ahead. With a groan, Leighton took off at a better pace than his earlier complaints would indicate.

Beryl—careful not to be overheard—muttered a mild curse, picked up her skirts, and dashed after them.

* * * *

Laughing, the young men lounged against the bridge's sturdy parapets as she panted up to them. Both had their jackets draped over the stones, and Beryl spared a moment to envy their freedom from long skirts, gloves, and bonnets.

"Don't feel too smug," she said. "You try running in petticoats and heels and see how well you do." Leaning against the sun-warmed granite, she pulled a handkerchief from her sleeve and dabbed her damp forehead. At least they were out of the stifling lanes, and a breeze cooled her face.

George chuckled. "There was a time when you could keep up."

"Keep up? I could best you," she said, and at his indignant expression added, "at least some of the time. But that was five years ago when I was twelve and didn't wear a corset."

Leighton's eyebrows rose and his cheeks darkened. "Miss Mayhew!"

"Pay her no mind," George said, elbowing his friend. "You will hear more shocking words than corset during your stay."

"It's not a shocking word. It's simply an article of clothing." Beryl frowned. "Or are you so delicate you can't bear to hear of such a thing, Mr. Leighton?"

Leighton scowled. "I'm not *delicate*. I'm studying medicine, after all."

"Medicine?" Beryl stood and smoothed her gloves. "Will you specialize in research, or are you destined for a consulting room on Harley Street, catering to the wealthy?"

"There's nothing wrong with Harley Street."

Beryl's soft snort was response enough.

George laughed. "Again, don't mind my sister. She's a free-thinker and has been influenced by our aunt. She has no respect for my legal studies, either. Come. We're almost to Heatherington."

A faint caw sounded. Beryl looked up, shading her eyes with her hand. A dark speck headed toward them.

"Wait!" she said.

George followed her gaze. "Is it Hermes?"

"Hermes?" Leighton squinted up at the sky. "Who or what is Hermes?"

Beryl stripped off her gloves and walked over to the grass along the river's banks. She squatted down and rooted in the green blades and wildflowers. "He's my pet crow. Or was, for the first year of his life. Ah!" She stood, holding a fat worm.

Leighton backed away. "Disgusting!"

"Disgusting?" Beryl raised one brow. "And you're going into medicine? How will you manage your anatomical studies?"

Lifting his chin, Leighton said, "I will do perfectly well."

Beryl didn't bother to reply. She placed the worm on the bridge's parapet and collected two good-sized stones, then waited until the crow circled closer.

He landed on the other end of the parapet, glossy black feathers shining in the sun. Tilting his head to one side, he regarded her with glittering eyes.

"Hullo, Hermes," she said softly. "Here's a worm and a puzzle for you."

Laying the stones close on either side of the worm, she stepped back.

"But the stones prevent it from reaching the worm," Leighton said. "I didn't take you for a tease, Miss Mayhew."

"Oh, don't fret. Hermes knows a few tricks."

Hermes hopped toward the stones, cocked his head the other way, and paused for a moment, as if studying the situation. Then he opened his wings and glided over to the grass beside the stream.

Leighton shook his head. "Your puzzle was too much for it."

"Not at all."

Hermes searched amongst the grasses until he gave a triumphant caw. He picked up a twig with his beak and flew back to the parapet. There he poked the twig into the crevice between the stones, pushing the worm out of its hiding place. Dropping the twig, he snatched up the worm and swallowed it.

Beryl smiled at Leighton's open-mouthed stare. "Good boy, Hermes."

With another caw, Hermes flew off.

George threw his arm over Leighton's shoulders and gave him a shake. "Close your mouth, Nigel, or something will fly in."

Leighton's mouth snapped shut and his face twisted into a reluctant smile. "Crows are more intelligent than I expected."

"Of course they are." Beryl pulled on her gloves and headed toward the village.

* * * *

As villages went, there was nothing memorable about Heatherington save its ordinariness. An Anglican church, a Methodist chapel, three shops including a bookseller, and a public house (with a parlor for ladies) lining the lane were the extent of its charms. Yet there was always a muted bustle in the street, and Beryl seldom visited without meeting a friend or acquaintance. Or even, as she could see before her, a handsome young man.

The handsome young man in question turned from the shop window and tipped his hat. "How do you do, Miss Mayhew."

She smiled. "I'm very well, Mr. Fitz-Clarence."

"Mayhew." He nodded to George.

"Fitz-Clarence." George nodded with all the insouciance he could muster.

Beryl added, "And this is George's friend from Cambridge, Nigel Leighton."

Leighton shook Fitz-Clarence's hand, and the warmth of his greeting made George's coolness all the more obvious.

"How d'you do, Mr. Leighton. Mayhew, it's good to see you again. So you're home for the summer. How are your studies?"

Beryl pressed her lips together. For heaven's sake, Fitz-Clarence always made it sound as if George were a child to be humored. After all, he was only three or four years older than George, not thirty or forty.

Color rose in George's face, but before he could reply, Beryl stepped over to the bookshop window. "We are here on an errand of mercy, Mr. Fitz-Clarence. My aunt has a touch of catarrh and must rest. We have come to find a book for her to read until she improves. You are usually *au courant* with the latest from London. Do you have any suggestions?"

Fitz-Clarence frowned thoughtfully. "I saw Mr. Trollope's newest book in Robertson's shop. And one by Miss Yonge, as well."

"Two excellent suggestions. Thank you." She favored him with a smile.

Across the road a shop door opened and three young ladies exited and hurried over. "Why, Beryl, we didn't expect to see you here," a pretty blonde said. "Mr. Mayhew, Mr. Fitz-Clarence."

There were more introductions for Leighton and the young ladies—sisters Margaret and Amanda Dole, and the speaker, Verity Plum. After Beryl explained their errand, Margaret giggled and said, "Oh, but Mr. Wilkie Collins has published another book! I know how much your aunt admired *The Moonstone*, and she would certainly enjoy one of his."

"So your aunt enjoys sensational novels?" Fitz-Clarence asked with a lift of his brow.

George laughed. "She adores them, as does Beryl."

"They're certainly more entertaining than some so-called edifying novels I could mention," Beryl said with a sniff. "Margaret, shall we see if Mr. Robertson has it in stock?"

Leaving their friends outside, Beryl and Margaret made their way into the stuffy little bookshop, and after a short discussion with Robertson, the owner, completed their transaction and emerged, flushed with success.

Only to find themselves deserted by friends and family. Beryl glanced up the road. There they were. As expected, George and Amanda walked together through the shaded churchyard, strolling along gravel paths beneath the plane trees, followed by Leighton and Verity, her hand on his arm. Fitz-Clarence trailed the other couples, swiping at clumps of tall grass with his stick.

"We have been abandoned," Margaret said, laughing. "Not that I blame them. The churchyard is far more appealing than this dreadfully hot pavement." Beryl could only agree.

Their friends turned at Margaret's hail and waited for them to catch up.

"Allow me," Fitz-Clarence said as he relieved Beryl of her parcel. "Did you decide on Wilkie Collins?" he asked.

She nodded. "*Man and Wife*."

Verity stumbled; Leighton caught her arm and steadied her.

"A…a pebble rolled under my foot," she stammered, "and my ankle buckled. I'm perfectly fine now."

"Have you seen Verity's new bracelet?" Margaret asked Beryl. "It's from a *secret admirer*."

"Don't be ridiculous." Cheeks aflame, Verity held out her left arm. A delicate gold chain, its links of fine filigree, encircled her wrist. "It was a birthday present from my grandmother."

"It's lovely but so fragile," Beryl said. "Be careful. If you catch it on something, the links will break."

"That's true, but it's so beautiful I don't want to take it off."

"What piece of frippery are you admiring now?" George said, peering over Beryl's shoulder. "Very pretty, but not as lovely as the one wearing it."

Verity's blush deepened, and she turned away.

"Goodness me," Beryl said, nudging George. "Aren't you the *preux chevalier*."

Fitz-Clarence laughed. "Quite so. Your aunt must be pleased that your time in Cambridge is not wasted."

George met his gaze. "*My* time there has not been wasted, unlike that of some others."

Silence settled over the group. Fitz-Clarence's sudden departure from Cambridge had been a subject of much speculation, but no one knew the true story.

"Touché," Fitz-Clarence said, sketching a bow to George. "Please excuse me. I have obviously overstayed my welcome."

"Not at all," Beryl said. "In fact, it is growing late, and I was going to ask if you would care to escort me to Ferndale, since my brother and Mr. Leighton appear to be otherwise occupied."

"It would be my pleasure." Fitz-Clarence offered his arm.

After a brief discussion regarding their plans, George and Leighton joined Beryl and Fitz-Clarence in saying good-bye to the young ladies. As they started down the lane, the two young men strode ahead, already deep in conversation. Beryl looked up; in the distance, a familiar black shape circled and swooped.

They were outside the village and approaching the bridge when Fitz-Clarence glanced at her. "You certainly took the wind out of your brother's sails," he said softly.

She laughed. "A salutary exercise. George is inclined to think too well of himself, and it's my sisterly duty to ensure that this does not last."

"I would say that you are doing a fine job, Miss Mayhew."

"You are too kind," she said, her cheeks warm. He was indeed a charming man. "You recommended Mr. Trollope earlier. Have you read his latest?"

"I'm afraid not. The last I read was *Phineas Finn*."

Their conversation turned to books as they crossed the bridge and retraced her earlier path up the lane and through the field, finally reaching her aunt's home.

Too large to be a cottage and too modest to be stately, Ferndale comfortably housed Miss Eleanora Mayhew, as well as her niece and nephew. A façade of Portland stone provided a sense of permanence, and the gardens, while not extensive, offered privacy and shade in the summer.

When they reached the front door, Beryl retrieved her parcel and offered tea, which was politely refused. "I don't wish to impose, and you will want to check on your aunt."

Very true, yet it was with a small pang of disappointment that she watched him stride back down the gravel path before she turned and entered the house.

* * * *

Tap. Taptaptap.

Beryl sat up in bed, rubbing her eyes. Although early, there was just light enough to see.

Tap. Taptap.

Where on earth… The window?

Throwing back the blanket, she scrambled out of bed and crossed to the open window. Hermes perched on the outer sill.

"What do you want?" she asked, holding out her hand. He hopped on the sill but did not enter. Something gleamed in his beak. "What's this?"

She gently caught the chain, and he opened his beak. She peered at the gold in her hand. Verity's bracelet.

"I told her to be careful. Where did she lose it?"

Hermes tilted his head and emitted a soft caw. He spread his wings and glided over to the old oak tree at the edge of the garden. Two louder caws, imperious.

"Very well." Beryl sighed. That particular tone signaled she would have no peace until he had shown her whatever it was that had caught his attention. She quickly dressed.

She slipped out the kitchen door, avoiding the cook and scullery maid, and walked across the lawn. The grass sparkled with morning dew. Standing before the oak, she rested her hands on her hips and looked up at Hermes.

"Well?"

He ruffled his feathers, then swooped across the lawn and landed on a gazing ball. He turned to look at her, and she obediently followed.

* * * *

A quarter of an hour later she emerged, breathless and tousled, from the overgrown shrubbery. Hermes had led her to the artfully placed Gothic ruins built half a century ago by a romantic baronet. Beryl had always loved exploring the deliberately broken walls and intentionally tumbled stones scattered among the bushes. When she clambered to the top of the ruins she could glimpse the Fitz-Clarence house, its prim Georgian façade concealing the original rambling Jacobean structure, the roofs of various outbuildings clustered around it just visible among the trees.

Hermes perched on a rhododendron branch and cawed.

Beryl stared at the lush foliage. Why would Hermes have found Verity's bracelet here?

With an impatient croak, Hermes hopped to the ground and ducked under the bush.

She stepped forward and lifted the branches. Peering underneath, she could see little, for deep shadows cloaked the uneven ground. Hermes hopped beside her and pecked at a…

Stifling a gasp, she backed away, her heart pounding.

A leg. A trousered leg.

But whose?

He must be sleeping or perhaps passed out from drink. A tramp, taking shelter from the morning damp?

There was only one way to discover the truth. With shaking hands, she pushed aside the branches until the growing light illuminated a shock of fair hair. She bent and tugged at his shoulder.

"Hullo? Can you hear me…"

He rolled onto his back, and Beryl cried out.

Open eyes glazed, tongue protruding, Nigel Leighton was most definitely dead.

* * * *

"A pet crow showed you where the body was hidden," Constable Wright said, his voice flat. He stood beside the drawing room hearth, hands clasped behind his back, his helmet on a small table. Sunlight striped the patterned carpet and gleamed off his brass buttons.

"Yes." Sitting on the settee with George beside her, Beryl lowered her gaze to her clasped hands. It did sound improbable. "Hermes woke me early—he has done it before, when he wanted to show me something interesting—so I followed him."

Aunt Eleanora coughed gently from the wing chair she habitually occupied. Her gray hair was drawn into a severe knot at the nape of her neck, and she wore her usual black, relieved only by touches of white lace at throat and cuff. "Beryl speaks the truth, Constable. She raised Hermes from a fledgling, and I have often seen him demand her attention." She gave Beryl an encouraging nod.

Constable Wright frowned. "That's as may be, Miss Mayhew. But the superintendent won't take kindly to the notion that Miss Beryl discovered the body through the offices of a pet crow."

"Sir Denys knows of Beryl's pet," Aunt Eleanora said. "I'm certain that if the superintendent asked, Sir Denys would confirm her statement."

Constable Wright opened his mouth, hesitated, and closed it. The stuff of local legend, Sir Denys was a force to be reckoned with.

"Very well," he said, shoulders stiff.

George suddenly stood. "Who cares about a pet crow. What of my friend? The man who was killed…murdered!"

Beryl closed her eyes. She would never forget the sight of Nigel Leighton's face.

"George, no one has forgotten Mr. Leighton." Aunt Eleanora's voice was gentle. "I'm certain Constable Wright will do everything in his power to discover who is responsible."

With a stifled groan, George covered his face with his hands. Then he dropped his hands and nodded. "I apologize for doubting your devotion to duty, Constable."

Constable Wright coughed. "Very natural, sir. So the facts are that you and Mr. Leighton went for a smoke and a stroll before retiring. Mr. Leighton, not having finished his cigar, decided to walk a little farther while you returned to the house. You left the side door unlocked and did not hear Mr. Leighton return."

"Exactly."

"Would you like to add anything else, Mr. Mayhew? Miss Beryl?"

"No," George said.

Beryl hesitated. Should she tell of the thin gold chain in her pocket? If she did, what would become of Verity? At the very least, her reputation would be in tatters, and she might even be falsely accused of this dreadful crime. No, Hermes had given her Verity's chain and entrusted her to discover the extent, if any, of Verity's involvement with Nigel Leighton's death. She glanced at the constable and shook her head.

"Very well. And now if you'll excuse me, the superintendent is waiting for my report." Wright gave a stiff bow, collected his helmet, and left.

Glancing at Beryl and George, Aunt Eleanora said, "Well, my dears, after that I would very much like a cup of tea."

* * * *

"There is no need for you to escort me, George," Beryl said three hours later. She reached the stile to Young Tom's field and turned to her brother. "I am simply going into the village."

"And I am simply accompanying you."

Beryl sighed. When George thrust out his chin like that, he would not be moved. "Very well. But do not complain of boredom if I linger in the shops."

They crossed the field in silence; a faint caw came from the trees ahead. Beryl shaded her eyes and scanned the branches until she spotted a familiar form circling toward them.

With a flutter of black feathers, Hermes landed on the stile. He waited until Beryl and George approached, then flew off with a croak.

"What has he left you this time?" George asked as Beryl picked up the small item.

"It's a button."

George laughed. "Another treasure for your hoard. You have collected dozens of buttons, courtesy of Hermes."

Beryl examined the button with a frown. "It's rather fine. For one thing, it's not brass. It's silver, engraved with a crest of some sort." She turned it over. "Look. It has been pulled from the cloth. See? A few threads of blue serge are still attached."

"You make too much of a random button when more important matters should occupy your thoughts."

Laying her hand on his arm, Beryl replied gently. "I'm sorry about Mr. Leighton, of course I am." But important matters did occupy her thoughts. For one thing, her trip into the village was not frivolous. She hoped to discover where and when Verity lost her bracelet, and that might provide a clue as to who killed Leighton.

"I still don't understand," George said. "How did Hermes know where to find Nigel's body? He's a crow, not a hound."

Beryl shook her head, her steps lagging. She didn't understand it either.

"And how did he signal you?" George continued. "Did he bring you something?" He peered at her face.

She turned away.

"He did." George grabbed her arm. "He did! What did he bring you? Something of Nigel's?"

"Stop that!" She broke free and glared at her brother. "It's… not Mr. Leighton's."

"Then what is it?"

Reaching into her pocket, Beryl slowly withdrew the gold chain and showed it to him.

A crease formed between his brows. "Whose bracelet is it?"

"Verity's," she said. "She showed it to us yesterday."

George picked up the delicate links and examined them. "It's broken."

"Yes. She must have caught it on something." She held out her hand, and he returned the bracelet. The gold puddled in her palm. She contemplated it for a moment before shoving it into her pocket.

"Perhaps she didn't notice when it broke," George said. "But Hermes brought it to you and then took you to Nigel's body."

"Yes. So it's possible that Verity was with Mr. Leighton before he was killed."

George met her gaze. "Or *when* he was killed."

* * * *

As Beryl and George approached, it appeared that every resident of Heatherington—stolid, sleepy Heatherington—had congregated in front of the shops, talking in low voices and glancing about, as if expecting…something.

With a cry, Margaret detached herself from a knot of women and ran to Beryl. "Oh, my dear!" She took Beryl's hands. "We heard about Mr. Leighton's death. Such a pleasant young man, and how very tragic."

"Yes, indeed. We are all very—"

"But have you heard?" She leaned close and lowered her voice. "Verity has gone missing."

"Missing? What do you mean?" Beryl exchanged a glance with George.

"The maid went to wake her this morning, and her bed hadn't been slept in. Even before hearing of Mr. Leighton's death, her father was quite wild with fear for her safety, and a number of men have gone out to hunt for her."

"Where are they searching?" George asked.

"I don't know," Margaret said. She looked up. A man on horseback was nearing the village. "Look! It's Mr. Fitz-Clarence. He's been out all morning. Perhaps he knows more."

A disheveled Fitz-Clarence rode up and leapt from his foam-flecked horse. Throwing the reins to a boy, he gave a curt order to water his mount. "Where is Mr. Plum?" he asked, glancing at the villagers crowding around. "He was not at home."

"He's still out searching. Any sign of Miss Verity?" one man called.

"No," Fitz-Clarence said, smoothing back his windblown hair before settling his cuffs. "But perhaps one of the others has had better luck."

Beryl pushed her way through the crowd toward Fitz-Clarence, George on her heels.

"Mr. Fitz-Clarence, where were you searching?" she asked.

Giving a little start when he saw her, Fitz-Clarence inclined his head. "Miss Beryl, Mayhew. I am so very sorry to hear about your friend. It is a great tragedy."

"Thank you," George said. "But we have just heard the news about Miss Verity. Have you looked for her in the area where Nigel was found?"

Fitz-Clarence shot him a glance and slowly nodded. "Yes, I have just come from there. The police examined the immediate vicinity, of course, but I widened the search all the way to my house, in case she…" His voice trailed off, and he cleared his throat.

"In case she had met with Mr. Leighton and was trying to escape his killer and find a safe haven with you?" Beryl said briskly, ignoring Fitz-Clarence's discomfort. "Yes, that is certainly one possibility."

"A possibility, perhaps, but there was no sign of her anywhere in the area." Fitz-Clarence sighed. "I can only pray she is safe."

"Amen," Beryl and George said together. Beryl hesitated, then continued. "Who else is participating in the search?"

"A dozen local gentlemen, along with any farmers who can spare the time." He gave her a brief smile. "Anyone able would of course wish to provide assistance to such a lovely young woman."

A hubbub arose near the churchyard as two other riders appeared, but their solemn expressions quieted the bystanders. They had been looking along the main road, but neither had seen any trace of Verity. A few pessimists frowned, and one pointed to the family headstones that stood nearby, as if Verity were already laid to rest.

From the other direction another horse and rider flew across the bridge and into the village. The dappled gray pulled up as it reached the shops. "Has anyone seen her?" Young Tom Perkins cried, dismounting and leading his horse over to the trough.

Fitz-Clarence shook his head and turned away. Perkins groaned.

Beryl and George hurried over to the newcomer.

"Where were you looking, Young Tom?" George asked.

"Around my property, along the lanes," he replied. "I searched every hedge, every ditch. She's not there."

"Well, she cannot have gone far, since she is probably on foot. I shall join in the search," George said. He led Beryl away from the others and spoke softly. "Hermes could have found the bracelet anywhere. Although he took you to Nigel's body after bringing you the bracelet, it does not necessarily follow that Miss Verity was there with Nigel."

"Not necessarily, but—"

"But nothing, Beryl. Hermes is a remarkable crow, but he is still a bird. I will trust in man's intelligence rather than a bird that brings you shiny treasures."

Beryl did not agree but would not argue the point—not this time. "Good luck to you. The shops hold no interest for me now. I am going home."

George smiled. "A sensible decision. Wait with Aunt Eleanora, and I will send word as soon as we have found her…" He leaned closer. "Hopefully alive."

Beryl returned his smile. Yet as she walked over the bridge, she scanned the sky for a familiar black shape.

* * * *

She did not see Hermes until she strode up the drive leading to Ferndale. Then he swooped down and settled on the grass before her.

"Hullo." Beryl took the bracelet from her pocket and held it out. "The lady who wore this, do you know where she is?"

Hermes cocked his head to one side and regarded her. He hopped forward and cawed softly. Then he turned, swiveled his head to glance back at her, and flew to a branch in the tree across the garden.

Beryl pocketed the bracelet and followed.

* * * *

Beryl looked around at the Gothic ruins and scowled at Hermes, who sat atop a half tumbled stone wall. "She can't be here! The constables combed the area when they retrieved Mr. Leighton's body this morning, and Mr. Fitz-Clarence looked as well."

Hermes let out a loud croak.

"What do you want to show me?"

With another caw, Hermes soared to a thicket of trees and perched on a branch. He cawed again. Muttering a curse and not caring if Hermes heard, Beryl pushed her way through the undergrowth. Whenever she paused to catch her breath or pull her skirts from a briar, Hermes flew back and encouraged her with calls and croaks.

Finally she emerged into a small, isolated clearing. Trees and shrubbery rose like ramparts around a grassy glade, and Hermes alighted at the far end, in front of a thatched cottage. According to village gossip, it was built eighty years ago for a Fitz-Clarence ancestor who enjoyed playing carefree yeoman on sunny afternoons. The thatch was old and wanted repair, but the granite walls and oak door remained solid, and iron bars had been installed over the tiny window to keep out vagrants. Beryl walked slowly toward the cottage. What were those muffled sounds? It almost sounded as if someone was crying out…

With a sudden piercing caw, Hermes flew off and Beryl turned, startled, as a man strode into the glade.

"Oh!" She pressed her hand to her chest, her heart beating rapidly. "You surprised me, Mr. Fitz-Clarence."

Fitz-Clarence stared at her for a moment, then glanced up at the branch where Hermes perched. His face twisted into a scowl. "That damned bird. He sees far too much."

"I beg your pardon?"

"I watched him approach and knew you would be close behind. It is *his* fault you are here, and you leave me no choice." With a much-put-upon sigh he stalked toward her, and she could not help but take a step back. The glitter in his eye and set to his jaw sent a chill down her spine. He looked…dangerous.

As she turned to flee, he sprang forward and caught her arm, spinning her around to face him. She cried out, but his other hand clamped around her throat, his fingers pressing into the soft hollows beneath her jaw. Her vision dimmed. She clawed vainly at his tightening hand and kicked, her boot connecting with his shin. He jerked and lost his grip on her throat.

She staggered, gasping. He struck her on the chin and her knees buckled, sending her to the ground. In a second Fitz-Clarence knelt beside her, both hands reaching for her throat again. She grabbed his wrists, but he pressed his advantage and broke her hold. His clenched fist struck her temple twice, and she lay dazed beneath him.

An unearthly screech pierced her stupor. Suddenly a demon with black feathers appeared before Fitz-Clarence, cruel beak pecking at his face, wings beating, talons lashing out.

Hermes!

With a scream, Fitz-Clarence rose, flailing at the crow. Hermes flew beyond his reach, then swooped and tore at his back, battering his head with beak and wings.

Bending over to protect his face, Fitz-Clarence grabbed Beryl's arms and dragged her across the grass toward the cottage. Hermes continued to rake his back. Dizzy and nauseated, Beryl dug in her heels, tugging against his inexorable grasp. With a curse he kicked her in the ribs, then hoisted her upright, gripping her hard around her waist. She cried out as pain sliced through her.

Fitz-Clarence fumbled an old iron key from his pocket and unlocked the door.

"A shotgun will take care of that damned bird before he rouses the entire village," he said. "And then I shall take care of *you*."

Throwing open the heavy oaken door, he shoved Beryl inside. She stumbled and reached out for support, landing hard against another body. They both tumbled to the floor. Fitz-Clarence slammed the door shut. The lock clicked.

With a groan, Beryl blinked and focused on the face beside her. "Verity?"

A tousled, tear-stained Verity embraced her. "Oh, Beryl! I am so happy to see you."

Outside, Fitz-Clarence screamed again, a bestial cry of rage.

"Hermes must still be on the attack," Beryl said. She scrambled to her feet and helped Verity up, pulling her to the tiny window. In the clearing, Hermes continued to swoop at Fitz-Clarence like a dark, avenging spirit. Fitz-Clarence struck at the crow, missing him, and the key dropped to the ground. He reached for it, but Hermes landed, covering the key with his body and croaking loudly. Fitz-Clarence retreated, nursing bloodied hands and head, then turned and ran into the trees.

Vision clearing, her dizziness retreating, Beryl moved from the window and looked around. The cottage consisted of one room containing a small table, a rumpled bed, and the shattered remains of a wooden chair. "Did Fitz-Clarence destroy the chair in his anger?"

Verity shook her head. "No. I did, to provide myself with a weapon. I would have attacked him when he opened the door, but—"

"But I knocked you down," Beryl finished. "Did he hurt you?"

"A little," Verity said. She raised her hands; her wrists were bruised and swollen. "He tied me up, but I managed to free myself. But Beryl, he killed Mr. Leighton!" Her voice broke.

"Why? And why imprison you?"

"I have long known that he admired me, and there were times when I…" She bowed her head.

"You encouraged him?" Beryl said gently.

Verity nodded.

Beryl stifled a sigh. "You are not the first to fall under his spell."

"Perhaps not, but my behavior was thoughtless. I will have to live with the fact that an innocent man paid a terrible price thereby. Yesterday Fitz-Clarence told me he had urgent news, news that would change my life, and that I must meet him at the ruins last night. I foolishly agreed." Verity chafed her wrists. "He said he… was mad with desire for me," she whispered. "He could fight it no longer and would take me to a place where we could be alone, where he would show me what it was to be loved by a man."

"How horrible! What did you say to that?" Beryl asked.

Verity shuddered. "I said I loved another, and he told me I did not know my own mind and he knew what was best for me. He raved that we were destined to be together and that nothing should part us, even if I did not realize that now, even if it took time—days, weeks, months—for me to see he was in the right. I replied I could never love one who treated me so. The banns would be read soon, and I would be the wife of a man who respects me and has more honor and integrity in his little finger than Fitz-Clarence has in his entire body. I spat in his face, and he could not contain his rage."

"You were very courageous to brave his anger." Had Verity lied about loving another, or was she genuinely engaged to someone? Beryl's curiosity was piqued, but now was not the time to inquire. "How did he respond?"

"He grabbed me, and I screamed once before he struck and stunned me. Mr. Leighton must have heard my cry, for within a few moments he appeared and flew at Fitz-Clarence. I was too addled to see much in the moonlight, but I could hear everything…. The sounds Mr. Leighton made as the life was choked from him… I will never forget." Tears rolled down her cheeks, and she covered her face with her hands.

Beryl pulled Verity close in a comforting embrace. "Fitz-Clarence has gone to fetch his shotgun, but we can try to overpower him as he enters. Let us each wield a chair leg—"

A fusillade of imperative raps on the window interrupted her.

There, on the windowsill, sat Hermes. Beryl quickly unfastened the latch and opened the window.

Hermes held the key in his beak.

"Oh, you wonderful creature!" Reaching careful fingers through the bars, Beryl grasped the key and pulled it inside. "Verity," she said, holding up the key. "Do you think you can run?"

Verity wiped away a tear and nodded. "Like the wind."

Beryl unlocked the door with shaking hands. "Then let us go." As they left the cottage, Beryl closed and re-locked the door, pocketing the key. "That might give us more time."

"We will need it." Verity grabbed her hand.

Despite their bruises and pains, the two women darted across the glade and into the trees, trying to make as little noise as possible as they pushed through the shrubbery and ducked under low branches. Safety beckoned; Ferndale was only minutes away.

"Hush." Beryl lifted her head. The faint sounds of someone crashing through the undergrowth increased. She held her finger before her lips. "Keep moving quickly and quietly."

"He will hear us," Verity whispered, trembling.

"We must chance it." Beryl gave her hand an encouraging squeeze.

They moved carefully through the thick undergrowth, but at every brush of cloth or crack of twig, Beryl flinched. Surely he would be upon them at any moment! At last a familiar open lawn was visible through the thinning trees. It provided no cover, but Ferndale lay just beyond—their safe haven, if they could only reach it.

The sounds of pursuit drew nearer.

"Run!"

Beryl and Verity broke from the trees, almost flying as they dashed across the grass toward the house.

A raucous caw cut through the quiet.

Heart pounding, Beryl glanced around. Hermes would not be so foolish as to call attention to their vulnerable position…or would he?

Hermes was nowhere to be seen, but Fitz-Clarence erupted from the wood with a shout. Shotgun in one hand, he pounded after them.

A caw sounded again as a black shape arrowed from the trees toward Fitz-Clarence. With a croak, another crow joined him, then another. A veritable chorus echoed through the wood and across the lawn as a feathered black cloud descended on Fitz-Clarence.

Beryl and Verity stumbled and slowed, staring.

Fitz-Clarence screamed, dropped the shotgun, and raised his arms to shield his head from the onslaught. He fell to his knees, then collapsed to the ground.

The din increased, the whirlwind of crows intensified, and his shrieks rose in pitch.

Unable to look away, Beryl stood frozen, her mouth dry with horror.

"That's enough!" George shouted as he ran across the lawn from the house, waving his arms at the black maelstrom that engulfed the fallen man.

Beryl started, her paralysis broken; she picked up her skirts and ran after him.

"Hermes!" she cried. "Stop! We are safe!"

Gradually the flying crows quieted and slowed, many settling on the lawn around the huddled shape, while others retreated to the wood, perching on branches. The noise abated, her ears rang in the quiet.

Beryl hurried to the bloodied body. George stood before Fitz-Clarence, face impassive, staring down at the battered man. He glanced at her.

"He's still alive."

She nodded and her hand crept up to her bruised throat. She would not, *could* not, bring herself to touch him. He would have to wait for the doctor.

George lifted his hand and gently touched her bruised chin and temple, then studied her throat. "*He* did that?"

"Yes. Hermes led me to where he had hidden Verity." Where was Verity? She glanced over her shoulder and breathed easier. Verity was still safe, standing on the terrace. She turned back to George. "Fitz-Clarence tried to kill us, but Hermes intervened."

"Hermes deserves as many worms as he can eat for the rest of his life," George said. "How is she?"

"Frightened but basically unharmed. He had not had time to do…anything."

George turned from Fitz-Clarence and offered his arm. "Shortly after you left for home I thought about the etched silver button Hermes brought to you this morning and remembered where I had seen silver buttons engraved in such a manner."

"On Fitz-Clarence's blue serge coat." Grateful for the support, Beryl leaned on him.

"Exactly. When you said you were returning home we could see Hermes following you, and Fitz-Clarence disappeared. He must have taken fright and wanted to ensure Hermes didn't lead you to Miss Verity."

"Which he did."

"Yes. I gathered together a few of the locals, including the doctor, intent on combing the areas that Fitz-Clarence claimed to have searched. But you and Hermes were a step or two ahead of me."

They started back toward the little group of people standing in front of the house, passing several men, including Dr. Sayre, who trudged toward his patient, carrying his black bag.

Beryl glimpsed Verity standing with the others by the house and breathed a sigh of relief. Verity was unharmed, held closely in the arms of…Young Tom Perkins? When Verity had said she loved another, Beryl had not guessed this.

"Did you know about Verity and Young Tom?" she asked.

"Not until he came to me, frantic with worry, and insisted on accompanying our search party. He needed someone to confide in, I suppose. They have been in love for years and secretly engaged for the past several months. Her father would not permit the match until Young Tom's prospects improved."

Beryl nodded. "Hence the reason for expanding his dairy."

"They will be calling the banns now."

"Did Fitz-Clarence know of this match?"

"Not until yesterday. Young Tom apparently let something slip about their plans, and that might have precipitated Fitz-Clarence's actions."

"Perhaps." Beryl gave her brother's arm a gentle squeeze. "Or perhaps he had already planned it. But one fact is certain: if Nigel

Leighton hadn't been outside last night and heard Verity's scream, Fitz-Clarence would surely have harmed Verity. As it was, he did not have time to do more than truss her up and stow her in that little cottage near his home. Although she broke from her bonds and was ready to defend herself, Mr. Leighton's actions helped save her, and he will always have my gratitude."

George nodded and cleared his throat. "At least his death wasn't meaningless."

Beryl didn't agree, but she certainly wasn't going to contradict her grieving brother. "That must be some comfort," she said.

Fending off the questions and remarks of the others, she and George made their way over to Verity and Young Tom. His strong arm supported her, and she pressed against him.

"You must be exhausted," Beryl said to Verity. "Come inside and rest until we can arrange a carriage to take you home."

"In a minute." Verity looked at the small group of men on the lawn. "Is he…"

Beryl shrugged. "Alive but badly injured. He will answer for his crimes." She reached into her pocket and drew out the bracelet. "I wanted to return this. Hermes found it and brought it to me." Had it only been this morning?

"Thank you." Verity took the delicate chain. "But I won't… I *can't* wear it again."

A soft caw caught their attention. Hermes circled overhead, then swooped down, landing on a stone wall and staring at them.

Holding out the chain, Verity slowly walked toward Hermes. "Thank you for all you have done, Hermes. I'd like you to have this." She placed it on the stone before him and stepped back.

Regarding her intently, Hermes let out a gentle croak, then picked up the chain in his beak. With a flap of his wings he lifted and soared, disappearing into the trees.

Beryl shepherded Verity, Young Tom, and her brother toward the front door. "Let us go into the house while we wait for word from the doctor. I, for one, could use a cup of tea."

She heard a distant caw and smiled.

Carla Coupe's short stories have appeared in several of the Chesapeake Crimes series, and most recently in Malice Domestic's *Mystery Most Historical*. Two of her short stories were nominated for the Agatha Award. She has written a number of Sherlock Holmes pastiches, which have appeared in *Sherlock Holmes Mystery Magazine*, *Sherlock's Home: The Empty House*, *The MX Book of New Sherlock Holmes Stories, Part VI*, and *Irene's Cabinet*. Her story "The Book of Tobit" was included in *The Best American Mystery Stories of 2012*. www.carlacoupe.com

RASPUTIN

BY KM ROCKWOOD

I heard tires on the gravel driveway. Lifting my head, I sniffed hard, but I couldn't get a good scent of whoever it was. Not that it mattered. My tail thumped on the floor.

The vehicle continued up to our trailer, which is at the end of a long driveway, back in the woods. The people got out, and I could hear their bootsteps on the uneven concrete blocks that led up to the front door.

Company! I was so excited, I twirled in circles, barking and wriggling my rear. I jumped at the closed door to greet the visitors. People don't come often, but I love it when they do. It does get a bit lonesome, just me and Larry. Larry's my person.

Once I found another dog in the woods and brought him home with me. Larry said we could keep him, but someone came looking for him, and of course he wanted to go with his own person.

Larry got up and went over to the door, but he didn't open it.

Standing in front of the door but not opening it is the kind of thing that infuriates me about Larry sometimes. He won't join me doing some of my favorite things, like digging through the garbage or rolling in the mud or bringing home a road-kill skunk. He spends most of his time in front of the TV with a beer and a joint, doing nothing. But he's my best friend, and I love him.

Now he leaned against the door and said, "Go away or I'll set the dog on you."

I barked louder.

"Hush up, Rasputin," Larry said.

Rasputin's my name. I hear people talking all the time, but I don't pay much attention to it unless someone says my name. Then I listen to see if I'm being told to do something. Or, more likely, not to do whatever it is I'm doing.

I learned long ago that it's hard to make sense out of all that yakking, so most of the time I don't even try.

"I'll shoot the dog," someone on the other side of the door said. "And you, too, if you don't let us in."

"What'd ya want?" Larry shouted through the door.

"The boss wants to know what you're doing. He sent us to find out, and maybe bring you over to talk to him."

With a sigh, Larry grabbed me by the collar and pulled me back so he could open the door.

Three people tumbled in, two men and a lady.

I tried to leap up to kiss the visitors—who doesn't like to be kissed?—but Larry held tight to my collar.

"Keep that mutt away from me," the man said, "or I'll shoot it."

I inhaled deeply. The man smelled like dirty socks, tobacco smoke, and cooked onions. Not bad, although I could do without the onions.

"Aw, Vern." The lady pushed past him and held out a hand for me to sniff. "He's just being friendly. He won't hurt you, will you, boy?"

She had a chemical odor, like fake flowers. Maybe some kind of perfume. Underneath, though, I could detect that delicious female smell. She hadn't taken a bath in a while. I yipped my approval.

She walked in little mincing steps, like a bitch in heat. I think it was that her pants were too tight. I pulled away from Larry to latch onto her leg and started humping.

"If that dog bites you, Ginny, don't come crying to me," Vern said.

"Ha. Scared of dogs, are you?" Laughing, she pushed me down and tickled my ears.

Everybody crowded into the tiny living room and sat down. Larry shrugged and went over to open the refrigerator door. He tossed cans of beer to the visitors.

I don't drink beer. Usually.

Vern pulled out his cell phone. He looked at it, frowned, and got up to walk down the hallway.

I sat next to Ginny and laid my head on her lap.

"What's his name?" she asked Larry.

"Rasputin."

"Rasputin? Wasn't that some kind of demented Russian genius?"

"Yeah. The dog's mother was a purebred black Russian terrier. And look at his eyes."

Ginny lifted my head and scratched under my chin. "That blue is a funny color for a dog's eyes, isn't it? And they're awfully close together."

"Kind of makes him look demented. But he's no genius."

She laughed again and rubbed my head.

Definitely my kind of visitor.

"I can't get no signal on this phone," Vern called from the end of the hallway.

"Not surprising. It can be hard to get a signal out here," Larry said.

"What the…? I was supposed to call the boss as soon as we got here. He was gonna tell me what he wanted us to do. Besides have a look around." Vern started opening doors in the hallway.

There wasn't much down there. A closet, a bathroom, a space for a washer and dryer hookup, but Larry didn't have a washer or dryer. And the plant room.

"What the hell is this?" Vern asked. I peered down the hallway. He'd found the plant room.

"Just my little garden," Larry said.

"Maybe that's what the boss is worried about. You're dealing your own stuff."

"Nah. That's just for my personal use."

"You must have, what—forty or fifty plants in here."

"Yeah, well, I figured once I got the lights on timers and the space heaters going, I might as well grow as many as I can fit in there."

"And you don't sell any?"

"Nah. But sometimes I give some to friends. You want some?"

Vern coughed. "Sure. But not now. Is there anywhere around here I can get a cell phone signal?"

"Not really." Larry drained his beer. He smelled sweaty. Funny. I couldn't see that he was doing anything to make him work up a sweat. "Sometimes up the road on top of the hill, but not always."

"Well, then, if I can't talk to him, I guess we're gonna have to go see the boss."

"You just do that."

"And you're gonna come with us." Vern put the cell phone back in his pocket.

Larry shook his head. "Not gonna happen."

Vern planted himself in front of Larry. "I wasn't asking you if you were coming with us. I was telling you."

"You can't make me."

"Wanna bet?"

The other guy stepped over and seized one of Larry's arms. Vern took the other one.

I stared at them. What kind of new game were they playing?

The two men started pulling Larry toward the door. He struggled.

People didn't usually play this rough. In fact, Larry yelled at me when I tried to play wrestling games inside. But if they were going to, I wanted to be part of it. I stood up and barked.

Vern swung his foot at me.

I could play that game! I seized the leg of his overalls in my teeth, shook hard, and snarled. He tottered on one foot, leaning on Larry.

What fun!

Vern reached into his pocket and pulled out a gun. He aimed it at me.

Ginny grabbed my collar, pulled me back, and stepped between Vern and me.

Larry and the other guy were falling over, pulling Vern with them. As he fell, Vern turned the gun toward Larry.

"Don't shoot him!" Ginny shouted.

"Huh?" Vern glanced at her.

The three men tumbled into a pile on the floor. The gun went off, sending a bullet through the sagging ceiling of the trailer.

A big drop of water plopped onto the floor beneath the hole. It turned into a steady drip.

Vern was on top. He turned and pressed the gun against Larry's neck.

"The boss wants to talk to him," Ginny said. "He can't talk to a dead body."

"She's right." The other guy was on the bottom. "He won't like it if we bring in a dead guy."

"I guess." Vern struggled to his feet and shoved the gun back into his pocket. He held out a hand to help the other guy up.

Together they pulled on Larry. He didn't want to get up.

Vern smacked Larry on the side of his head. "Stop it. You're coming with us. Where's your truck key?"

Larry shook his head, but he stopped pulling. "I'm not gonna let you use my truck."

"We can't all fit in the cab of my truck," Vern said. "So I guess we're just gonna have to hog-tie you and put duct tape on your mouth and dump you back in the bed."

"It's in my pocket," Larry mumbled.

"Ginny, get the key. You can follow us in Larry's truck."

She let go of my collar and reached into the pocket of Larry's jeans, pulling out the key.

We all headed out the door.

"Aren't you gonna shut that mutt up inside?" Vern asked Ginny.

She looked down at me. "How long are we gonna be gone?"

"I dunno. It's up to the boss."

"Well, I'm gonna leave the door open a little. I don't know how long it's gonna be before somebody gets back here. There's a bag of dog food by the sink he can knock over if he wants, and he can get out to poop."

Vern shrugged. "Suit yourself. But if it gets real cold and the door's open, the pipes might freeze. Not to mention all those lovely plants. Shame if they froze."

"It's not supposed to get that cold tonight."

They headed toward the trucks. Vern climbed in behind the wheel. Larry and the other guy got in the passenger seat.

Vern was right. There really wasn't room for another person.

Ginny got into Larry's truck and started the engine.

I stood by the front steps, trying to figure out what to do. If Larry didn't want me to go with him someplace, he'd say, "Rasputin, you be a good dog and stay home and mind the trailer." Some of the saddest words any dog ever heard.

But nobody said that. So it must mean I could go, too.

I leapt into the back of Larry's truck. Usually I sat in the cab, but sometimes he'd have me ride in the back. The best thing to do then is to curl up right against the cab and keep my head down. I missed some of the wonderful smells carried by the wind, but if I stood, or even sat up, I might fall over.

We lurched down the driveway and onto the road. I like riding in the truck, so I was happy we drove on for a long time.

By the time the truck stopped, the sun was going down and a light drizzle was falling. We were at an old farmhouse at the end of a driveway even longer than ours.

A strong odor filled the air. It almost smelled like a million cats had peed all over. But it was a sharper smell, and had other things I didn't recognize mixed into it.

Ginny got out of the truck and went toward the house.

I stood in the bed of the truck, watching. The men had climbed out of the other truck, with Larry between the two big men. Kind of like how he held me when he didn't want me to run off, but he didn't have a collar, so they held his arms, pushing him ahead of them onto the front porch and into the house.

Too bad he didn't run off. I would have gone with him. We could look for a deer to chase or something.

The door to the house slammed shut. I jumped out of the truck and went up to sniff it. The cat-pee odor was even stronger there. I shook my head and sneezed.

They weren't letting me in.

The rain came down harder. The wind was chilly. It was suppertime, but no one seemed to be in any hurry to feed me. I sniffed around, but in the end I curled up in a corner of the porch, out of the wind and rain, wrapped my tail over my nose to keep it warm, and dozed off.

* * * *

I woke up when someone opened the door and stepped onto the porch. It was a woman, but not Ginny. Too bad. I liked Ginny.

She stood at the edge of the porch, smoking a cigarette and flicking the ashes into the rainy night. She had one of those tiny flashlights that just give a pinprick of light, and she was shining it at the floor.

Maybe she'd like some company. I stood up, stretched, and yawned.

The woman jerked the flashlight around so the light hit my face. It hurt my eyes a little, but she couldn't help that. I wagged my tail hard to show her I was being friendly and opened my mouth in a big grin.

She screamed.

Startled, I jumped off the porch and ran over to Larry's truck.

People came pouring out of the house. Vern was first.

Last ones out were Larry and someone who was pulling him by the arm. Larry swayed a bit and stumbled.

"A wolf!" the woman hollered. "Right up here on the porch."

"A wolf?" Vern said doubtfully. "I don't think there are any wolves around here."

"Well, something. Something with big teeth and beady eyes."

"Where is it now?"

"I don't know. It jumped off the porch and ran away."

Vern leaned back. "A coyote, I could believe. A wolf, no."

"Coyotes are tan-colored," the woman insisted. "This was dark gray. And bigger than a coyote."

"Yeah, right. I bet it just looked that way in the dark."

"Whatever." The woman finished up her cigarette and tossed the butt onto the ground. "We can't have a wolf around here. Or a coyote. You gonna do something about it?"

"Which way did it run?"

"That way," the woman said, pointing off into the woods instead of toward the parked vehicles, where I cowered against the truck. I hadn't seen anything myself, but the smell of fear was in the air.

I crawled under the truck. It was out of the rain, and if whatever they were afraid of tried to get at me, at least I could run out the other side. I peered at the people gathered on the porch. They were all staring off into the woods where the woman had pointed.

One guy lifted up a rifle and let loose with a shot in that direction. "That ought to scare it off, whatever it was."

Vern pulled his handgun out of his overalls and shot twice in the same direction.

The noise seemed to jerk Larry fully awake. He shook his head.

No one was looking at him. Even the guy who was holding onto his arm wasn't paying much attention to him.

Larry pulled his arm free and jumped off the side of the porch.

"Hey!" Vern twisted around. "Get him!"

But Larry had a good head start.

Vern lifted his gun and fired at Larry.

Larry tripped and almost fell, but he got his feet under him and kept going.

I was surprised. Larry usually doesn't like the rain. And he wasn't wearing his heavy jacket. Why was he coming out in this weather?

Not paying any attention to me, he ducked around the corner of the house. I followed him.

We pressed up against the wall. He held his left arm snuggled up against his chest. I heard people on the porch, so I crept back to where I could see what was going on.

A few people stood there, looking around.

"Where'd he go?" someone asked.

"I dunno. It'll be hard to find him in the dark, though."

"Did the shot hit him?"

"I think so. I saw blood on his shirt."

"What are we gonna do?"

"Not much to do."

"So we let him go?"

"The road's over two miles away. He's not gonna get far in this weather. Especially not if he's losing blood. We can find him in the morning."

"Suppose he dies?"

"So what? Then the boss doesn't have to decide whether to off him or not."

They turned around and trooped back into the house.

I trotted back to Larry. He looked down at me. "Rasputin? Where'd you come from?"

I wagged my tail and did a little dance, showing him how happy I was that he had decided to come out and play with me.

With the rain lashing at our faces, we crept around to the front of the house. He was careful to avoid the pools of light spilling out of the uncurtained windows of the house, so I was, too.

Four trucks and an old car sat in the driveway. Larry went over to them, keeping them between himself and the house. He stood for a minute, looking around.

I crawled under a high truck to get out of the rain.

Larry went to his truck and tried the door. It wouldn't open.

One by one, he tried the other vehicles. None of the doors would open.

He turned to walk behind the house again. I came out from under the truck and went along.

It was hard to see much.

A few old outbuildings leaned at precarious angles. I sniffed at them. One had definitely been a chicken coop at some point. Another had an oily smell and a few rusted tools lying around. A third had housed goats. It still had an open bag of goat feed and some old straw up against the far wall.

Larry stepped inside. The roof leaked a little, but most of the interior was dry.

I went up to the bag of goat feed and sniffed it. It didn't smell all that good, and it was moldy. I took a tentative mouthful, but it was scratchy and tasted terrible. I could eat it if I got hungry enough, but I wasn't that hungry yet.

When were these people going to fix some real food? It was way past suppertime.

Larry turned and walked out. "Come on, Rasputin. We need to get away from here."

He led me around the house once more, past the trucks, and we started down the driveway. It was uneven and muddy. Hard enough to walk with my four legs. Larry only had two. He kept tripping.

Most of the gravel had washed away. Even if we could see well, which we couldn't, we couldn't have avoided the holes. Each one was filled with water, and whenever we stepped in one, our feet got wet.

I trotted from one side of the driveway to the other, sniffing. The rain had intensified but scattered the smells, making it hard to tell where they were coming from.

Larry walked down the center. He was pretty unsteady on his feet. He fell a few times and had trouble getting back up. Then he went down again and could only get to his knees. I went up to him and whined, trying to ask why he didn't just go back to the house. He grabbed onto me for support and turned to look at now-distant lighted windows, showing through the bare trees.

The rain beat against us and the wind whipped my fur and his shirt.

Leaning heavily on me, he stood and turned back the way we had come.

It took us lots longer to get back. By the time we got near the house, I wondered if Larry would be able to get up the steps. I figured I could go up and scratch at the door. Surely one of the people would come out and help him in.

But he stopped short of the house. We crept around back, to the goat shed, and went in. With his wet boot, Larry tried to pull some of the straw away from the wall.

Was he making a bed? Using my front paws, I dug into the pile and kicked it out on the floor. Larry tried to flatten it down, so I got onto it and turned around a few times, making a nest for us.

Larry collapsed onto it. I stood there for a few minutes, trying to decide what to do. Sometimes Larry let me sleep in bed with him. I shook the water from my fur as best I could and lay down next to him.

He was shivering.

I crawled my torso over his chest and lay my head next to his, being careful not to lean on the bloody spot on one side. That might be sore.

He moaned softly. I gave him a quick kiss.

It seemed like a funny place for him to choose for the night, but it would do.

Gradually his shivering stopped. We were still wet, but between the straw and our combined body heat, we got warmer. His breathing became slow and regular.

We slept.

* * * *

The rain was still coming down at dawn but not quite as hard. A cold wind blew between the warped boards covering the walls and through the open door.

I had to pee. And since no one had to open the door for me, I could just go out and do it. Why didn't Larry just leave the door open like that at home? It would be much easier. Then I'd never have to wake him up or whine at the door to be let out.

The ground outside the shed was a sea of mud. I found a higher patch near a big tree and let loose. That taken care of, I trotted through the drenched grass to see if anyone was up in the house.

No one had fed me my supper, and it was getting to be time for breakfast.

Ginny, the nice lady, was standing under the roof on the back porch, smoking a cigarette, and peering at one of those plastic rectangle things that light up and sometimes talk. Larry had one, but he didn't use it much. Only sometimes when we were out in the truck. What's so fascinating about a little piece of plastic, even if it can talk? It didn't even taste good. I'd tried both licking it and chewing it.

I went over to the edge of the porch and stared up at her, but she didn't look my way. I thought about going up on the porch and humping her leg or licking her hand or something, but to tell the truth, I hadn't known her long enough to tell how she'd react. Maybe she'd get mad and send me away.

Larry might be waking up soon. I slipped back into the decrepit goat shed to see. He was still lying there, breathing heavily. Didn't he have to go pee, too? Although he didn't usually go outside to do it. Just used that big white bowl in the house that's usually filled with drinking water.

No, he was still asleep. Not much fun at all.

I went back to see what Ginny was doing. Shouldn't someone be fixing breakfast soon?

She was still looking at that little plastic thing.

The smells coming from the house didn't seem breakfasty. In fact, they were rank. Some new chemical smells, worse than the cat-pee odor, burned my nose.

Ginny rubbed her nose. I know humans have a terrible sense of smell, but really, this was foul. And irritating.

Sure enough, she coughed and rubbed her nose again. Then she looked down at her cigarette and sniffed it.

It wasn't the cigarette. It was the smell coming from inside the house. But how could I make her realize that?

I jumped up on the porch and gently grabbed her hand in my mouth, pulling her toward the stairs.

She started to jerk her hand back, then looked down at me. "Rasputin! How did you get here?" She tossed the cigarette and rubbed behind my ears with her other hand. "Did you play wolf last night and scare the living bejesus out of everybody?"

Now, I love to have my ears rubbed as much as the next dog, but the smell was burning my throat. It couldn't be doing Ginny any good. I tugged.

"You got something to show me?" She laughed and came down the steps with me.

When she was a little ways away from the house, I dropped her hand and ran into the shed to see if Larry was awake yet. He might be waking up soon. He was still lying there, breathing heavily, but he moved a bit when I licked his face. Wasn't he going to get up?

Next thing I knew, a huge explosion shook the air. I turned and ran out to look.

The windows in the house had blown out. Smoke was billowing through the empty holes. Someone inside was screaming.

Ginny was lying on the wet ground.

In the shed, Larry was trying to get to his feet, holding onto the rough wall with one hand. The other was tucked into his chest. When he saw me, he said, "You are here, Rasputin. I thought I must have dreamed seeing you."

Wagging my tail furiously, I rubbed my head against him. He almost fell over.

"You're all wet!" he said.

Well, it was still raining.

He leaned on me and struggled up. "Let's see if we can get out of here."

We went around to the front of the house. Smoke was still pouring out of the windows, and bright tongues of flames reached for the roof. Whoever had been screaming was quiet now.

Larry stumbled over to his truck and tugged at the door handle. No one had unlocked it overnight.

I went over to where Ginny lay and sniffed at her. She was getting pretty wet. I nudged her, and she rolled over and threw her arm over her face.

Still unsteady on his feet, Larry joined us. He reached down and grabbed Ginny's shoulder, but he almost fell over. "Where's my truck key?"

She moaned.

He shook her shoulder. "Where the hell is the key to my truck?"

"I dunno."

"You drove the truck here. You must have had it. Where is it?"

"Maybe in my pocket?" She tried to sit up.

Larry rolled her over on her stomach and patted the outside of the back pockets of her jeans. The he reached in front and felt the front ones. "Damn."

He pulled her onto her back and tried to reach a hand in her pocket. The jeans were too tight for him to get his hand in.

"Help me get up," she said, shaking her head.

Holding onto me and each other, they both managed to stand. Ginny slipped her slender hand into a pocket and pulled out the key.

Larry tried to snatch it from her.

She jerked her hand back, keeping the key away from him. "Take me with you."

"Why the hell should I do that?" Larry asked.

She held her hand behind her. "Because otherwise I'll throw this key into the woods as far as I can, and you'll never find it." She looked up at him. "So please?"

Larry ran his hand through his hair, which was now soaking from the rain. "Okay. But let's get going."

We all headed for the truck, me dancing ahead and the two of them staggering, holding onto one another.

Ginny opened the passenger door. I jumped in. Then Larry grabbed the key and headed around to the driver's side, holding onto the bed of the truck to keep from falling. Ginny clambered in, leaning her head back with her eyes closed.

Larry managed to get in, but since he was still holding his left arm close against his chest, he had trouble closing the door. He finally managed and started up the truck.

"What the hell happened?" he asked as he yanked the truck into gear and turned it toward the potholed driveway. He had to let go of the steering wheel to switch gears, so we drifted toward the side of the driveway.

"They were cooking up a batch," Ginny said.

"Meth?"

"Yeah."

"And it blew up?"

"Sure looks that way, don't it?" she said.

It was Larry's turn to say, "Yeah."

We were all wet. The windows were streaked with moisture, inside and out. Larry turned on the wipers. "Look," he said to Ginny. "Could you turn on the heat? And the defrosters? I can't see where I'm going. And I can't use my left hand."

She leaned forward and fiddled with the buttons on the dashboard until a blast of cold air shot up by the inside of the windshield. "It'll have to warm up," she said. She pulled her sleeve over her hand and rubbed at the windshield in front of Larry. "That any better?"

"A little."

He rolled down the side window and stuck his head out.

We bounced down the driveway, reaching the end. "Which way?" he asked.

Ginny shrugged. "Prob'ly the best bet is to go away from town. Right. Somebody's gonna call in the fire. And we want to be as far away from that as we can."

"I just want to get back to my place," Larry said.

"Yeah. Well, you can go around and come in from the other side."

"You think I have enough gas?"

"Maybe."

We had only gone a little way along the road when we heard sirens. A huge pickup with flashing blue lights dashed past us, coming from the other direction, and whipped around the turn into the driveway so fast it slipped into the ditch.

"Damn volunteer firefighters," Ginny said. "Some of them are good guys, but they have their share of cowboys."

Larry started to pull the truck over to the side of the road.

"Are you crazy?" Ginny said. "Put as much distance between that house and us as you can."

"But that guy might be hurt."

"The whole damn fire department's on their way. If he's hurt, they'll take care of him. We don't want to be around for them to ask any questions."

Nodding in agreement and letting go of the steering wheel to shift, Larry stepped on the accelerator. Steering and shifting and accelerating were enough to handle. Adding the nodding wasn't such a good idea. The truck swerved toward the ditch, and he had to wrench it back onto the road.

Gradually the blast of air by the windshield grew warm, then hot. The glass cleared, at least on the inside. Larry rolled up the window.

"You hurt bad?" Ginny asked him.

Gingerly, Larry moved his left shoulder. "I don't think so. I think the bullet nicked my rib and kept going. It's sore as all hell, and it bled a lot, but it don't feel like a cracked rib. I've had them before. How about you?"

"I dunno. That blast knocked me off my feet. I don't think anything's broken. I'm gonna be pretty stiff. And I maybe got a little concussion. But I think I'm okay."

"What about the others?"

Ginny turned her head and looked out the window. "It was an inferno in there. I don't see how anybody could have survived."

"Is that where you lived?"

"Yeah. With Vern. A lot of people would've said he wasn't much of a boyfriend. But he wasn't so bad. At least to me." She wiped her eye with her hand.

I laid my head on her arm and looked up at her. She scratched behind my ears. I sighed happily and dozed.

I woke up when Larry opened the truck door. We were in our own driveway. We climbed out and splashed up to the trailer.

"Might as well come in and see if we can find something to eat," he said. "And feed Rasputin."

Yes!

"And see how badly we're hurt," he continued. "I'm gonna take an oxie and get some more sleep. You can, too. Then we can decide what to do."

I bounced ahead of them. Finally, I was going to be fed.

And Larry had brought Ginny home. Maybe we could keep her.

KM Rockwood draws on a varied background for stories, including working as a laborer in steel fabrication and fiberglass manufacture, and supervising an inmate work crew in a large state prison. These positions, as well as work as a special-education teacher in alternative education and a GED instructor in correctional facilities, provide material for numerous short stories and novels, including the Jesse Damon Crime Novel series. www.kmrockwood.com

BARK SIMPSON AND THE SCENT OF DEATH

BY ALAN ORLOFF

"Three more weeks before you're put out to pasture," I said to my partner, Gerry O'Brien. "Gonna be nice. Sleeping late. Pina coladas. Thirty-six holes a day."

"Maybe only twenty-seven holes. I'm no longer a young man." O'Brien sighed. "Thirty years on the job. Seems like just yesterday I got my gold badge. Hard to believe I was once like you, Rook."

"Like me? You mean handsome?"

"No. I mean a newbie."

I'd been on the force for six years before I got the recent bump to detective. "I'm not so new."

"Face it kid, you're green."

From the back seat of our unmarked car, the dog started yipping. "Tell me again why we're driving around town with a mutt?" I said, raising my voice to be heard over the racket.

"He's not a *mutt*. He's a Shih Tzu, and his name is Bark Simpson. Belongs to my son. My grandson Sean named him. Technically, I suppose he's my great-granddog."

I refrained from rolling my eyes. "Okay. So why the pooch?"

"You'll see, Rook."

"This rookie has a name, too. It's Willis," I said, maybe a little too forcefully.

"Yeah, I know." O'Brien paused for effect. "*Rook.*"

"Listen, I—"

"Red!" O'Brien ordered, and the dog stopped in mid-yap.

"How'd you do that?" I asked.

"Do what?"

"Make him stop barking."

"He's exceedingly well trained."

Enough about the dog. Time to get down to business. "You really think Machete Morris and his crew killed Tommy Page? And his murder is connected to the Archer kid's death three years ago?" I knew the Archer case was firmly stuck in O'Brien's craw—an innocent fourteen-year-old kid in the wrong place at the wrong time. O'Brien had been talking about clearing that one—on a daily basis—since I'd started working with him. The one case he felt he needed to solve before he could retire in peace. The white whale. Right now, we were headed to question Morris at the body shop where he worked.

"I don't *think* Morris did it. I *know* so. We've picked him up for half a dozen things over the years, never nailed his ass. Today, I feel a disturbance in the Force. In a good way. We're going to get him."

"How is that going to happen? Some new evidence get discovered?"

"Oh, ye of little faith. I've got something up my sleeve." He started humming under his breath, effectively cutting off any further conversation.

I stared out the passenger side window, imagining all the wild things O'Brien could have up his sleeve. He had the reputation as an out-of-the-box thinker, a creative genius with a badge, and I'd seen flashes of it during my short time with him. Three weeks ago, he'd taken a Ouija board into the interrogation room and had come out with a confession after convincing the suspect that if he didn't own up to the crime he'd committed, evil spirits would punish him worse than the criminal justice system ever could.

As we closed in on Morris, the neighborhoods got seedier. More empty storefronts, more disenfranchised people wandering about, searching for something—anything—to give meaning to their lives.

A few minutes later, O'Brien hung a left off the main drag, and we wove our way through a maze of warehouses and light industrial operations, many out of business. He pulled into a vacant parking lot in front of a boarded-up dry cleaners and killed the engine.

"Where's his shop?" I asked.

O'Brien pointed across the street, one block up. "There. With the green roof."

The dog, who I figured had gone to sleep, started barking again. High-pitched yipping, enough to give someone a headache.

"Red," O'Brien said, and the dog shut up.

"What did—"

O'Brien said, "Green," and the dog began barking.

"Red," he said again, and the dog stopped again. "Grandkids thought it up. Pretty cool, huh?"

"Nice parlor trick. Nice dog, too. But what are we going to do with it?"

"He's not an *it*, he's a *him*. And he has a name." He glared at me. "How would you like it if I called you Rook all the time?"

"You do."

"'Sides the point. How about showing this K-9 a little respect?"

I stared at him a beat, and when he didn't crack a smile, I said, "Sorry."

"Don't apologize to me," he said, tipping his head toward the back seat.

I swiveled in my seat and faced the dog. Bark Simpson was about a foot long, covered in whitish fur. He looked like a dirty mop with a black nose and even darker marble eyes. He bared his teeth, and I was reminded of an angry ex-girlfriend. "Sorry."

The dog barked once.

"He accepts your apology," O'Brien said.

I faced my partner again. "Fine, fine. So, Bark Simpson accepts my apology. Are we just going to leave him in the car? What if he, you know...does his business?" I hoped Shih Tzu was the name of his breed and not descriptive of his actions.

"I told you, he's well trained. Better trained than you, in fact."

I let it slide. Only three more weeks of putting up with O'Brien's insults.

"And it's not too hot, either. He'll be fine here." O'Brien picked up his cell, punched in a number. "You guys ready?" he said after a moment. "Okay. Yeah, two minutes." O'Brien hung up and faced me. "Backup's in place. An alley behind the shop, in case we get a runner. Ready?"

"Ready," I said.

He unbuckled his seat belt. "Let's go, Rook," he said. "Be a good boy."

I assumed that last part was meant for the dog.

Leaving the dog behind, we got out and strolled up to AAAA Auto Body. Only a blind man couldn't tell we were cops. We entered the dingy office and asked the stringy-haired guy behind the counter playing Candy Crush on his phone if Morris was around. Without uttering a word, he nodded at a doorway leading out to the garage bays.

O'Brien flashed a smile, and we followed the guy's nod into the garage proper. Six heads swiveled our way. The guy closest to us put down the buffer in his hand, grinned broadly, and swaggered over.

"What can I do for you, Detective?" he said. "Bang out a few dents?" Immediately, his five grease-stained buddies closed ranks behind him. Several brandished lug wrenches and crowbars. I unsnapped the retention strap on my holster.

"Afternoon, Morris." O'Brien smiled for the second time since entering the garage, which was exactly two smiles more than I would have predicted. "Gentlemen."

Morris's goon squad postured and flexed, but kept quiet.

"We have some questions. About Tommy Page."

"Tragedy." The way Morris said it made me think he wasn't that broken up about what happened to Page.

"You know him?"

"Small neighborhood. Everyone knows everyone," Morris said. Behind him five heads nodded. I had a feeling Morris would be doing all the talking while the others would take care of the posing.

"Heard he ran with you. There was a dustup. Then he turns up face-down in a dumpster."

"Coincidence." Morris shrugged as he said it.

"And is it also a coincidence that you were spotted arguing with Lil' Will Archer right before we found his body, too?"

"Just an unfortunate coincidence." One side of Morris's lip curled up. "But that was years ago."

O'Brien stepped forward, got right up into Morris's face. The goons behind him also moved closer. I tensed, ready.

"Archer was only fourteen years old. A good kid." O'Brien clenched his jaw so tight I could see the ripples from where I stood, six feet away.

"Detective O'Brien," I said, gently. "Easy, now."

O'Brien froze for a long moment, face still just inches from Morris's ugly mug. Then he eased back. "I can prove you killed Tommy Page."

Morris laughed. "Bullshit."

O'Brien turned to me. "Go get Officer Simpson."

Officer Simpson? And was it a good idea to leave O'Brien by himself? "Now?"

"Sure. I'm fine here." O'Brien gave me a little nod of reassurance. "We'll just catch up a bit, talk about the weather, until you return."

I hustled out of the garage and jogged to the car. Bark Simpson was waiting patiently in the back. "Okay, boy. Let's go." I grabbed the leash off the seat and reached for the dog's collar, but he started yipping again, snapping at me whenever I tried to corner him.

"Red," I said, but the dog kept barking. "Red. Red. Red." The yips and yaps continued, and the mutt threw in a few snarls and growls and yelps, too, whenever I got close. "Red. Red. Red. Red. Red."

More barking.

"Orange. Blue. Black. White." I paused to catch my breath, then dove back in. "Chartreuse. Tangerine. Mauve."

The barking continued.

I had visions of Morris and his crew subduing O'Brien and carving him up while I tried every color in the rainbow. "Please stop, Bark Simpson. Please."

The dog sat and barked twice more. I could have sworn it sounded like *Okay*. Then he went quiet.

Seriously? I attached the leash and we trotted back to the garage. As soon as Morris and his gang saw us enter, they started laughing and pointing and falling all over themselves.

"That's Officer Simpson?" Morris managed to spit out between howls. "No wonder crime is up around here."

I handed the leash to O'Brien and he waited patiently for the commotion to die down. Then he spoke calmly. "This is Officer Simpson. He's a cadaver dog."

"He looks alive to me." Morris started sniggering again. Behind him, his crew echoed his laughter.

O'Brien didn't react, merely waited for things to settle. When they did, he cleared his throat. "Once given the command, cadaver dogs can locate dead bodies. They smell death. They can detect the scent of death on a killer's hands. Even months after they've come into contact with a dead person."

All of a sudden, Morris's crew got quiet. Real quiet. Nervous eyes glanced around.

From time to time, our department worked with a cadaver dog, but it wasn't Bark Simpson. In fact, if Bark Simpson could really locate dead people, I'd eat a bag of Alpo. Dry.

"Ready?" O'Brien asked. Without waiting for a response, he bent over and snapped out a command to Bark Simpson. "Go, boy. Green!"

The dog started barking like he'd been poked with a stick, and after about five seconds, the tallest guy in Morris's posse threw a crescent wrench at me and bolted for the back of the garage. I dodged the wrench and sped in pursuit, and when he stumbled into a stack of tires, I tackled him. After cuffing his hands with a zip tie, I hoisted him up and brought him back to where the rest of the group stood. O'Brien had Bark Simpson's leash in one hand and his weapon in the other, trained on Morris's crew.

"Assaulting a police officer with a wrench is a crime," O'Brien said, clearly proud that his ruse worked. "Call backup to come get this guy."

I alerted our backup. A minute later, two uniforms arrived, and one of them hauled the guilty party away.

Morris smirked. "That has nothing to do with me. I told you I was clean, and I am."

Now it was my turn to step forward. "I don't think so. When Detective O'Brien said that cadaver dogs can smell a scent on a killer's hands, I noticed you shoved your hands into your pockets. Like they were covered with the stench of death and you thought stuffing them into your pockets would keep the dog from smelling them."

"You can't prove it."

"We've got your accomplice. I don't think it will take much to get him to roll over on you," I said. "Enjoy your last few breaths of fresh air while you can."

"He's not going to rat on me," Morris said. "No way."

"You don't know Detective O'Brien too well, do you? He can be very persuasive." I glanced at O'Brien, who gave me a small smile and a curt nod, then walked Bark Simpson outside, leaving me with Morris.

"You want to come with me now? Or later? It's just a matter of time before we haul you in for murder."

Morris didn't answer, unless you counted a scowl as an answer.

I left him to stew and joined O'Brien just outside the garage. He was on one knee, ruffling Bark Simpson's fur. "Well done, boy, well done. That's my big fella." He stood and chucked me on the shoulder. "You did a nice job, too, Rook. Or should I say *Detective Willis*?"

Bark Simpson barked twice, and it sounded exactly like *Good boy*.

I bent down and scratched behind his ear. "Right back atcha, Officer Simpson."

Alan Orloff's debut mystery, *Diamonds for the Dead*, was an Agatha Award finalist. His seventh novel, *Running from the Past*, was an Amazon Kindle Scout selection. His short fiction has appeared in numerous publications, including *Jewish Noir*, *Alfred Hitchcock's Mystery Magazine*, *Chesapeake Crimes: Storm Warning*, *Mystery Weekly*, *50 Shades of Cabernet*, *Shotgun Honey*, *Noir at the Salad Bar*, *Black Cat Mystery Magazine*, *Windward: Best New England Crime Stories 2016*, and *The Night of the Flood*. Alan lives in Northern Virginia and teaches fiction-writing at The Writer's Center (Bethesda, MD). He loves cake and arugula, but not together. www.alanorloff.com

A SNOWBALL'S CHANCE

BY ELEANOR CAWOOD JONES

Gabriel the angelfish swam to the front of the tank, wiggling excitedly in anticipation of a delicious fish flakes dinner.

"Are you hungry, Gabriel?" Cindy cooed, lifting the top of the tank. She sprinkled high-protein fish food liberally over the water and watched as Gabriel quickly rose to the top to snatch his food as soon as it hit the surface. "Do you want some dinner? Here you go, buddy. Good boy. So pretty."

From atop the ladder where he was carefully faux painting the wall above the fireplace, Bede grinned at her, his teeth startlingly white in his dark face. At well over six feet and not a thin man, his figure on the ladder was imposing.

"I tell you what, young lady," he said in his musical Jamaican lilt. "If you ever meet a mon, and you treat that mon even half as well as you treat that feesh, that will be one *very* lucky mon!"

Cindy grinned back—and up—at him. "You think so?"

"I know so." His dark eyes twinkled.

"I don't know why you say that. I'm just giving him his dinner." Gabriel was still wigwagging around his tank. His little molly brothers and sisters darted under him trying to catch the flakes he'd missed as they floated to the bottom, where they covered a hodgepodge of colorful castles and chess pieces like snow, drifting pinkish-white against the shiny blue gravel.

Cindy cocked her head and admired her angelfish. "Still, he is gorgeous, isn't he?" Gabriel swam about majestically as if sensing that the shadow who brought him food on a regular basis was talking about him. At least Cindy assumed Gabriel was a "him." He was about five inches tall as well as long—not counting his flowing fins above, below, and behind—soft black with silver stripes, and the usual perky fish lips. Gabriel was a stunning example of piscine health.

Grinning, she told Bede exactly that. "I know he's just a fish, Bede, but he's so handsome. And so responsive. Don't tell *me* fish can't recognize their owners."

Bede's smile grew wider. "I'd pay attention to you, too, if you fed me twice a day like clockwork, hired someone to clean my house every week, and made sure I always had fresh water. And bought me castles."

Cindy laughed. "Hey, that wall over the fireplace is looking good." She hadn't been sure about the faux brick design that her artsy cousin Bettina had talked her into trying, but Bede was turning her into a believer. "I might even build a fire next winter under a wall like that."

"Oh, yes? Make sure you consult with young Gabriel here before you do," Bede teased her. "You don't want heem to be too warm, do you now?"

If Cindy consulted with anyone, it would be her brother, Geoff. She'd been housesitting his 1950s-style, split-level house in Northern Virginia while he was managing construction projects in California. Two years before, he'd been kind enough to take her in. She'd been looking for a job after grad school while at the same time coming off a bad breakup that didn't bear thinking about. She'd landed her dream job at the Library of Congress the year before, and since her brother refused to charge her any rent, she was putting some of her income into his house, getting it rehabbed inside and out, as a thank you.

He'd given her his full blessing as long as anyone she hired came with a license and recommendation and, of course, a full background check. She was his only baby sister, he often reminded her. She was in her late thirties now, so that always made Cindy smile.

Bede had come highly recommended by the neighborhood homeowners association, and she was enjoying his company as well as the work he was doing. He'd been there every weekday for more than three weeks, and she was already dreading the time when he would complete the work and move on to the next lucky homeowner.

"Now that you've fed your gentleman feesh, you should get ready for your gentleman human date," Bede told her, raising an eyebrow and flashing his infectious grin.

Cindy sighed. "I don't know if I even want to go, Bede."

"Why, what is it, young lady?"

"I don't know. Doug's nice and all, it's just that, well…"

"No chemistry, perhaps?"

"Maybe. But it's something else too. Something's, I don't know, *off.*"

"Ah." Bede nodded wisely and patted himself on the stomach with the hand not holding a paintbrush. "It's your gut. Always trust your gut, girl. Your gut instinct. It does not lie."

And just like that, with a jolt, Cindy remembered Snowball, her pet bunny from childhood. She quickly brushed the memory aside; what on earth had brought Snowball to mind? There was barely time for a shower and to throw on a dress and sandals before Doug would come knocking at the door. She wasn't looking forward to it.

She heard Bede's voice behind her as she headed down the hall to her room. "Let him down easy, my young friend." He paused. "Feesh aren't the only creatures with feelings, you know."

* * * *

That night, after taking Bede's advice and gently breaking things off with Doug, Cindy slept restlessly and dreamed about long-forgotten events. A vivid and disturbing dream woke her. It was about the time her white rabbit, Snowball, had gotten out of her hutch, and Cindy had gone searching for her beloved pet when she wasn't supposed to leave the house. About a man with a gold tooth who helped her. And a man named George Ramsey, who had gone missing the same day Snowball did. And about George Ramsey's distraught wife, who'd been a friend of Cindy's mom. Cindy remembered how much she had liked her.

There was no more sleeping for Cindy. Drenched in sweat, but entirely awake, she lay in bed long before her alarm went off, thinking, remembering.

* * * *

"Snowball! Where are you? Come home!" A skinny eight-year-old in shorts and a Boston Celtics jersey dragged the toe of her sneakered foot across the asphalt on the driveway. Cindy had already caught Frisky Bunny, who never strayed too far from home but still managed to chew his way out of the hutch occasionally. He had paused under the sweet gum tree in the backyard just long enough for her to scoop him up and deposit him inside the garage next to a bowl of raw carrots.

But Snowball Bunny, his sister, had made a beeline down the driveway and into the road. The previous month she'd made it all the way down the street to the park, but Daddy had been there and they'd found Snowball in the undergrowth among the crocuses, having a fine time exploring and eating green plants. Together they'd cornered Snowball and borne her, reluctant and wiggling, back to the safety of the backyard hutch.

Cindy sighed. Daddy had sworn he'd gotten the hutch door back on tight, too. And she'd been careful to latch it just right. But Frisky the escape artist had sharp teeth, strong back legs, and a lot of spare time. And now his sweet, pink-eyed sister was missing.

Cindy sniffed, the tears starting. Daddy was at work and Mom had started back to school. Cindy wasn't supposed to leave the yard by herself for any reason. If only her brother Geoff were here, but he'd gone off to college again. She didn't understand why anyone would want to be an engineer, especially if it meant leaving her behind.

There were cats and dogs in the neighborhood, and Daddy had warned her about hawks, too. Snowball's rescue was more important than getting in trouble, she reasoned. Besides, she would have the bunny back home eating carrots before Mom or Daddy got home. Nobody would be the wiser, not even the horrible babysitter who lounged around inside the house eating doughnuts and watching soaps.

Just a few minutes, Cindy promised herself, deciding. She took off at a dead run toward the forested paths that made up little Mastenbrook Park.

Cindy was almost to the park when she heard the scream. She speeded up, almost choking on her tears. Rabbits screamed like people, she knew. Frisky had once been cornered by a big gold dog; the poor rabbit had screamed so loudly she'd dreamed about it for weeks.

"Snowball!" She ran deep into the park, down the paved path where the brush had grown so thick you couldn't see far.

She heard the screaming again and this time something worse—dogs snarling and barking.

She dodged right, off the path and into a thicket of shrubs, tripping over a stump. She struggled to her feet, crawled over the trunk of a fallen tree and a pile of rocks, and stopped short. Poor Snowball was stuck in a bush, struggling, caught in the crotch of a branch near the ground. Four dogs had surrounded the bush, barking, growling, lunging. Snowball fought to escape and screamed again.

It was too much to bear. Legs bleeding from her struggle through the undergrowth, Cindy dashed forward to save her pet, only to be stopped in her tracks when something grabbed her from behind, catching her shirt and practically lifting her off the ground. Now her own screams joined Snowball's.

"No!" A man's voice behind her. "Stay here! Stay back! I'll get him!"

She could smell him now. Mothballs and sweat and stale beer. "Let me go!" she screamed. "The dogs are murdering Snowball! Let me go!"

He shook her, turned her around, and bent down to her face. "Stay still. I'll get him. Stay here! I mean it!"

She sniffled, nodded, and stepped back. He let go of her shirt and waded into the fray, snatching up a large branch as he went. He swung at the dogs, connecting with the largest two, normally friendly black labs Cindy knew belonged to the Ramseys, her neighbors on the next block. Chastened, the labs whimpered and backed off. A little tan-and-white mixed breed that Cindy didn't recognize backed away as well, but continued to bark. The man reached in and snatched Snowball by the scruff of her neck, but not before Benji, the little yappy terrier from down the street, dashed in and bit the stranger deeply on the hand.

The man swung his branch at the dog, hard, and connected. Benji yelped and ran, limping.

Suddenly everything was quiet and the smelly man was putting Snowball into her arms. She could feel Snowball's heart beating impossibly hard, her pink eyes wide, her mouth open, gasping for breath. Her white fur was filthy.

"Just hold him still for a minute," the man told her. "Till he figures out he's safe." He dropped the stick and pulled a grubby handkerchief out of his coat pocket, wrapping his bloody hand in it.

Cindy tried not to clutch the panting bunny too hard even though her instinct was to hold Snowball tight. "Thank you," she managed to whisper through grateful tears. "Snowball's a she, though."

"Not a problem, little lady."

Cindy stared up at his dirty, wrinkled face into the brightest pair of blue eyes she'd ever seen.

"Are you the homeless?" she asked the old man.

He smiled, then threw his head back and laughed. "*The* homeless? Yes, I guess I am at that. Oh, well. It beats being called a tramp."

"Like *Lady and the Tramp*?"

He smiled again, and a single gold tooth flashed in the sunlight. "That's right, honey, exactly like that. Now you get that she-bunny home and give her some food and water. Tomorrow she'll be right as rain."

Cindy had never seen a gold tooth before, nor stood next to someone quite so smelly, but she wasn't afraid of the man at all. She adjusted Snowball in her arms. "Thanks again, mister." She looked again at his hand wrapped in the dirty handkerchief. "I'm sorry Benji bit you."

"It was my pleasure to help. And I'll be fine. Keep her locked up tight, you hear?"

"I will. Promise."

"Oh, and little girl? Don't blame the dogs or be mad at them. It's their nature."

Cindy, thinking that over, nodded reluctantly. Then she turned and headed for home without stopping.

Hoping none of the neighborhood busybodies were watching, Cindy lugged her heavy but calmer pet home and put her in the garage with Frisky. After a bit, she went into the house—ignoring the snoring babysitter on the couch—and grabbed a roll of paper towels. She filled a saucepan full of warm, sudsy water to take to the garage. Snowball was going to have a bath, and that was that.

Although she worried that someone might question her absence or ask how her pet got so dirty, it turned out the town had more important things to worry about that night than an eight-year-old truant and her pet rabbit. Mr. Ramsey, the man who owned the black labs, had gone missing and it looked like someone had broken into his house. He hadn't returned to work after his lunch hour and no one, not even his wife, knew where he'd gone. Even though it was too soon to file a missing persons report, a uniformed policeman showed up at their door in typical small-town fashion, asking neighbors when they had seen Mr. Ramsey last. Cindy, holding Daddy's hand, told the policeman she didn't remember the last time she saw Mr. Ramsey.

"But I visit Mrs. Ramsey every Saturday," she volunteered. "She gives me cake. Then we watch TV and talk while she's ironing. She irons all the time." Cindy wrinkled her nose at the thought of being cooped up inside with a hot iron. "I get to play with the dogs, too. She lets me throw balls for them in the living room."

The young blond policeman smiled at her.

"The Ramseys don't have any children," Mom explained. "Mrs. Ramsey is always telling me how much she enjoys Cindy's visits because Mr. Ramsey works at his car dealership all weekend."

Cindy knew her parents would never allow her to visit the Ramseys if Mr. Ramsey was in the house. Cindy's instincts told her he was not a good man. She didn't understand why gentle Mrs. Ramsey had such a mean husband. One day Mr. Ramsey had come home early from work, yelled at his wife for having company, and scowled at her with his dark eyes. Mrs. Ramsey, who seemed frightened, had sent Cindy straight home. She hadn't even gotten cake or played with the dogs, and she didn't like leaving Mrs. Ramsey, but she went.

And now mean Mr. Ramsey had disappeared. And Cindy wasn't the least bit sorry.

Despite what Daddy thought, Cindy was old enough to understand what was going on. Between sneaking peeks at the newspaper and overhearing what her parents discussed in hushed voices, she knew Mr. Ramsey was still missing several days later, and on the day he disappeared blood had been found in the Ramseys' kitchen. Money was missing from its hiding place in the cookie jar. Chairs were overturned. Mrs. Ramsey had been questioned at length.

Mom and Daddy talked quietly at night about homeless vagrants. Surely a stranger had done this horrible thing, Mother said.

Cindy knew she wasn't supposed to know about the blood so she didn't talk about it. And she didn't dare admit that she'd been in the park near the Ramseys' house and talked to a homeless man with a gold tooth on the same day Mr. Ramsey disappeared. She knew how much trouble *she'd* be in. Somehow she knew the smelly man was a good man, even if he did need a bath and a haircut—and maybe a better dentist. She wondered if he'd taken care of his hand where Benji had bit him. Her grandmother had read *Old Yeller* to her and she knew about rabies. It worried her.

The following Saturday, Mom and Cindy took a casserole over to Mrs. Ramsey. "Oh, Margaret!" Mom said, hugging her friend. While Mom comforted her, Cindy hugged the dogs, who couldn't help their nature.

There was no ironing board in sight.

After that, the weekly visits to Mrs. Ramsey tapered off. Cindy still saw her at the market, out walking the dogs, and at church. Mrs. Ramsey's footsteps seemed lighter, Cindy noticed, and she smiled more often.

Then something happened to make Cindy forget all about the Ramseys. Something that changed her life forever in the saddest of ways. That fall, Daddy was killed on the way home from work when a truck overturned right in front of him. With Daddy gone, Geoff took the semester off from college and came home.

Her brother helped Mom sell the house, and they all moved to a smaller place nearby, but the ache of missing Daddy went on. Cindy tried not to let Mom and Geoff see how sad she was, especially when there was no room for Snowball and Frisky in their new home. Her beloved pets went to live at a farm owned by one of Geoff's college friends, and he reported they had settled in fine. Mom let Cindy get an aquarium for her bedroom, though, and thus began her lifelong affair with owning—and pampering—all kinds of small fish. Two years later, Mom married the new minister at their church. Life was good for the family. Slowly the memories faded.

* * * *

Until last night. Tired of tossing and turning in bed, racked by nightmares, Cindy got up, made a pot of coffee, and switched on her computer. Wondering what had happened to George Ramsey, she powered up Google. He had never turned up, she learned. His body had never been found, and the blood on the kitchen floor of his house was the last evidence that he had ever existed. Thirty years later it was a case so cold she could find no articles about the crime in the last ten years. Mr. Ramsey was all but forgotten.

Searching county real-estate records online, she learned that the Ramsey house hadn't changed hands since the time Mr. Ramsey went missing. She wondered if Mrs. Ramsey was still there. Mrs. Ramsey was so nice, and the cake was always good, and the dogs were fun to play with. But something nagged at Cindy. Something about Mastenbrook Park. She felt uneasy, haunted by the image of a pile of rocks at one end of a fallen tree, near where the man with the gold tooth had saved Snowball. Why were rocks stacked up there at all? Was the rock pile real, or had she dreamed it?

"Trust your gut, girl," Bede had said.

Cindy got up from her computer, took a shower, and dressed quickly in jeans and an old blouse she normally wore only when she did housework. She brewed a fresh pot of coffee, washed last night's dishes, and put some food in the fish tank, greeted as always by the wriggling and appreciative Gabriel. Just before eight a.m. she poured two cups of coffee and got out sugar and half and half, and when Bede arrived, she invited him to join her at the kitchen table to tell him, from an adult's viewpoint, and from her gut, about her childhood memory. All about Snowball, the park, the man with the gold tooth, and her old friend Mrs. Ramsey.

The coffee was long gone, and the rehab work forgotten, when Cindy and Bede left the house and drove away in her car.

* * * *

"So you don't think your gold-toothed friend did thees." Bede was sweating. He'd just helped her move a backbreaking pile of very real rocks from underneath the root end of a fallen tree. They never would have seen the rocks if they hadn't been looking for them, almost hidden in old undergrowth and new trees.

Cindy had a sense that she had stepped back in time. She remembered the look and smell of the strange man, the stains on his coat, and, mostly, the amount of blood on his hand as he wrapped it in his dirty handkerchief. Way too much blood, it occurred to her suddenly, for a little yappy dog to have drawn with a single bite.

"No, I don't think the gold-toothed man did this. But I blame *you* for my even being here," she said to Bede. "You woke something inside me last night. You said to always go with my gut, and my gut said to come back here. Now I know the rock pile from my dream is real."

"What's under it is new to you, though, young Cindy." Bede sounded sad.

Together, they had moved the rocks and dug beneath them. Several inches down, they unearthed a bundle the size of a duffle bag, sealed up in a triple layer of garbage bags. Bede used his utility knife to slice the bags open, and the dank, mildewy smell made Cindy wince. She watched, hardly daring to breathe, as Bede peeled back the layers to reveal an ancient, rust-covered steam iron whose cord had rotted to the bare wires; a wadded-up, soiled apron and a housedress; and darkly stained and soiled men's pants, dress shirt, and underpants. Cindy wondered if the dark stains were blood, especially the splatters on the shirt collar. There were several similarly stained towels as well.

Cindy closed her eyes and took a deep breath. "I'm sure this was the apron Mrs. Ramsey used to wear when she was ironing and baking," she said. "It had little blue birds embroidered on the pockets, just like this one."

She opened her eyes. "I don't know what to do. I feel eight years old again."

Bede studied her carefully. "There's no body, but I think we can assume there was one and that it was put elsewhere. Do you think your lady friend with the iron could have done thees?"

"I don't see how. Her husband was big and strong and intimidating. Mrs. Ramsey was always so gentle, almost mousy."

"Even the gentlest among us can be driven to great anger, Cindy."

Cindy sighed. "You think we should go to the police, don't you? I'm sorry I put you in this situation." She straightened her spine. "I don't want to do anything about this right now. I need to think. It's been almost thirty years. A few more days won't matter." She paused and glanced up at his worried face. "Will you help me put the rocks back?"

"Child." Bede patted her on the arm. "I've seen worse and dealt with worse." Cindy saw untold sadness and wisdom in his eyes.

As carefully as possible, they returned the bundle to the hole and restacked the rocks on top. Together, they climbed through the underbrush back to the path. It was early in this bedroom community and they hadn't encountered anyone, not even a solitary jogger, by the time they reached Cindy's car.

Bede didn't ask any questions when they pulled up in front of a neat brick ranch-style house not far from the park. Cindy sensed him behind her, following as she trudged up to the front door, each step propelling her forward feeling like a mile. When no one responded immediately to her knock, she rang the doorbell.

Mrs. Ramsey, looking sweet but decades older, answered the door, still in a robe, carrying an almost empty cup of coffee. Her soft white hair was in disarray. Her gentle brown eyes met Cindy's, and recognition slowly dawned. Wordlessly, she opened her arms and Cindy walked into them. They held each other for some time before Mrs. Ramsey noticed Bede and opened the door wider.

"I'm Margaret Newman, although Cindy knows me as Margaret Ramsey," she said. "And if you're a friend of Cindy's, you're a friend of mine." She stood back. "Won't you come in? We'll have coffee."

Bede followed Cindy into the front hall.

Cindy went straight to the living room, feeling almost like it was a homecoming. "Where's the ironing board, Mrs. Newman?" she called after their hostess, still adjusting to her old friend's new name.

"I made sure my second husband was willing to take all his shirts to the dry cleaner," came the answer from the kitchen. "I'm sorry you missed Fred, actually. He's on the golf course today." Mrs. Ramsey—regardless of her new last name, she'd always be Mrs. Ramsey to Cindy—entered the living room and carefully placed a loaded tray in the center of the coffee table. "Won't you both sit down, and Cindy, you can introduce me."

"This is my friend, Bede. He's an artist."

At that Bede grinned widely, reached out, and shook Mrs. Ramsey's hand.

"Nice to meet you, Bede," she said. "And Cindy, considering you're all grown up now, why don't you call me Margaret?"

Cindy smiled gently at her old friend. "Margaret it is. But I wish I'd come by for a more pleasant reason."

Margaret set her coffee cup down carefully on the table. "Oh? Why is that?"

"When I was a child," Cindy said, "I lost my pet rabbit, Snowball. I wasn't supposed to go out of the yard, but the rabbit liked the park, and I sneaked down there to find her. She was being attacked by dogs, but a kind, homeless man with a gold tooth saved her. He might have been scary to other people, but he was a hero to me. I never told a soul. And I had pretty much forgotten all about it until last night when I dreamed about it as clear as if it was yesterday." Cindy paused and took a deep breath. "It was the same day Mr. Ramsey disappeared."

Margaret's eyes filled with tears. "I always wondered if you'd come back to see me one day. You were always a bright, perceptive child, observing things other people didn't see."

"Did you know—" Cindy began.

Mrs. Ramsey raised a hand. "That homeless man was my grandfather. I never told anyone that either. I was ashamed of him. He'd always been unstable, and it got worse as the years went by. It was a huge point of contention in my first marriage. George was big on appearances. When he'd catch Grandfather coming to visit me during the day, he would blow his top. George was a tightwad, too. Didn't like me sharing our food with bums, he said."

She grimaced. "Remember the constant ironing? He wouldn't let me spend the little bit of money it would have taken to have the dry cleaner launder his clothing, even though business at the car dealership was good. Besides, women were placed on this earth to serve their husbands, he always said. Cooking and cleaning were part of the job description." She shuddered.

All of a sudden, Cindy couldn't speak. She looked over at Bede pleadingly. Bede nodded, then reached out to take Margaret's hand.

"In the park where Cindy lost her rabbit, we found a fallen tree with a hole under it. The hole was filled with rocks, but we dug them out and found a garbage bag."

Margaret clutched his hand and closed her eyes. "Tell me. I need to know."

"We found stained men's clothing, towels, a housedress, an apron Cindy says she remembers you wearing, and a heavy steam iron."

"George…?" her voice faltered.

Bede shook his head. "There was no body."

Tears slipped down Margaret's face. "I never knew what Grandfather did with the iron and the clothes. I never knew what he did with the body. I never saw him again after the day he saved my life."

She opened her eyes, let go of Bede's hand, and settled her hands carefully in her lap. "George liked to hit me. I tried to hide it in all the usual ways. Long-sleeved shirts, not leaving the house if the bruises were too bad, avoiding close friendships in case people asked too many questions. Your mother suspected, Cindy. She was always good to me. She knew that your visits meant the world to me because while you were with me, George wouldn't come home and…" She let the thought die. "George and I couldn't have children. Maybe that was just as well."

"What happened that day, Mrs. Ramsey?" Cindy asked, forgetting to call Margaret by her first name or new last name.

"Grandfather stopped by unexpectedly at lunchtime. I never knew when I was going to see him. I put the dogs outside, made him a sandwich, and was sitting with him in the kitchen. Just sitting, talking, that's all. George came home for lunch, walking over from the dealership like he did once in a blue moon. I hadn't expected him either. He found Grandfather with me and lost his temper. He shoved me aside and threatened Grandfather with a knife."

More tears ran down her face, and neither Cindy nor Bede moved or spoke.

"He cut Grandfather badly on one hand. That's when I lost it. My grandfather never hurt a soul. I was afraid George was going to kill him. I rushed to the living room, got my iron, and hit George in the back of the head with it as hard as I could. And when he fell down, God help me, I kept hitting him—over and over and over—until Grandfather stopped me, pulled me away.

"Grandfather spread towels on the floor so I could step away from the body without leaving footprints. He sent me upstairs to shower and waited outside the bathroom door as I stripped, and handed my blood-splattered clothing out to him. After my shower, he sent me to bed, almost like a child. Told me to stay there while he 'took care of things.' He promised he was going to give me my life back."

She sighed deeply. "I'd never seen him so lucid, so focused. When I came back downstairs, my clothes were gone, the iron was gone, the body was gone, and Grandfather was gone. In spite of our best efforts, there were still bloodstains on the floor. Earlier, I'd been working in the garden in the empty lot down the street, so I went back there, muddied up my shoes, and tracked dirt into the kitchen, especially on top of where the blood was, as if I'd come home and found the blood that way. Then I called 9-1-1, told the operator that there was blood and broken things in the kitchen, that there had definitely been someone in the house, and that I was frightened." She paused. "I *was* frightened. That much was the truth. Then the operator told me to get out of the house right away and run to a neighbor's, and I did. The rest you know."

Margaret reached over, picked up her coffee cup, and took a sip. "I swore, Cindy, from that day on, if I didn't go to jail, I was never going to iron another blessed shirt in my entire life. And I haven't. And I have missed my grandfather to this very day."

She put the cup down and stood. "I'm ready to go to the police station with you."

"Sit down, Margaret," Cindy said. "We're not going anywhere right this second."

Margaret sat. "Why ever not?"

"Because when you grow up not everything is black and white," Cindy said. "You've lived a good life. I know all about your work with the young people in your church because I read up on you last night online. You were always good to me. You were defending your grandfather. Your first husband, from what I understand, was a horrible, horrible man."

Bede nodded. "A clear case of self-defense. I told Miss Cindy thees would be her call, no matter what. She and I, well, it turns out we operate on the same wavelength, especially where justice is concerned."

Cindy managed a smile. "The only time I ever met your grandfather he waded into a pack of frantic dogs to save a beloved pet for a scared little girl." She paused. "I lost my father later that same year. I'm glad, looking back, that your grandfather did that great kindness for me and kept me from losing my pet as well. Snowball was a stupid, fat rabbit with no sense at all." Her eyes filled with tears. "But I loved her."

Cindy gestured around the house. "It's been thirty years, Margaret. Look at your home, at the life you've built with the man who loves you. Okay, so now I know. And Bede knows. But as far as I am concerned, it stays here and it ends here."

Bede nodded and they both stood up.

"I don't know what to say." Margaret sat still on the couch, her hands in her lap, looking small and frail.

Cindy leaned over to hug her. "Sometimes you have to do the right thing. This is the right thing. Your husband was a cruel man. That was his nature. You killed him defending your grandfather. Try as I might, I just can't see the crime in that." She glanced over at Bede. "Call it gut instinct."

"Will you be all right, mees?" Bede studied Margaret with concern.

"I'll be fine, I think. Just fine," Margaret answered. Cindy leaned over and hugged her once more, then she and Bede let themselves out.

They were quiet during the drive back to Cindy's house. She didn't know what to say. Somehow thanking Bede didn't seem to cover it. But she knew in her heart he would never breathe a word about Margaret and her secret, and right now that was all that mattered.

Cindy jumped when Bede spoke. "You've met my wife?"

"Your wife? Yes, I've met your wife. What about her?"

"She's Irish. Got herself a son with red hair. My redheaded stepchild." Bede grinned. "She's gotten it into her head that you two might like each other. She's invented an excuse for the boy to come over with my lunch today, so he can check you out."

"Dear God, Bede, how can you think of that at a time like this?" Cindy wanted the silence to continue. In a way, she felt like she was grieving. Not the loss of that horrid man, George Ramsey, but something different. Her father, maybe; her childhood, definitely; innocence, perhaps.

Bede patted her hand where it rested on the steering wheel. "Dear girl," he said, "the living should go on living, take each day that is given to them, make the most of it. Suppose you like our redheaded boy. Suppose you go to dinner and a movie with him as a favor to your friend Bede, help keep peace at Bede's house with his lovely wife. Suppose you find something new to think about."

Cindy thought about it. She thought about going home, taking a shower, rubbing Neosporin into the scratches on her hands from the undergrowth at the park. She thought about watching Gabriel swim happily in his tank, living in this moment and anticipating that everything would be fine in the next. She thought about Margaret, wrestling with her ghosts, living with her new husband, and making regular visits to the neighborhood dry cleaner.

"We solved a cold case today, didn't we, Bede?"

"We did. We dealt with a cold case, but you have a warm heart, my girl. Your feesh knows it, your family knows it, I know it, and Margaret always knew it. Now do an old man a favor, and go out with my boy."

Slowly, without taking her eyes off the road, Cindy nodded. The past hadn't been so bad, all in all. The future might be even better. She was ready to take a chance.

Eleanor Cawood Jones is the author of *A Baker's Dozen: 13 Tales of Murder and More* and *Death is Coming to Town: Four Murderous Holiday Tales*. Her story "Killing Kippers" appears in *Malice Domestic 11: Murder Most Conventional*. She began writing in elementary school, using a Number 2 pencil to craft stories starring her stuffed animals. A former newspaper reporter, Eleanor is a travel consultant in Northern Virginia who spends her spare time telling people how to pronounce Cawood (Kay'-wood). She's working on several crime-centered short stories and a cozy mystery series, and intends to write romances, but her characters won't cooperate. Learn more at www.GirlsGoneChillin.com.

HUNTER'S MOON

BY ROBIN TEMPLETON

"It isn't almost heaven, Rupert, it *is* heaven." And then to myself I added, "I hope."

Rupert poked his nose through the cedar rails of our cabin balcony. I'd already taken my Irish setter for a chilly predawn romp, and he was going to have to put off any further mountain exploration until I'd finished my coffee. A mid-October Virginia sunrise over the Shenandoah River was not to be missed. Red and gold trees were on fire with the morning light, and a pine-scented, westerly breeze mingled with the pleasure of sipping my favorite dark roasted brew.

I smiled affectionately at my cup and at Rupert. The coffee mug had a Hogwarts crest on it, and my daughter had named her puppy after Rupert Grint, the English actor who played Ron Weasley in the Harry Potter movies. In the early morning light, Rupert's coat did look like Ron Weasley's tousled red hair. But the dog was ten now, Lindsey was a sophomore in college, and I was trying to begin a new life without Lindsey and without her dad.

"It's just you and me, Rupert." He wagged his tail, and pushed his head under my hand so I could scratch behind his ears. I put my coffee on a wicker end table, kneeled down, and buried my face in his fur. More tears? Damn. Hadn't I cried enough? When Lindsey left for college, and then, the very next week, when Mark left to live with his executive assistant?

Clearing out our Arlington home had been the worst. Alimony and my part-time job as a librarian didn't provide enough money to hang onto the house. It took me over a year to sort through the belongings and the memories of a twenty-year marriage. Neither Mark nor Lindsey seemed to care about any of it. They had already moved on. Only Rupert was there to witness my constant anguish: what to keep, what to give away, what to sell—and what to burn.

I gave Rupert one last pat and picked up the coffee mug again. Lindsey had kept her drawing pens in it when she was a little girl. She no longer wanted the mug, but I did. I wanted the memory of my daughter transported by the magic of the J.K. Rowling books. And I desperately needed a little magic of my own.

"Come on, Rupert. The sun is up. I'm ready to explore."

* * * *

Raven Valley in the Blue Ridge Mountains was a far cry from Washington, DC, and its suburbs. But the very good news was that even after the 2008 housing crash, selling our home in Arlington gave me the means to take a year's lease on a beautiful little cabin, and still have plenty of money to live on until I decided what I wanted to do after my midlife crisis. Many people considered me a fairly youthful and even attractive forty-two-year-old—I could tell that by how Keith Renwick lit up whenever I walked into his general store.

"Hello, Carolyn! It's a fine day, isn't it? Did you see the sunrise this morning? You've got the best view on the mountain."

Keith was not only the owner of the general store, he was also my landlord. And my insurance agent. In a pinch he could probably set a broken leg, birth a calf, and pull a rabbit or two out of his ever-present porkpie hat. But Keith wasn't the kind of magic I was looking for.

The store owner extracted a dog biscuit from a large glass jar. Rupert dutifully sat and put one paw out. Keith laughed appreciatively and gave him the biscuit. "Good dog! He sure is one smart pup."

I let Keith and Rupert bond over tricks and biscuits while I put groceries into my basket. Shopping was easy when I only had to feed myself and a dog. I selected a dusty bottle of overpriced shampoo, and paused before adding a medium-brown hair dye to my purchases. I kept thinking I'd let my natural hair grow out, but every time I saw a widening band of gray at my scalp, I chickened out. Mark's thirty-year-old trophy babe was already making me feel old before my time. I didn't need to see my mother in the mirror.

Next to the hair dye was a display of earrings unlike any I'd ever seen. They were made of copper and feathers and beads, but the designs were—I don't know—almost otherworldly. As I rotated the display, each pair seemed more fascinating than the next. But one pair held my eyes.

The artist had created a copper heart, then cut the center out so that one earring was the outline of the heart while the other was the cutout center. A piece of turquoise hung from the tip of the smaller heart, almost like a dewdrop or a tear. The larger heart had turquoise and a tiny black feather hanging through the cutout portion. Onyx and turquoise beads decorated the wire that fit into the ear.

As I looked in the nearby mirror and held the earrings up to my face, I liked how the turquoise made my eyes look blue instead of gray, and the copper brought out the red in my hair. After putting the earrings in my basket, I even exchanged my usual mousy-brown hair color for one with auburn highlights.

After tallying my selections, Keith pointed to my jewelry purchase. "I'm glad somebody likes these. I thought they were fishing lures when she first brought them in."

I pulled my wallet from my purse. "She?"

"Haven't you met Crazy Marla yet? Hell, she lives just down the road from you."

"What makes her crazy?"

"She likes animals better than people. Talks to them more, too."

I patted Rupert's head. That didn't seem crazy to me.

"Well, I like the earrings. Maybe I'll pay her a visit. I'll let Rupert introduce us."

Keith laughed. "Well, you know mountain folk." He tapped his hat to communicate that "mountain folk" were all a little crazy. "I've only lived here eight years, but old Sam who delivers our firewood swears Marla's grandma was a witch and a shapeshifter."

I'd read Native American folklore about shapeshifters—Navajo skinwalkers or the Ojibwe Deer Woman. "Does Marla seem friendly?"

Keith's brow furrowed. "I can't say I really know her. But, yeah, she's sometimes friendly. I even asked her out to dinner one time. She didn't talk much, didn't ask questions. But it was like after a half hour she knew me better than I knew me. Spooky. Now I just see her when she drops off things to sell or picks up supplies.

Sometimes she makes extra money by leading groups of hikers, or hiring herself out as a fishing guide. Nobody knows these mountains like Marla."

A denim-clad man carrying an open beer can pushed through the door. He didn't seem drunk, but he didn't seem quite right either. I noticed a leather-sheathed hunting knife on his right hip. His dirty-blond hair was cut close to his head with the exception of one thin, long braid, decorated with what looked like an eagle feather. A small black swastika was tattooed on the side of his neck. Lovely.

"Hey, Pops! How much for a six-pack of Bud?"

Keith gestured toward the beverage section. "We have different types and different sizes. The prices are on the case."

Feather Braid sauntered forward. I pulled back and Rupert barked a warning. The man grinned and made his way around me to the refrigerator.

I wanted to leave, but something told me there was safety in numbers—for me, for Keith, and even for Rupert. An Irish setter was known for being friendly, but Rupert's tail wasn't wagging. I set my groceries down and held Rupert's collar with my right hand.

Still grinning, the man slid an eighteen-pack of Budweiser Select on the counter. Winking at me, he said, "I could use a little company. Get rid of that mutt of yours, and we can have a party."

Rupert let out a low growl. Feather Braid laughed, pointed at a pack of Marlboros, and pushed two twenties across the counter. Keith's hands shook as he handed the customer his cigarettes and counted out the change.

The man seemed to be enjoying the tension. Instead of leaving, he ripped the cigarette pack open with his teeth, pulled a book of matches from his breast pocket, tapped out a single cigarette, lit it, and inhaled deeply. On the exhale, he threw the matches into my grocery bag and leered at me. "Suit yourself, sugar, but if you change your mind, the address of my motel is on the matches—room fourteen."

Rupert growled again. As the man picked up his beer, he added, "I'd keep that mongrel at home, lady. Hunting season is already open in these parts—somebody might just mistake him for a deer or a coyote."

His laugh went through me like an icicle. I kneeled next to Rupert and held him close while I watched the odious jackal set off on foot toward Route 32.

Keith helped me to my feet with still-shaking hands. "Carolyn, are you okay? I'm sure sorry about that. I was afraid if I said something, he might pull that gutting knife on one of us. But I think he was all talk."

I didn't know what I thought. For the first time since I'd arrived in Raven Valley, I was missing my pretty little Arlington house, where I'd known and trusted everyone in my neighborhood. And where there were regular police patrols. I didn't even know how far away the sheriff's office was from my cabin. Crazy Marla was probably my closest neighbor.

"Well, Rupert and I are going to lock our doors. That's for damned sure. I thought hunting season didn't open until November."

Keith shook his head. "Guns are in November. Archery season opened yesterday."

* * * *

I was grateful when it rained later that afternoon. With a log burning brightly in my fireplace, a pot of tea on the stove, and Rupert at my feet, it seemed cozy and safe inside. I'd used the stranger's matches to light my fire, and then Googled the location of "Hunter's Haven Lodge and Tavern." It was over three miles from my cabin—I would have preferred fifty miles, but at least it wasn't next door.

While still at my computer, I realized I was curious about "Crazy Marla," who really was my neighbor. I had put on my new earrings as soon as I got home and loved them. They reminded me of my teenage years—before I'd married Mark, and *long* before I'd become president of the local PTA and an expert at coordinating bake sales for any occasion. Marla's website address was on the back of my earring packaging, and when I pulled it up, I laughed out loud.

Marla's site was as delightful as her earrings. She clearly liked to feed the impression that she came from a magical and mysterious lineage. At the top was a holographic impression of the moon, with the image constantly changing phases and giving a corresponding calendar. The hunter's moon was due tomorrow night. I never paid much attention to such things in Arlington, but here in the mountains, a full moon drew you outdoors to watch the show—orange to yellow, yellow to white. It was magical.

In addition to jewelry, Marla McKenna created beeswax candles, tapestry purses, potions, natural honey, and venison sausage. She was also available, by appointment only, as a fishing guide, a massage therapist, and a tarot card reader. My neighbor's talents were so eclectic, and the illustrations on her website so whimsical, that I decided to call her right away. Except there was no phone number and no address.

I searched every page of her website, and the only way to contact her was through email. I briefly wrote that I'd purchased a pair of her earrings at the general store, and wondered if I could make an appointment for a tarot card reading. I hesitated for a moment. A tarot card reading? Really? But just as I'd felt attracted to the earrings, I felt drawn to this woman. The mountains were changing me. It didn't feel silly; it felt right. I hit the send button.

Rupert and I went out on the deck to get a few more logs for the fire. The rain had stopped, but the sky was still overcast. No moon tonight.

Over the ridge I heard a "yip, yip, yip" and a long, lonely howl. Rupert barked back, and I put my hand on his head to quiet him. It didn't sound like a coyote pack—just a lone hunter. The Shenandoah hills were home to a hybrid mix of coyote and gray wolf. The animals were much larger than western coyotes and more likely to hunt alone. A shrill, hollow scream sounding like a death cry pierced the night. It was better to be hunter than hunted. I grabbed the firewood and quickly herded Rupert into the safety of our cabin.

After getting a good blaze going on the hearth, I opened a can of Rupert's favorite certified organic beef dog food. He became glued to my leg while I scooped out fresh food and poured water in his bowl.

I made myself a salad, adding shrimp and avocado to the basic greens. I wanted something hot to eat, too. My kitchen cupboard was depressingly bare, so I ventured downstairs to see if there might be a stray can of chicken or vegetable soup in the pantry.

I wished I'd come downstairs earlier, while there was still daylight. My pantry adjoined the sunporch, and at night it felt like being in a goldfish bowl. Involuntarily, I thought of Feather Braid from the general store. As quickly as I could, I switched on the light, found a couple of cans of Progresso soup, turned the light back off, and raced back to Rupert and the comforting fire.

* * * *

I was surprised to wake up fully dressed and in my living room. I hadn't done that since my first week here. The fire had long gone out. After turning off the television, I squinted at the clock: 4:23 a.m. Too early—the sun wouldn't be up for hours. But my being awake was enough of an alarm clock for Rupert. I heard him scratching at the front door. I couldn't be angry at him. The poor dog was probably desperate.

"Coming, boy!" I flipped on the porch light and opened the door. He rushed by me, but stopped to examine a brown woven basket sitting on the stoop. After a few sniffs, he trotted to a nearby bush, did his business, then circled back to the basket to sniff some more.

First pulling on a coat, I kneeled down and opened the lid. Inside was a jar of honey, a black velvet pouch, and a note written with blue ink on pale blue, lavender-scented stationery.

"Welcome, neighbor. Many thanks for buying the healing heart earrings. I'm glad you found them. Consider this jar of honey and your first card reading a welcome present from me to you. I'll be back at ten with hot biscuits to go with the honey. We'll do your reading then. Marla."

I brought the basket upstairs to the kitchen and tossed a dog cookie to Rupert. When had Marla delivered this? Was it okay to open the pouch? As gently as I could, I untied the drawstrings and peeked inside.

It was a pack of cards, and they were beautiful. The backs were a shimmering midnight blue with the imprint of a silver wolf in front of a full moon. And on the front of each card was a painting of an animal, or a bird, sea creature, or reptile. There was even a painting of a turtle with the words "mother earth" written underneath. I'd read that American Indians called earth Turtle Island. Along with the cards was a book of interpretation. According to the book, turtle was about deep creativity and protection—but I still had no idea what that had to do with me. "Rupert, it says here that dog medicine is all about loyalty. I can vouch for that."

At precisely ten o'clock, there was a light tap on my front door. I'd already made a fresh pot of coffee and heated water for tea. But even with the forewarning of the earrings, the website, and the basket, Marla McKenna was astonishing.

The woman didn't seem to walk so much as glide. Although she was slender, her swaying hips and full breasts exuded sensuality. I estimated that she was at least four inches taller than my five foot five, and in contrast to my medium-length, medium-brown hair, her hair was raven black and hung straight down her back, past her waist.

Despite the cool weather, Marla wore sandals, a turquoise cotton skirt, and a coral scoop-neck blouse. She was tanned—you could see the white of her skin when her blouse slid slightly off her shoulder. And her eyes were mesmerizing. Rimmed with long black lashes and framed by perfectly arched brows, the irises of her eyes were the same brilliant turquoise as her skirt. When she reached to shake my hand, I inhaled vanilla, coconut oil, and something else—something earthy and musky. It wasn't unpleasant, just very different from the Chanel and Calvin Klein scents that wafted off city women.

Even after we settled at the kitchen table, I truly couldn't tell how old she was. In some lighting, she looked like a child with an infectious smile around brilliantly white teeth. But when she stood after petting Rupert, she looked ancient—I had to blink twice to restore the image of the beautiful young woman.

Marla tapped my earring with her long right forefinger. "So you're the one in need of a healed heart. After we pour our tea and spread honey on a few biscuits, let's see what we can do about that."

Somehow she knew her way around my kitchen better than me: going straight to the cupboard housing the teacups, finding the silverware drawer at first try, and pouring just the right amount of cream in my tea. Maybe I should have been frightened by her clairvoyance, but I was having the opposite reaction. I hadn't realized how hungry for a friend I'd become. And Rupert never left her side during the entire visit.

After four hours, she knew just about everything there was to know about me, including my middle name, that I hated soggy brussels sprouts, every detail of my marriage and divorce from Mark, and my sadness over how distant I felt from my daughter. All I knew about her was that she was half Cherokee and half Scottish and that her family had lived in Raven Valley for a very long time. It wasn't like me to talk so much, but as my words spilled out, particularly the angry and bitter ones, I felt lighter—like my heart was being cleansed in those deep turquoise eyes. She held my hand while I sobbed over my wayward husband, simply nodding and saying, "Yep, menfolk keep having to spread their seed. It's just the way of it."

Reaching for my fourth honey-coated biscuit, I asked, "Do you have any children?" Her eyes darkened, and she shook her head. Scratching Rupert's ear, she said, "The critters are my children. And my art. I'll invite you over in a few days to see if I can tempt you with anything else."

I touched my ear. "You called these healing heart earrings. I already feel better."

Marla smiled. "Folks pick out what they need. When I made those, I used deer medicine—there's nothing gentler. And the feather is from a chickadee."

I thought of the man with the braid and the eagle feather and described him to Marla. She frowned. "Did he look like a Native American?" When I said no, she replied, "Eagle feathers are sacred. It's illegal for anyone to have them except indigenous people. I don't remember seeing anyone like him around Raven Valley."

As she gathered together her animal cards, I asked her if she'd like to go somewhere for dinner. "Maybe we could find a place with a band," I added hopefully.

She shook her head. "Not tonight. You need to stay close to home tonight."

"Me? Why?"

Marla studied me before answering. "I don't know why, but I know I'm telling you the truth. Call if you need me. My number is on the honey jar label."

And before I could ask any other questions, she was gone.

The rest of the day was routine. The sky had cleared, so I took Rupert for a long walk. I kept thinking about Marla and her card reading. She said that I was living too much in my fear—rabbit medicine—and I needed to develop my strengths using bear and hawk medicine. Her turquoise eyes looked through to my soul when she said, "A healing message is coming your way. Act without fear."

I didn't know why, but I believed her. She didn't seem at all crazy to me.

* * * *

Rupert and I sat on the river bank watching the late afternoon sun sparkle on the water. Two kayakers paddled by and waved. It made me feel the pangs of my loneliness again. I attached Rupert's leash and said, "Come on, Mr. Loyalty. It's time to head home. We don't want to get caught down here after dark."

By the time we got back, the sun was setting. I poured a glass of iced tea and grabbed my cell phone from the kitchen. What? There were twelve texts from my daughter asking me to call her as soon as possible. My hand shook a little as I pressed the call back button.

"Mom?"

"Lindsey. Thank God! Are you all right? What's going on?"

She started crying. Between sobs and hiccups I finally made out, "Jeff dumped me."

I bit my tongue to keep from saying, "Is that all?" I knew it was a very big deal. Lindsey and Jeff had been dating since high school. As much as she'd denied it at the time, I knew that Jeff was the reason Lindsey had chosen Cornell over Yale. He had been her first love and her heart was broken. I knew only too well how that felt.

"Oh, honey. I'm so sorry. Is there anything I can do?"

After another round of sobs she choked out, "Yes, I'm on my way down to you. My GPS says I should be there in an hour. But I don't know how to get to the cabin. I'll call you from the general store."

Ithaca, New York, was well over three hundred miles away. "How long have you been driving, Lindsey?"

"I don't know. Around five hours. I'm-I'm-*fine*." And the sobbing started again.

"Lindsey, listen to me. If you get tired, pull over at a rest stop or check into a motel. You don't sound fine." I envisioned her driving through the pitch black mountains while she was having an emotional breakdown. Dear God, please protect my baby.

"I-I will, Mom. I'll call you."

I kept myself busy for the next hour, but after that Rupert and I moved out to the deck, where the cell phone reception was better. I tried to quell all of my mom fears, but my only real comfort was in watching the gigantic hunter's moon rising over the trees. At least the narrow switchback roads wouldn't be completely dark. Finally after another hour, I broke down and called my daughter. Her voice mail picked up instantly. "Hi, Lindsey here. You know what to do."

"Lindsey, please call me as soon as you get this. You're over an hour late, and I'm beginning to think you've gotten lost."

I followed the call with a text message. Then I called Keith's store. Closed. Oh, hell! On Sunday, Keith always closed early. He and his son Tommy ate dinner at a cousin's house.

I started pacing. I didn't want to leave. If Lindsey made it here, she didn't have a key. Then I saw Marla's jar of honey sitting on the table. Tapping the number from the label into my cell phone, I prayed that Marla would be home. She picked up on the first ring.

"Hey, Carolyn. What's up?"

Now it was my turn to sob.

"Sshh, sshh. Hush now, Carolyn. We'll find her. Remember me? I'm the best guide in these woods. I'll pick you up in five minutes."

Hearing her voice helped to calm me down. I washed my face, threw on a clean sweater, and fed Rupert. But when I opened the door for Marla, I started crying all over again.

"It's okay. I'm going to drive, and you're going to keep calling. We'll leave the front door unlocked. Rupert's here to guard the place. Are you ready?"

Marla took the mountain road slowly, and I kept checking to make sure there were no signs of a car going off the edge. The hunter's moon had climbed high in the night sky. Although the bright glow helped to light the road, it cast menacing shadows through the trees and the underbrush. My morbid imagination had vaulted into overdrive.

"Carolyn, think like your daughter. Why wouldn't she call you?"

I tried to push the horrifying thoughts from my head. "Well, she could have lost her phone, or stopped at a motel or a rest stop and fallen dead asleep. Or the phone battery may have died. Or she's in a dead zone." I didn't like all the times I'd mentioned death in those last few sentences.

Marla pulled her car in front of Keith's general store and picked up her phone. "Keith? Carolyn Holloway and I have a little problem. Her daughter, Lindsey, was supposed to get into town almost two hours ago, and there's no sign of her. Did you see her? No, I'll put Carolyn on and she can describe her."

Describing my beautiful blond daughter with hazel green eyes and her dad's cleft in her chin brought back my tears. I almost missed Keith saying, "I saw her, Carolyn—over an hour ago. She was at the Hunter's Haven Tavern. But…"

"But what?"

"She looked pretty drunk. And there are a lot of men in town. I wouldn't waste any time getting over there."

I didn't have to repeat Keith's message. Marla had already thrown her Jeep in gear and was heading toward the motel and restaurant.

"Marla, that's Lindsey's car!" I pointed to a little white Audi convertible at the edge of the parking lot. "Do you see the Cornell sticker?"

We jumped from the car and headed into the tavern. Keith hadn't been joking. The place was wall-to-wall men. Where was my daughter?

I ignored the catcalls and whistles while I fought through the bar to get to the poolroom in the back. There she was, sprawled facedown on the pool table, cue stick in hand, with Feather Braid on top of her helping her with her "game." I screamed as loudly as I could, "Lindsey!"

Her head bobbed up, but her eyes didn't seem to focus. What was going on?

Marla stayed right by my side. I pushed the man off Lindsey, and he pushed me back. "Well, if it isn't mama bear coming for her cub. How about a threesome?" Then he looked at Marla. "Or a foursome. C'mon, boys, there's enough to go around."

Men began to circle us. I pulled my cell phone out to call 9-1-1 when I realized that a uniformed deputy was one of the men egging Feather Braid on. "Come on, Lindsey. We have to get out of here, *now*."

My daughter was as limp as a rag doll. She'd never been much of a drinker, but it couldn't just be alcohol. Had somebody drugged one of her drinks? I pulled her toward me one more time and Feather Braid gave me a hard shove into a pair of hairy arms. The strange man put his hands over my breasts, and I screamed.

That's when Marla stepped in. "Ah, Hank, what are you doing? Leave Mrs. Holloway alone. She wants to get her baby girl." Hank immediately dropped his hands. "Sorry, ma'am. We're just having a little fun."

Then Marla set her sights on Feather Braid. "And you, big boy, why don't you pick on somebody your own size?" She slid between the man and my daughter, and put her arms around his neck, tugging his braid playfully. She motioned for me to get Lindsey.

Marla was plenty distracting for Feather Braid. Lindsey slumped against the table when he dropped her. I managed to half drag and half carry her to a safe corner near the bar. "Lindsey, where are your car keys?" She still couldn't focus on me, but she pointed to her backpack underneath a barstool. When I pulled the backpack out, I called the bartender over. "There's a woman alone with a bunch of men in the poolroom. Please go back and help her."

The bartender pushed into the crowded back room while I tried to get Lindsey to drink some bottled water I found in her backpack. She kept passing out. "How many drinks did you have? Do we need to pump your stomach?"

She shook her head and held up two fingers as if to say she'd only had two drinks. Nobody gets that drunk on two drinks. What had that monster given her?

After about five minutes, the bartender returned. "There's no woman back there, lady. Somebody said she left with one of the hunters."

"But…could you stay with my daughter for a minute?"

I went to look for Marla. This time the men drew away and made a path for me. The menacing alcohol- and testosterone-fueled atmosphere had abated. “Where’s my friend? Did anyone see her leave?”

The men looked at the floor or shook their heads.

I fished my phone out and texted Marla. “r u ok?”

The answer came instantly. “Yes. Drive Lindsey home in her car. I’ll see you tomorrow.”

* * * *

Lindsey was still asleep at eleven the next morning. I didn’t sleep at all. Between checking in on her every fifteen minutes and hoping for a text from Marla, I was a wreck. When Lindsey finally did wake up, she had no idea where she was.

I got her a glass of orange juice and described the previous night’s events. Her eyes grew wider and wider. “Wow, Mom. I remember going to the bar, but that’s about it. I did stop at the store, but it was closed. My phone was dead, and there was no public phone. I flagged down a car—this guy with a braid and a feather was driving. He told me there was a place where I could call right down the road. All I had to do was follow him. There was somebody using the bar phone, and Larry—I think that was his name—said he’d ordered me a beer. That’s the last thing I remember, Mom. I’m sorry. I don’t know what happened.”

I did. It had happened to me once in college. I didn’t know what the drug was then or now, but I recognized the symptoms. But how do you report something like that when the damned deputy was in on the fun? Some “almost heaven” this was!

After bringing Lindsey coffee and toast, I tried calling Marla. No answer. When I left a text, she responded immediately. “Glad your girl made it through. I’ll be over at noon.”

I needed milk and eggs, but I didn’t want to leave Lindsey. The general store was number four on my speed dial. “Keith, Carolyn here. Could you send Tommy over with milk and eggs when he has a chance? Two percent—and if you have the large brown organic eggs, that’s my preference. Yes, we found Lindsey. Thanks for your help. I’ll tell you about it later.”

Marla arrived exactly at twelve. When she handed me a bouquet of late-blooming roses, I noticed a bandage on her right arm. “Are you okay? Did that Larry jerk get rough? I went back to look for you, but you were both gone.”

She didn't answer. "May I see your daughter?"

I led her to the spare room. Lindsey had fallen asleep again. Marla walked over to her, pulled the covers around her, and briefly touched Lindsey's gold hair fanned out on the pillow. Rupert was sleeping on the rug next to the bed, and Marla leaned down to pat his head. "Good boy. Keep her safe."

Marla tiptoed out of the bedroom and sank into a kitchen chair. "You asked me if I had children. I had one daughter. Somebody just like Larry raped her and left her to die by the side of the road. She was twelve, Carolyn. Just twelve years old. I couldn't let that happen to your daughter, too. Let Lindsey sleep. She'll be fine."

The story about her daughter was horrifying. I tried to say how sorry I was, but she shook her head and raised her hand to stop me. Then Marla rose to leave.

"But what happened last night? Are you okay? What happened to Larry?"

Marla lowered her eyes and smiled sadly. When she looked up, I could have sworn her eyes glowed amber. I looked again and they were back to turquoise. She turned abruptly, waved as she glided toward the door, and said, "I'm fine. We're all fine. It's just the way of it."

A half hour later, Tommy banged on my front door, and I ran to stop him. "Shhh, Tommy. My daughter's trying to sleep."

He handed me my grocery bag and took off his cap. "Sorry, Ms. Holloway. Did you hear the news? A coyote got one of them drunken hunters last night—ripped his throat right out. The doc says he's never seen nothin' like it. Looks like the man tried to fight back—his knife was right next to him, and it had blood all over it. But it didn't do him no good."

My heart began banging against my rib cage when I thought of the bandage on Marla's arm. Trying to keep my voice calm, I said, "Tommy, did the man have identification on him?"

"Oh, it was nobody you'd know, Ms. Holloway. He wasn't from around here. Larry something, Larry Naston or Napier. I dunno, Larry something."

"Did he have a braid?"

Tommy gave me a long look. "Now that's weird. Dad said a man with a braid had come in the store. With an eagle feather.

I know from Boy Scouts you're not supposed to have an eagle feather. Not unless you're an Indian."

My hands trembled as I pulled a twenty-dollar bill out of my purse and handed it to the boy. "So did the man have a braid and an eagle feather?"

Tommy shook his head. "Not exactly. Doc said there was a blond braid next to him. He thought maybe the man cut it off himself when he was trying to fight off the coyote. But there wasn't an eagle feather around." The boy held up the twenty. "I don't have change, ma'am. Dad said you can put it on your account."

I closed my purse and took a deep breath. Exhaling slowly, I said, "That's okay, Tommy. Keep the change. And Tommy?"

"Yes, ma'am?"

"When you grow up—when you become a man—please promise me you'll never forget how to be a good Boy Scout."

Robin Templeton is a Virginia-based writer. Her long-time career as a professional photographer and experience as a private investigator formed the basis of her work-in-progress, *Double Exposure*. She was awarded the William F. Deeck-Malice Domestic Grant for Unpublished Writers, and an early version of *Double Exposure* was a finalist in the Minotaur Books/Malice Domestic Best First Traditional Mystery Novel Competition. Her story "The Knitter" appeared in *Chesapeake Crimes: Storm Warning*, and she was thrilled when "Hunter's Moon" was selected for *Furs, Feathers, and Felonies*. You can find out more about Robin's writing and photography adventures at www.robintempleton.com.

TILL MURDER DO US PART

BY BARB GOFFMAN

Murder's always a sin. But it especially feels like sacrilege when I get called from church on a Sunday morning because a body's been found.

Today's killing proved once again the sad wisdom of why my husband and I always drove everywhere separately. I left him behind in the air-conditioned comfort of Countryside Fellowship, turned the siren on in my rig, and headed the ten miles out to Bob and Lilly Novinger's farm. I didn't actually need the siren. My county's so rural, I wouldn't see another car for half the trip. But I wanted to give a shout-out to God. Was Bob's death really a part of your plan? And if not, could you pay a little more attention to what's going on down here?

Good Lord, we're boiling.

We were in the middle of the worst heat wave since the state began keeping records. The temperature hadn't dropped below ninety in more than a week and was expected to hit 108 degrees this afternoon.

Extreme weather could make people testy—especially people who hold a grudge. Like Bob Novinger's neighbors. The question for this morning: which one of them had finally boiled over and bumped him off?

They'd all had it in for him ever since he renovated his old dairy barn last year and began renting it out for weddings. Bob was cashing in on a trend—city folk coming to the country to start their married lives with rustic charm. But the neighbors hadn't found it charming. They'd made a huge fuss at the county council, trying to shut Bob down. There was too much noise, they said. Too much traffic. Too much everything.

But Bob had prevailed. Until now.

It was hard to believe God would let a man be murdered over holding weddings. Yet I knew I shouldn't be surprised. In the eleven years I'd been county sheriff, I'd encountered enough despicable behavior to conclude that God allows people to make their own choices, with the prospect of punishment waiting in the wings. Perhaps punishment would come from God eventually. But it would definitely come from me first.

As I pulled up to the crime scene, my chief deputy, Jackson Garrett, emerged from the barn, tugging a surgical mask off his lean face. My deputies often wore peppermint-scented masks when dealing with dead bodies. Considering the heat, Bob might already have been emitting an awful smell.

"Hey, boss," Jackson said when I stepped onto the dirt road. "Someone strangled Mr. Novinger in the barn there. Left him sitting at a table, a laptop open in front of him. He's already stiff, so it must have happened last night, after the wedding festivities ended."

Our crime-scene tech and the medical examiner would get us more details, of course, but I never liked waiting. "Strangled him with what?"

"Twinkle lights. They've got 'em strung all over the barn. Makes it look festive. Or at least it used to."

Twinkle lights. That was a first.

"What's on the laptop?" I asked. "Can you get into it?"

Jackson nodded. "It's not password protected. Mr. Novinger was looking at a spreadsheet that lists his upcoming barn rentals. I haven't had time to study it yet, but it seems business was good."

Just what the neighbors had been afraid of.

"Witnesses? Suspects?" I asked.

"No witnesses so far. Mrs. Novinger said she found her husband just a little while ago. She came out looking for him when she woke up and realized he'd never come to bed."

"Find out who got married here last night. Maybe someone didn't want to pay their bill. And get a list of all the wedding guests and personnel—wait staff, caterers, photographers—everyone who worked here last night. And we need the names of the neighbors who complained at the county council meetings last year. The two families in the immediate vicinity were vocal, I know, but there were others just as unhappy." Speaking of unhappy, I looked around for the widow. "Where's Lilly?"

Jackson nodded at the old clapboard house across the field. Its peeling white paint shone in the sun, which was beating down so hard, I felt sweat beading up on the back of my neck.

"You know if she's told anyone about what happened here?"

"Just their daughters. After I questioned her, I told her not to tell anyone how Mr. Novinger died. She said she needed to call her girls, but she'd just tell them that he died, not how. They didn't need the image in their heads."

Agreed. I hadn't seen Bob's body yet, but no child should have to view a parent after they'd been murdered.

"Anyway, I didn't want her contaminating the crime scene any more than she had," Jackson added, "so I told her to go on home."

"Any *more*?"

"When she found Mr. Novinger, she thought he'd had a heart attack, so she rushed over and tried to help, but rigor mortis had already set in. I think she was pretty shook up when she realized what had happened."

Who wouldn't be?

But was it from finding her husband dead? Or from strangling him herself?

While I figured a neighbor had done Bob in, I knew I shouldn't overlook Lilly as a possible suspect. First rule in homicide: the spouse probably did it. Still, I had a hard time believing Lilly could have done this. I'd known her all my life. In the winters, she used to waitress at the diner in town to help make ends meet. She was cool. Unsentimental. Strangling someone is the act of an enraged person. I doubted Lilly could ever muster that much emotion.

Jackson and I walked to the barn. He slipped his mask back on and returned to work with the other deputy and our tech, while I stood in the doorway, glancing around. It looked as if wedding cleanup had been completed the night before. No dishes or glassware lay out. A large pile of tablecloths sat on one of the round wooden tables, apparently waiting to be washed. And there was Bob sprawled in his chair. His abundant salt-and-pepper hair had gotten mussed as he apparently tried to fight off his assailant. The twinkle lights still hung around his neck.

I said a quick prayer, then headed over to the house. "Lilly," I called, knocking on the door. "It's Sheriff Wescott." It felt odd using my title, considering how long Lilly and I had known one another. But this was a business call.

The door creaked open. Lilly's gray hair, usually pulled into a tight bun, was loose. Unkempt. The wrinkled edges of her lips tried to rise into a smile but failed. Lilly was in her late fifties, but grief had added a decade to her face.

"Hello, Ellen." She sighed, as if saying my name had drained her last bit of strength. "Please come in."

She led me into the living room, which had a leather couch and recliner—both looked and smelled new. A big flat-screen TV hung over the fireplace. Their wedding business must have been doing well. Folks around here often didn't have the money to spring on new furnishings, and Bob was known for being frugal.

After Lilly offered me something to drink, which I declined, we settled on the couch. "I'm so sorry for your loss," I said. "Can you tell me what happened?"

She frowned, the skin on her face pulling tight. "Bob was out in the barn last night, overseeing a wedding, as usual. I turned in around eleven. Slept like a log. When I awoke this morning, I realized he hadn't come to bed. The blanket on his side was smooth. I called for him, but he didn't answer, so I threw on clothes and went looking. I about had a heart attack when I found him."

"Is it typical for you to turn in while the parties are still going on?"

"Oh, yes. I have no interest in watching people celebrate their love." She stretched out the last word, as if it were a bad thing. "Waste of money, if you ask me. When Bob and I got married nearly thirty-five years ago, we had a short church ceremony, followed by a luncheon at my mother's home. Small, inexpensive, and simple."

"Small and intimate," I countered. "Sounds romantic."

She snickered. "I wish. Everybody thinks Bob was Mr. Romance 'cause he started the wedding business. Bunch of fools. Bob wasn't romantic. He was pragmatic. We're getting older. Farming's hard work. We needed an easier way to make money. Weddings are it.... Were it." Her eyes watered. "I don't know what I'm going to do now."

"Bob have problems with any of his clients?"

She shook her head.

"Any enemies?"

"Sometimes customers didn't like Bob's prices, and he could be a tough negotiator. But enemies?" She shook her head faster. "No."

I leaned forward. "I have to ask. How were things between the two of you?"

"They were fine. The same as ever."

"Money problems?"

"The new business had solved our money problems. We're making more than enough to cover the loan Bob took out to rehab the barn and save for our retirement."

"I'm sorry I have to ask this, but can anyone vouch for your whereabouts last night?"

Her eyebrows rose. "No. I was asleep. Alone."

Lilly's lack of an alibi didn't bother me. People are alone a lot of the time, with no one to verify it. It's the people with ready alibis for odd times who worry me. I asked a few more polite questions, explained what would happen next with Bob, and headed out.

I'd spent less than twenty minutes in the house, yet the day felt even hotter than before. As I wiped my forehead, I noticed that the medical examiner had arrived. His car was parked outside the barn. I hoped he'd figure out something useful fast. Seconds later, a car came careening down the driveway, straight at me, skidding to a stop in a cloud of dust. Lilly and Bob's girls, Natalie and Andrea, flew out.

"What the hell happened?" Andrea stormed up to me, her dark blond hair streaming behind her.

"Hey," Natalie scolded. "Show some respect."

I'd known the girls all their lives, and they hadn't changed. Andrea, the younger one, was tall and curvy, all fire and passion, studying to be a paralegal last I heard. Natalie, an accountant, was more serious, like Lilly. She looked like Lilly, too, with her sharp brown eyes, lanky frame, and ashy blond hair pulled up in a bun. They'd always been mama's girls through and through.

Andrea rolled her eyes. "Fine. I *respectfully* ask what the hell happened? Mom called and said Dad had died, but we're driving over and that busybody Teresa Templeton said on the radio that he'd been murdered."

So much for keeping things quiet.

"She didn't say murdered," Natalie corrected. "Stop jumping to conclusions. She said that a body had been found on the farm and a neighbor had reported hearing gunshots last night."

Gunshots? That was news to me.

Natalie drew a shaky breath. "We're guessing Dad was the body?"

This was never easy. "Yes. I'm sorry to inform you that your father was killed last night in the barn. I can't tell you any more than that right now. We're doing everything we can to find out what happened."

"Who would kill Dad?" Andrea asked.

"That's a good question. You know anyone who had a beef with your father?"

Both girls shook their heads.

"When was the last time you saw him?"

"We came over for dinner last Sunday, as usual," Natalie said, while Andrea nodded.

"Things okay between him and your mom?"

Andrea rolled her eyes again. "Of course."

It was amazing how many children think their parents' marriages have no problems, considering how many marriages went kaput these days.

I thanked the girls, headed to my rig, and radioed my dispatcher. "You get any calls about gunshots last night?"

"No," she said. "Why?"

"The radio is supposedly reporting someone heard gunshots out here."

"First I've heard of it. I'll keep an ear out."

"Thanks," I said before signing off.

Minutes later I pulled up the long drive to Curtis and Debra Randall's farm, passing wandering cows and a barn that had seen better days. The Randalls lived next door to Bob and Lilly—though the term "next door" could be misleading. While the Randalls' property line ran near Bob and Lilly's house, their homes were separated by a quarter mile. The Randalls' house sat at the top of a rise, though, so they had a clear view of the Novingers' house and barn.

As soon as I opened my truck door, a rancid smell hit me, making me gag. It was like a combination of excrement, raw eggs, and ripe, dead meat. Holding my breath, I hurried to the house and banged on the door. Debra opened it, winced, and waved me quickly inside.

"Ellen," she said, once she shut the door. "What can I do for you?"

I panted for a moment. With the air conditioner running full blast, the air was better inside, but the horrendous odor did linger a bit. "What was that smell?"

"Cow." She shook her head, her dark hair swishing against her slim shoulders.

"Cow?" I blinked at her and then realized. "Oh no."

"Oh yes. This damn heat is killing 'em. Curtis, the boys, and our workers are out there now, trying to keep 'em cool and watered. We've had three die from heat exhaustion this week. The one that died last night exploded. The guts must have flown twenty yards. That's what you're smelling." She sighed. "If she'd died during the day, we'd have noticed and could've dealt with the body. But that poor cow must've been lying dead in the field for hours while we slept, her body gasses expanding in the heat until . . . boom."

I shivered. Dead-cow explosions were an unfortunate happenstance during heat waves in farm country. Sometimes they made the news, serving as a source of amusement for folks in other areas. But here, heat-related cow deaths could be a major financial loss. And dealing with scattered guts wasn't something anyone wanted to do.

Debra gave me a weak smile. "But you probably didn't come here to talk about exploding cows," she said, leading me to her big kitchen. "So how can I help you?"

I was surprised she didn't know what had happened at the Novinger farm, considering her proximity and how word had already spread—especially since we didn't have that many murders around here. Or did she know about it and was just being sly?

"Can you tell me what you did last night?" I asked as we sat at the table.

Her eyes widened. "Why? Did something happen?"

I kept my mouth shut, figuring she'd talk if I didn't. After a few seconds, she proved me right, saying, "We were here, dealing with the cows."

"Can anyone vouch for that?"

"The children." She had four boys, all teenagers. "And some of our workers stayed late, helping. We didn't head in till nearly eleven."

"Did you see or hear anything unusual last night?"

"No."

"Nothing from the Novinger farm?"

"No. Why?"

"How have things been between your family and the Novingers? Curtis made quite a ruckus last year over their wedding business."

"You can say that again. He was certain we'd lose our peace and quiet. But it hasn't been bad like Curtis had expected. Why? Is someone saying we've complained recently? Because we haven't. In fact, I took Lilly and Bob a pie just last month, trying to be neighborly."

"How'd that go over?"

Debra shrugged. "Lilly was polite, but I got the impression I was interrupting. She had travel magazines spread out." She leaned forward. "She and Bob are going to renew their vows and have a big party when their anniversary comes up in the fall. Can you believe it? Then they're taking off to someplace exotic. Hawaii, I think."

"Bob Novinger is paying for a big party and a trip to Hawaii?" His business must have been doing really well.

"The first weekend in November, Lilly said. Anyway, when she accepted my pie, I thought she was accepting my apology for Curtis causing such a fuss last year. Though, come to think of it, she didn't offer me any of the pie. And she never returned my plate, either."

The back door opened, and Curtis walked into the kitchen, wiping sweat off his brow with the back of his hand. His clothes were dirty, he had deep bags under his eyes, and he reeked of cow guts. I tried not to cringe.

"I saw your truck, Sheriff. Is everything all right?"

Debra opened her mouth, but I jumped in first. "Can you tell me where you were last night, Curtis?"

He squinted, appearing confused. "Sure. I was here with the team, trying to keep the cows safe."

"All night?" I asked.

He walked closer, and I shifted away from the smell. "Yeah, all night," he said. "We were out in the field with the cows till late. Then I woke up early to check on 'em." He shook his head. "We lost one overnight, between the time I came in to get some shut eye and got up. It's a shame. She was a good milker."

"Can anyone verify all this?" I asked. "Outside your family and the people who work for you, I mean?"

He sputtered. "What the heck is going on?"

"I've been asking that same question," Debra said.

I stared Curtis down. "No," he finally said. "Well, maybe Bob Novinger. On party nights, I often see him coming and going from his house to the barn. Given the traffic last night, I assume he had another wedding going on. So he might have seen us last night."

How I wished Bob Novinger could alibi anyone this morning. After Curtis said he hadn't seen or heard anything odd last night, I broke the news of Bob's murder. Their shock appeared genuine. They couldn't suggest anyone who might have done it, saying the rest of the neighbors had also grown to accept Bob's business, that it wasn't as disruptive as they'd feared.

"Though Mac Tucker has had a bit of trouble," Curtis said. Tucker's farm was directly across the road from the Novingers'. "At least twice, idiots attending weddings in Bob's barn have snuck onto Mac's land and tried to tip his cows. Only someone not raised on a farm would think you can tip over a twelve-hundred-pound cow by giving it a push. All you get is an angry cow."

And maybe an angry farmer.

I thanked Curtis and Debra and headed out to see Mac Tucker. He ran a bigger operation than Curtis did, with a large number of workers. I thought Mac would be slogging in the fields, so I was surprised to find him rocking on his porch, flipping through a copy of *Rack* magazine, which—despite its name—is actually about hunting.

"Sheriff." He nodded at me as I approached. He had a gray five o'clock shadow coming in early. "I sure am popular today."

"How so?"

"First that lady reporter from the radio called me, and now here you are."

Wow, was he a throwback. He probably thought of me as the lady sheriff.

"So someone finally plugged Bob Novinger," Mac said. As my eyes widened, he added, "Naw. I didn't do it. But with all the cops at the barn this morning, and then the medical examiner driving up, stands to reason."

I stepped onto the porch, getting out of the direct sun. Unfortunately, the air was so thick, the shade barely helped. "I heard you've had trouble with some of Bob's guests."

Mac set the magazine down and spit tobacco juice over the porch rail. "Stupid city kids think it'd be fun to try tipping my cows. The last pair I put a good scare in, shooting my shotgun into the air. They ran like hell for the fence. One of them fell climbing over it and ripped his fancy suit. I'd say we was even."

"And last night? Did you have problems then?"

"Other than having to listen to that danged 'Celebration' song again? It used to be quiet out here at night. Peaceful. Now there's music and hollering till way too late."

"You can hear the noise up here?"

"When the wind carries a certain way, I can."

"You hear anything last night? Besides Kool & the Gang?"

Mac spit again. "I was awoken by a loud noise at some point. Didn't realize it was a gunshot till I saw all the police cars pull up this morning. That's what I told that lady reporter."

So Mac was the source of the shooting rumor. I'd have Jackson check if there's any evidence of shooting in the barn, but chances are, Mac was just jumping to conclusions. Or maybe Mac was trying to throw my suspicions elsewhere by pretending he didn't know Bob was strangled. Maybe the loss of his peace and quiet had stuck in his craw far more than he wanted me to believe.

"Can anyone vouch for your whereabouts last night?"

"Nope. I was sleeping by my lonesome."

There was a lot of that going around. I thanked Mac and left. As soon as I got in my rig with the blessed air conditioning, my phone rang. Jackson.

"I've got something," he said.

Thank the Lord. My interviews had yielded some suspicions but not many answers.

"Where are you?" I asked.

"I'm sitting in my truck outside the Novingers' barn."

"I'll be right there. Oh, by the way, you see any evidence of gunfire in or near the barn?"

"No. Should I?"

"Not necessarily. But ask the team to keep an eye out."

"You got it, boss."

A couple of minutes later, I joined Jackson in his truck, adjusting his air-conditioning vent so the cool air blew right at me. He'd ditched his face mask but now wore latex gloves.

"I was talking with one of the men who worked for Mr. Novinger," Jackson said. "He helped him set up tables and chairs, things like that. He said some rich guy showed up a few days ago to check out Mr. Novinger's barn. The guy's daughter attended a wedding there and loved it so much she wants to be married there, too. But Mr. Novinger wouldn't take the guy's reservation."

"Why not?"

"The date he wanted was already booked. The guy tried to give Mr. Novinger extra money to dump the existing reservation, but Mr. Novinger wouldn't do it. So the guy left. Mad."

"Mad enough to kill?"

"I don't know, but it probably doesn't matter because the guy ultimately got what he wanted. He wouldn't take no for an answer. Kept calling Mr. Novinger and offering more and more money, until Mr. Novinger caved and accepted the reservation. This all happened right before last evening's guests began arriving."

My eyebrows climbed toward my hairline. "Bob always knew the value of a dollar, but he also was a man of his word. I'm surprised he'd cancel an existing reservation like that. Who'd he screw over? That's probably our culprit."

"I don't know that either." Jackson opened the laptop that had been sitting between us. "Here's the list of reservations. It appears Mr. Novinger already updated it. But once we get his phone records, we can see who he called and disappointed last evening."

I reached into Jackson's glove compartment for a pair of latex gloves. My deputies always carried spares; you never knew when they'd be needed. After snapping the gloves on, I picked up the laptop and scrolled down the screen. Bob's business had been booming. He had nearly every Friday, Saturday, and Sunday booked through the end of the year with hefty down payments.

"There." Jackson pointed. "That must be the wedding for the guy who weaseled his way onto the schedule. You see Mr. Novinger typed yesterday's date with the notation 'waiting on deposit.'"

I stopped scrolling at the autumn listing for the Rachel Simmons/Liam Ryan wedding. I could hardly believe it, but I knew who'd killed Bob Novinger.

* * * *

A short while later, I returned to Bob and Lilly's house. I was glad I hadn't changed out of my church clothes before heading out on the investigation this morning. My blouse and skirt were more appropriate than a uniform for paying a condolence call.

"Ellen, you're back soon," Lilly said, opening the door. "Have you learned anything?"

"I think so."

"Please, come in."

We went to the living room, which was hopping with people. Word about Bob's "shooting" had spread all over the local grapevine thanks to Mac's chat with that reporter. So folks had come out, as expected, to pay their respects. In addition to Lilly's daughters, there were several cousins, nieces, and nephews, as well as friends and neighbors, including Debra and Curtis Randall. The room got quiet, everyone staring at me expectantly.

"Maybe we could talk privately, Lilly."

Natalie and Andrea rose, evidently expecting to join in on this conversation.

"I'd like to talk to your mom alone for a few minutes if you don't mind," I said.

Her full lips pursed, Andrea clearly minded. "You sure you want to talk to the sheriff alone, Mom?"

"Of course. It's fine." Lilly shooed the girls back to the couch. "We can talk in the kitchen, Ellen."

I watched Curtis Randall eyeing me as I headed out of the room, down a short hallway. When Lilly and I entered the kitchen, my mouth watered. Food lay everywhere. Cakes and casseroles and what smelled like chicken parmesan. I understood why folks brought food after a death. They wanted to help. To do something. But so much food always felt a little unseemly, as if the death was being celebrated.

"Can I get you something?" Lilly asked.

It was even more unseemly for a widow to be offering *me* food on the day her husband died. And worse that my stomach gurgled in response. But it was past lunchtime. I sheepishly helped myself to a cookie and sat at the kitchen table.

"It's nice so many people have come over today," I said, swallowing the last of the crumbs. I could hear someone talking about Bob in the other room. "Sharing memories must be comforting. I remember, must be twenty-five years ago now, when Bob got into a fender bender down on Main Street. He'd been turning left, and someone clipped his back bumper. The darn thing fell off. I was on patrol, and I had to give Bob the ticket because the other guy had the right of way, even though Bob was adamant he hadn't been at fault. Boy, was he angry."

"I don't remember the incident, but I'm not surprised. Bob pinched every penny he could."

"Even now? That's some nice new furniture you have in the living room."

She glowered. "After we started doing well with the wedding business, Bob decided he didn't want a saggy couch anymore. And he wanted a big TV to watch the games."

"What did you want?"

"Me? Nothing. This wasn't a time to dip into our savings. We still needed to keep putting money away for a rainy day. We still had to pay off that loan."

I nodded. "It's funny, isn't it? You were finally doing okay financially because of all these short-sighted people, spending a king's ransom for weddings. You and Bob did it the right way. A church ceremony, followed by a small, inexpensive luncheon at home."

"That's right."

Sighing, I shook my head slightly. "Of course, a small luncheon at home didn't allow you to have all the guests you probably wanted."

"Well, no."

"And you didn't have the chance to pick out flower arrangements and a band and all that fun stuff. And you probably didn't go on a big honeymoon, did you?"

"Honeymoon? We had two days at a bed-and-breakfast an hour north of here. It wasn't even that nice."

"Which must be why you wanted to make your next anniversary special. It would have been your thirty-fifth, right? I heard you were planning a big ceremony where you'd renew your vows and then take a trip to Hawaii."

She blinked. "That's true, we were." She paused. "Not that it makes any difference now." The next words seemed to catch in her throat. "Ellen, do you have any idea who killed Bob?"

Oh, I did, but I wasn't going to say so. "Who do you think did it?"

"I can't even guess. You asked about enemies this morning. The neighbors are the only people who've been upset with us. They were worried about the noise when Bob started the business. But surely none of them are responsible. They've all come around. We were going to invite them all when we renewed our vows in the fall."

"I bet that would've been nice, being the center of attention after all these years. Finally having money spent on something special for you." I leaned forward and grasped Lilly's hand. "Folks have always called you unsentimental, but you were just saving face, weren't you, because Bob would never spring for nice dinners or flowers or anything to show you he loved you." My mouth twisted in a grimace. "But he could buy that big-screen TV out there."

Lilly stared down at the wooden table.

"So it must have made your day when Bob agreed to have a big party to celebrate your upcoming anniversary. It was finally going to be your turn."

"That's right." She glanced up, her eyes watering.

"Except you weren't going to get your turn after all, were you, Lilly? Bob chose money over you again, didn't he?"

She paled and pulled her hand from mine.

"I saw his bookings spreadsheet," I explained. "The first Saturday in November's going to be the Simmons/Ryan wedding, not your vow-renewal ceremony."

She shook her head no repeatedly. "I can see where you're going with this, Ellen, but you're wrong."

How I wished I were. It didn't feel right, thinking Lilly had killed Bob, but the pieces fit.

"Am I wrong?" I asked as the landline phone rang once, then stopped. "I saw the down-payment amount Bob listed on the spreadsheet. It was ten thousand more than he required of everyone else. That's what he sold you out for. A measly ten thousand dollars."

Lilly kept shaking her head. "No. I never—"

"I'm sorry to interrupt," Natalie said, walking into the kitchen with her sister in tow. "Mom, that was Harlow Springer from the funeral home on the phone. He heard about what happened to Dad and wanted to know if you feel up to dealing with the funeral details. He said Dad told him a while back that you'd both use him," she took a deep breath, "when the time came, but you never made any actual plans."

"That was just something your father said at a Rotary meeting to get Harlow off his back," Lilly said. "Besides, we never thought the time would come so soon." She blinked several times. "I can't deal with this now. You girls take care of it, all right? Just be careful with the money. Stay middle of the road. Nothing too expensive."

"Sure, Mom," Natalie said in a quiet voice. "We'll choose the casket and all that stuff. And don't worry. We won't go too fancy. Just something with a pretty lining so Dad'll look right for the viewing."

"The viewing?" Andrea said. "We can't have a viewing. Then everyone would see the marks on Dad's ne—" She stopped short, her eyes wide. "I mean the mole, that ugly mole on his neck."

Oh my God. I should've listened to my gut. I'd pinned this on the wrong person. The only way Andrea could know about the marks on Bob's neck was if she'd made them. Everyone else thought Bob had been shot.

Lilly jumped up, her mouth hanging open. She clearly was as surprised as I was. "You girls go on." She tried unsuccessfully to push them from the room. "The sheriff and I have things to talk about." Lilly turned to me as I stood. "You were right, Ellen," she said, talking rapidly now. "Bob chose money over me again. When we were struggling I could understand. But now we're doing okay.

Okay enough that he spent money on himself, but my dreams, those were disposable. I got so mad that I…I killed him."

"Mother!" Natalie cried while Andrea's face paled.

It was admirable how Lilly was trying to protect her child. And disturbing how Andrea was keeping her mouth shut.

"I knew it," I said in my sternest tone. "But I need to hear it from you, Lilly. All the details. The judge will want to know everything before he sends you to prison."

Her lips quivered at the word *prison*. "Well, Bob came into the house as I was about to go to sleep," Lilly said. "Told me how that spoiled girl was getting my party date. I couldn't believe it. He went back out to the wedding, while I…I stewed for hours, waiting for the party to end so I could tell Bob what I thought of him."

Her voice had gone up half an octave after she paused. That was probably where the lie began.

"Finally I heard the last of the cars leave," Lilly said, "and I stormed out. And there he was, sitting there, playing with his computer like he didn't have a care in the world. My face got so hot, I thought I'd have a stroke. So I grabbed the twinkle lights, and I killed him."

I glanced at Andrea. Her lips were clamped shut. She was actually going to let her mother take the rap for her.

"Okay," I said. "Lilly Novinger, you have the right to remain silent—"

"No!" Andrea yelled. "You can't arrest her. She didn't do it. I did. She's covering for me."

Lilly narrowed her eyes. "Hush up."

"No." Andrea crossed the kitchen straight to me. Finally her conscience had woken up. "Mom called me late last night, upset because Dad had given away her party date, just like she said, but it was me who went into the barn to talk to him, not Mom."

"Andrea, be quiet," Lilly said.

"No, I won't. Dad said he couldn't pass up that much money, that Mom could have her event some other time. Like it was nothing. I began telling him what I thought of him, how he was a selfish, money-grubbing jerk, and he told me to calm down, that I was being hysterical. I hate it when men tell women they're being hysterical. It's so sexist. And then he turned his back on me and sat down at the computer. I wanted to squeeze the living daylights out of him. So I did. I grabbed some of those damned twinkle lights—twinkle lights Mom was supposed to have at her party—and I choked him from behind."

"She's lying," Lilly yelled. "I did it."

Andrea sighed. "I'm not lying. Mom's trying to cover for me, and I appreciate that, Mom, so much." She grabbed Lilly's hand. "But I can't you let you do it. Sheriff, you'll find my fingerprints on the twinkle lights. Not Mom's. She's never had anything to do with the business."

I noticed how quiet the house had become. The kitchen had afforded just the right amount of privacy. Clearly all of Lilly's friends and family had heard the confession, as I'd hoped. It's always nice to have witnesses.

Including Jackson. "Boss, you want me to do the honors?" he asked, stepping into the room.

I nodded. I'd asked him to come over a few minutes after I did so he could be here at the appropriate moment. My church clothes didn't have a place for hiding handcuffs.

Andrea stood tall, as if trying to prepare herself for what was to come. Lilly fell back into her chair, tears flowing down her cheeks, while Natalie leaned against the counter, looking sucker-punched. I felt sorry for all of them. Lilly had waited so long for so little, and now she'd lost her husband and one of her daughters just like that. Andrea would probably be going away for a long time.

After Jackson read Andrea her rights, he led her out of the house. Everyone in the living room followed, got into their cars, and drove away, giving Lilly and Natalie their privacy. Debra and Curtis Randall walked with me to my truck. I fanned myself with my hand. The heat was unbearable.

"If I hadn't heard that with my own ears, I wouldn't believe it," Debra said.

Neither would a lot of people, which was one reason I'd been glad to see all those folks in the living room when I arrived—all the better to have the confession overheard, even though I'd guessed wrong about who had done it. But, hey, not every sheriff could get two confessions for the same crime.

"And all along I thought Bob had been shot," Curtis said.

"Nope," I said. "I'm pretty sure the noise that woke Mac Tucker last night wasn't a gunshot at all. It was your cow exploding."

"Wow," Curtis said. "Talking about the cows, we better get back home to check on—"

Boom! An explosion erupted from the Randalls' farm. I turned toward the blast and saw chunks of something flying right at us. Holy cow! It was cow! I ducked, covering my head and face, trying not to vomit, as the pieces rained down on us and a rancid smell whooshed our way.

Really, God? Really? I caught a murderer and this was the thanks I got? Cow guts all over me?

And these were my church clothes, too.

Barb Goffman has won the Agatha, Macavity, and Silver Falchion awards for her short stories, and she's been a finalist for national crime short-story awards nineteen times: ten times for the Agatha (a record in that category), four for the Macavity, three for the Anthony, and once each for the Derringer and Silver Falchion awards. Her book *Don't Get Mad, Get Even* won the Silver Falchion for the best collection of 2013. Barb runs a freelance editing and proofreading service and is a coeditor of the Chesapeake Crimes series. She lives with her dog in Winchester, Virginia, and has never actually seen—or smelled—an exploding cow. She blogs at www.SleuthSayers.org and www.PensPawsandClaws.com/blog. Learn more at www.barbgoffman.com.

YOUR CHEATIN' HEART

BY MARIANNE WILSKI STRONG

On Halloween night many years ago, my mutt Buddy, part Jack Russell terrier and part only Buddy's mother knows what, discovered that Ditch Vlatek was a corpse.

I was twelve. I spent most of the afternoon helping my mother arrange little baskets of yellow and purple pansies for All Souls' Day. We didn't know at that time that we should have made one more basket, for Ditch Vlatek, the town's reigning black sheep.

I worked sullenly because Mom refused to let me dress up as Superwoman for the evening of trick or treat. Aunt Sophie had called to advise Mom that Josephine—on the phone, she always used my full name instead of Jo—should stay home because the weatherman had predicted a cold and sleety evening of about thirty-five degrees. So Mom insisted that I wear my great-uncle Dick's altered, heavy World War I uniform. I didn't put up too much of a fight because the uniform was always a big hit with the guys at the saloons, and that meant big-time money, at least big-time for a twelve-year-old girl.

You see, in Scranton, back in the fifties and sixties, we kids went trick or treating in the saloons. No silly knocking on doors of homes, squeaking out "trick or treat," and opening a bag for somebody to drop in a peanut butter cup. In the saloons, we kids earned money by a performance of our choice.

I, befitting a kid who got A's in English class, recited A.E. Housman's "On Moonlit Heath and Lonesome Bank." I can still recite a stanza of that poem:

So here I'll watch the night and wait
To see the morning shine,

When he will hear the stroke of eight
And not the stroke of nine.

Well, Ditch never even heard the stroke of eight. He was occupying his usual chair in the saloon, but he was dead though nobody realized it.

At Mr. Joseph Bednar's saloon, I was first in line. Buddy, who always came with me and howled to accompany my recitation, giving it a melancholy aura, sat by my feet, his white body quivering in anticipation. But then he began acting strangely. He kept getting up and straining on his leash toward where Ditch was sitting, apparently asleep, his hunter's cap pulled low over his forehead. I'd pull Buddy back into place, and he'd start growling, a low, steady growl, like some alarm gone off.

When I began reciting, Buddy began to howl as usual. But then he stopped and started growling again. I was so upset, I forgot the line about the dead man standing on air, and had to recite stanza two again. Humiliated, I got back in line, yanking Buddy to my side.

Carl Staski was next. He began singing "Your Cheatin' Heart." Buddy got up and pulled me toward Ditch again, straining at his leash and growling. Carl threw me a dirty look. I pulled Buddy away from Ditch, glad he hadn't woken the mean sucker up. Among his other amusements, like cheating Ms. Shilski, his landlady, out of rent money, cheating the saloon patrons at cards, pilfering money from his girlfriends, putting slugs instead of quarters into our trick or treat bags, and dreaming up ways to cheat the government out of taxes and welfare money, Ditch liked pulling the ears of dogs till they whined. He especially enjoyed pulling the ears of Mrs. Bednar's poodle, Frenchy. Ditch would sit in his usual chair underneath the shelf where Mrs. Bednar, the saloonkeeper's wife and Ditch's cousin, occasionally stored a small pan or two when all her other shelves were jammed with pots and pans and dishes for cooking the bar's famous kielbasa and potato pancakes. Ditch would rock forward to pull Frenchy's ears, then slam the chair back against the wall, pitch forward again, then back, laughing so hard he'd almost fall out of the chair. If a pan were on the shelf, it would shake and rattle as if frightened of Ditch, then settle down until Mrs. Bednar rescued it.

Unlike Frenchy, who was a sucker for Ditch's offer of a piece of beef jerky, Buddy had never tolerated Ditch. In fact, two Halloweens ago, he bit Ditch, leaving a nasty little scar on Ditch's left thumb.

I was horrified when Buddy pulled again, this time so hard I lost control of his leash. Buddy scrunched down and scrambled toward Ditch. I tried to grab the leash. We were all better off when Ditch was sleeping, as he usually did after a night of carousing, when he would let himself into the saloon with his key, then slump into his usual chair in the bar from about two in the morning till about six in the afternoon when either Mr. Bednar or Mrs. Bednar officially opened the place for the evening.

Well, Carl had just finished belting out words about crying and sobbing all night when Buddy reached Ditch. Buddy's tail rose up like a warning flag on a coast guard station when a storm is approaching. He started growling and pawing at the floor, like some miniature bull.

"Ditch must be dead drunk again," somebody said.

Mr. Bednar went over, stood a moment looking at Ditch, then reached out and shook Ditch's shoulder. "Ditch?" he said.

Ditch slipped further down in the chair.

Buddy jumped away, then scrunched down again and crawled toward Ditch, sniffing. Mr. Bednar knelt down by Ditch. "Holy Mother," he said. "Call an ambulance," he yelled to Mr. Peleski, who stood staring for a moment, then headed for the phone. Mr. Bednar pushed Buddy away from Ditch. "Get your dog away, Josephine," he said.

I grabbed Buddy and scurried back to my place, mortally embarrassed by Buddy's behavior.

We all strained to see what was happening.

Mr. Bednar lifted Ditch's left hand by the wrist, then dropped it. He lifted Ditch's hat a little, then yanked it back into place. "Never the mind the ambulance, Peleski," he yelled. "Call the cops."

Nobody else said anything. Nobody moved.

Then everything happened at once. Somebody said they'd better go to the kitchen to tell Mrs. Bednar and maybe even call Ann, Ditch's ex-wife. Somebody else said Mrs. Bednar would be relieved to be rid of her cousin at last and Ann would probably celebrate. Mr. Peleski asked Mr. Bednar what the hell he had seen under Ditch's hat. Somebody else said something about Ditch's brains being bashed out. Somebody else said that was impossible because Ditch didn't have any brains. Mr. Bednar told Chester Krolski to get us kids out. Mr. Krolski came over, opened his big arms, and practically swept us toward the door. We all scuttled out backward, straining our necks to see Ditch.

Outside the bar door, Mr. Krolski told us all to get on home.

"I didn't finish 'Your Cheatin' Heart,'" Carl wailed.

"Well, Ditch's cheatin' heart is finished and that ain't a bad thing," Mr. Krolski said. "Damned if that dog didn't realize it before anyone else." He looked at Buddy with considerable respect. Then he waved his arms at us as if he were shooing away a flock of pigeons. "Get on home. Now."

I walked home a little shaken, but proud as punch, not even minding the sleet that had begun to fall. Buddy was a hero.

* * * *

A week later, Strut, our leader, called us kids to a meeting in Flynn's field. With his chest thrust out as usual, Strut, as we knew he would, had some information from his father, the chief of police. I was late because Mom had sent me over to borrow Aunt Sophie's big cast-iron pot and Buddy had yelped and strained all the way back, jumping up toward the pot like he always did when he thought he would get some of Aunt Sophie's cooking.

I got to the field just as Strut was getting to the key point. "Dad says that the coroner said that at about seven thirty in the morning, somebody bashed Ditch right smack on the top of his head with something heavy, but not sharp, and killed him."

"Was his head all bashed in?" Carl asked.

"Well," Strut said. "Dad said something about brain spots or clots. I think the blood and brains were all mashed into his hair and under his hunter's cap. That's why nobody knew he was dead."

"Bleah." Judy stuck out her tongue and held her stomach.

"Buddy knew," I said.

"Right," Strut conceded. "Buddy did real good. But we're going to find out who did Ditch in." We all looked wide-eyed at Strut.

Buddy yawned. I should have known then that Buddy had already figured it out.

"Dad says this is a tough case," Strut went on, "because half of Scranton wanted to bash in Ditch's head. Dad says everybody would rather see the murderer get a medal than get fried in the chair."

"Bleah," Judy said again.

"So," Johnny Reilly said, "if your dad can't find out who did it, how can we?"

Strut looked round, taking his good-natured time to keep us all in suspense. "I have a suspect. We are going to look for Marty Cranson's shovel."

We all stared at Strut.

Buddy yawned.

Finally Judy spoke up. "Who's Marty Cranson?"

Strut almost busted the buttons from his shirt. "Marty Cranson," he announced, "is the guy who owns the farm next to my aunt Catherine's place, down there by the river. Mr. Cranson said he was gonna crack in Ditch's head with a shovel the next time Ditch blasted away, shooting at deer near the farm. Dad says Ditch nearly blasted Mr. Cranson's wife once."

"Wow," Jimmy said. "So we gonna look on Mr. Cranson's farm for the shovel?"

"No use," Francis Zimowski said, adjusting his glasses.

"We are," Strut said, ignoring Francis. Francis was a pretty clear thinker, but he was as dull as ditchwater, so nobody ever paid any attention to him. "We're going up to the farm tomorrow morning because Mr. Cranson is going down to Bloomsburg for a farm machine auction. We'll search his three barns."

"Most men would have just shot Ditch. My advice," Francis said, "is *cherchez la femme.*"

Buddy stretched and wagged his tail.

"Who's that?" Judy asked.

"It's French," Francis said.

"We don't know any French guys," Jimmy said.

"I mean," Francis said patiently, "look for a woman. I've heard talk that Ditch's ex-wife and his current girlfriend had plenty of reasons to kill him."

Buddy yawned and Strut went back to his own theory, giving orders to the boys about where and what time to meet.

"What do Jo and me do?" Judy asked.

"No girls," Strut pronounced. "Too dangerous."

"Wait a—" Judy started.

I stopped her with a yank on her arm. I knew protesting wouldn't do any good. Besides, I didn't think Ditch got done in by Mr. Cranson's shovel. For once, I agreed with Francis.

* * * *

The next afternoon, Judy and I walked over to Scranton High School, where we waited outside for the cheerleaders, including Dottie, Ditch's stepdaughter, to finish their practice session. I figured Dottie's mother, Ann, might have done in Ditch.

Dottie came out in her blue captain's sweater with big gold letters spelling out SCRANTON HIGH. She looked real pretty, a lot prettier than she had five years before when she'd always looked skinny and sad. That was when Ditch was still living with Dottie and beating up on her and her mother.

I asked about the next basketball game and then jumped right into asking if she and her mom had heard about Ditch.

"Sure," she said. "Mom says she's glad Ditch got it. So am I. He was bothering Mom again."

Judy and I raised eyebrows at each other.

Buddy yawned.

"Eh, your mom over at the saloon anytime last week?" Judy asked.

I rolled my eyes at her.

Dottie laughed. "You two pint-size detectives trying to find out who killed Ditch?"

I was going to deny it, but Dottie was too smart to fool. "Yeah," I said. "Sorry, Dottie."

She laughed again. "I would have done in Ditch myself if I'd had the chance. As a matter of fact, Jo, I intended to turn Ditch in for welfare cheating. I got the idea from your favorite aunt."

"My aunt Sophie?" I asked.

"Yeah. Mom and I saw her two weeks ago after eight o'clock mass. Mom was pretty upset about Ditch harassing us because she poured out her heart to your aunt. That's when your aunt told Mom to turn him in for welfare cheating."

"She do it?" I asked.

Dottie shrugged. "No. She told your aunt she was afraid Ditch would go after her if he suspected she turned him in. Anyway, I don't have to do it now."

"Yeah," I said, "somebody saved you the trouble. Any idea who?"

"Not Mom. She wasn't anywhere near the saloon on Halloween. After mass, she went straight to the lady she takes care of."

"Oh," I said, relieved for Dottie, but a little disappointed. My chief suspect was innocent.

"I'll tell you what, Jo," Dottie said. "If you insist on finding the murderer, try Mrs. Krolski. She and Ditch were running around, but then Ditch beat her up and dumped her."

"Mrs. Krolski?" Judy asked, her eyes wide. "The lady at the powder and lipstick counter in Woolworth's? The one with the real blond hair and the big dark eyebrows?"

"That's her." Dottie laughed.

"Yeah," I said slowly. "Chester Krolski's wife. She's one mean lady."

Dottie laughed and gave me a friendly punch on the arm. "Go for it," she said and marched away to rejoin her friends.

"Mrs. Krolski is the one who chased us out of Woolworth's for opening the lipsticks, isn't she?" Judy asked.

"You bet she is," I said. This was perfect. I could get heroine status for revealing her as Ditch's murderer and get revenge for me and Judy at the same time.

Buddy yawned.

* * * *

I intended to go over to Woolworth's as soon as I had a chance, but the next morning I had the dreadful thought that maybe Mrs. Bednar, Ditch's own cousin, had bumped off Ditch. Maybe she had gotten sick of letting Ditch sit around the bar at all hours, eating the food she cooked for customers, drinking up the profits, and pulling Frenchy's ears. I felt real bad. I'd have been happy to turn in Mrs. Krolski, but I would have hated to turn in Mrs. Bednar. She was real nice to all us kids.

I decided to have a talk with her and settle once and for all whether she'd killed Ditch or not. Maybe murderers' tongues turned black, like Sister Angelica said in religion class would happen if you received communion in mortal sin. I headed for the saloon, Buddy trotting along beside me.

Mrs. Bednar was there, getting the kielbasa ready for the night's customers.

"Gee, Mrs. Bednar," I said, thinking myself super clever. "I bet it takes you a long time to package all that kielbasa. I bet you have to start work at eight in the morning or even earlier." I opened my eyes wide, determined not to blink. I'd have to look carefully to see if her tongue was black.

"Not that early." She laughed, revealing a pearly-pink tongue. Scratch that theory.

"But don't you always open the bar really early on Saturdays so people can come anytime to pick up their cases of soda or beer or their packages of kielbasa?"

"Of course we do, honey. We unlock the door, even if we're not in the bar until we open officially in the afternoon. Nothing ever happened until now. Not even a dollar stolen from the saloon." Mrs. Bednar put down a package of kielbasa and looked at me. "Jo, does this have anything to do with Ditch?"

"Well, uh, well, yes. I was just wondering what time the bar was open on Halloween."

"Joe opened the bar around six as usual, honey." Mrs. Bednar fed Buddy a piece of kielbasa. He wagged his tail and jumped up and down for a pat. Buddy, I thought, might recognize a victim, but he sure didn't seem to know a murderer.

"Well, uh, well." I gave up trying to be subtle. "Strut says Ditch was killed at about seven thirty."

"Yes, that's what the chief told us. Why?"

"Well, I was getting worried. Strut said it was real important for everybody to have an alibi for about eight or so."

Mrs. Bednar gave me a hug. "Why, sweetie, don't you worry about Joe and me. After Joe opened the bar, we went to All Souls' mass really early because Joe had to get ready to collect the offerings. After mass, we went to Joe's mom. We were there until late afternoon."

Jeez, I thought, the whole town has the same alibi. My mother and I were in trouble. We'd gone to the ten o'clock mass. "You see Mrs. Krolski at mass?"

"Irene Krolski?" Mrs. Bednar thought a moment. "Well, I'm not sure. At least, I don't remember seeing her? Why?"

My eyes narrowed. "Not at mass, eh?" I was brilliant. Darn, I should have had a raincoat, a badge, and one of those hats with a brim. "You see her anywhere near the saloon that day?"

"No, I didn't. As far as I know, poor Ditch was the only one in here during the day." Mrs. Bednar thought for another moment. "Except, now I think of it, maybe, for your aunt Sophie."

Buddy strained toward Mrs. Bednar and earned another piece of kielbasa.

My mouth fell open. "Aunt Sophie?"

Mrs. Bednar wrapped up another batch of kielbasa. "Uh-huh. I guess she was here. She must have come to pick up her pot."

"Oh," I said. "Yeah." Everybody knew that Aunt Sophie made the best pigs in a blanket in town, letting them simmer for hours in her big cast-iron pot on Mrs. Bednar's big coal stove. "So Aunt Sophie was here the day Ditch died?"

"Well, I don't know for sure. Your aunt Sophie made a batch of piggies for the church on Friday and said she was going to make another batch on Saturday, so she left her pot here. But I guess she decided against making more piggies because, now that I think of it, her pot wasn't here when I came to the saloon in the afternoon."

"Did Aunt Sophie see Ditch when she picked up the pot?"

"I don't know. Anyway, Ditch often slept all day in the bar so nobody would think anything about it."

"Anybody else come into the bar?" I asked.

Mrs. Bednar shook her head. "I don't think so. Just Frenchy of course." She sighed. "He just didn't know enough to stay away from Ditch."

Buddy growled.

"Well, Frenchy's sure not the killer," I said.

It occurred to me that Aunt Sophie might be able to finger Mrs. Krolski. Unlike Mrs. Bednar, Aunt Sophie would be sure whether or not Mrs. Krolski had been at mass. Aunt Sophie was like that. If you weren't there, she knew. If you were there, she knew. If you were supposed to be there and weren't, she'd check up, ready with an intimidating frown or with chicken soup, just in case you were ill.

I headed up to Aunt Sophie's.

When I got there, Aunt Sophie was baking a second batch of peanut butter cookies.

Buddy greeted Aunt Sophie with big sloppy slurps. He loved Aunt Sophie. He knew on which side his cookies were peanut buttered.

I started right in talking about Ditch.

Aunt Sophie shook her head. "I asked your mother to keep you home or at least near the house that night. I hope you haven't had bad dreams, Josephine."

"Nope," I said, reaching into the cookie jar. "It was kinda fun."

"Josephine," Aunt Sophie said, folding her arms over her quilted apron. "Someone getting killed is a very serious matter. A person has to think very carefully about it."

"I am," I said. "Aunt Sophie, do you know if Mrs. Krolski was at eight o'clock mass the day Ditch got it?"

"She was," Aunt Sophie said. "Afterward, she arranged to have a mass said for some relatives."

"Somebody shoulda kicked her out," I said, chewing my cookie disconsolately, disgruntled at losing my prime suspect again. "She's mean and, besides, she was Ditch's girlfriend. For a while, anyway."

Aunt Sophie gave me her sternest look. "Josephine, when a person comes to mass, they may be seeking forgiveness, and that's something we must all be ready to give."

I had a brilliant insight then. "Say, Aunt Sophie. Ditch was killed around eight or so, maybe a little earlier. Maybe Mrs. Krolski did him in, then hurried to mass to get forgiveness. Sure she didn't buy a mass for Ditch?"

Aunt Sophie folded her hands across her apron again.

I braced for a sermon.

"Josephine, first, we do not sell masses. We accept donations. Secondly, people like Ditch Vlatek bring disaster on themselves because God watches everything and he is just."

I opened my eyes wide. "You mean God killed Ditch?"

Buddy yawned.

Aunt Sophie tilted her head and nodded. "Yes, Josephine, I believe he did. I believe God put him right in the way of justice."

"Then why doesn't God zap Barbara Kulitski?" I asked. "She cheats on all the tests, and, besides, just because she's pretty she can get the boys to do her math homework, and that's cheating if I ever heard it."

"Now, Josephine, you just stop worrying about Ditch Vlatek and go downstairs and fetch a jar of canned plums to take home for yourself and your mother. And take a jar of red beet soup for Mrs. Garner next door. She's feeling poorly." Aunt Sophie rose and patted Buddy, who looked up at her adoringly.

I went down the cellar, feeling sorry for Mrs. Garner. Bad enough to feel sick, but to have to eat red beet soup on top of it.

Buddy came with me, hopping down Aunt Sophie's big steps on his little white legs.

I went to the storage room where Aunt Sophie kept all her canned goods and utensils. I looked around for the plums. I'd just spotted the jars of purple fruit when Buddy started growling.

I frowned at him. He sniffed the air.

Then he crouched down and crawled over to the low shelf toward Aunt Sophie's big cast-iron pot, which Mom had returned. When he got there, he stood up and started growling, his tail and ears straight up in the air, just like when he'd spotted Ditch for a corpse.

I watched him, hardly believing what I was seeing.

I approached the pot slowly, as if it were about to explode. I looked inside. Empty. I don't know what I expected to find. Half of Ditch's head, maybe. I stepped back, Buddy crouching and growling by my side, then stepped forward and looked into the pot again. It'd been scrubbed clean, but that certainly wasn't unusual for Aunt Sophie. She scrubbed everything.

I tried to think. Strut had said that Ditch was conked with something pretty heavy, but not sharp. The pot fit the bill. Had Aunt Sophie conked Ditch? But then I remembered. She couldn't have. She had been at eight o'clock mass and had gotten there early and stayed late to sell, uh, to accept donations for mass cards.

Aunt Sophie must have picked up the pot sometime after mass. Ditch would already have been dead. I pictured Ditch slumped in his seat beneath the shelf in the saloon.

I thought some more. "Holy Saint Thomas," I muttered. Mrs. Bednar had said that Frenchy had been in the saloon. I was willing to bet that Ditch offered him some beef jerky. Stupid little Frenchy fell for it, and Ditch yanked his ears. Ditch would have slammed back against the wall, then leaned forward, laughing. His last laugh. If Aunt Sophie had put her pot on that shelf right above where Ditch sat, it might have tipped and come down on Ditch's head, just as he was slamming back again. The pot must have bounced off the top of his head and hit the floor. He must have slumped back into his seat, looking peaceful. Maybe he was. For the first time in his life, uh, for the last time.

Then Aunt Sophie must have waltzed in, found her pot on the floor, realized, sharp cookie that she was, that the pot had bounced off Ditch's head, leaving a considerable dent.

"Holy Saint Catherine," I muttered, realizing why Aunt Sophie had tried to persuade Mom to keep me away from the saloon. She hadn't wanted us kids to see Ditch.

I thought some more about how she'd told Dottie's mother to put a stop to Ditch's harassment and how Dottie's mother had said she was too afraid. So maybe Aunt Sophie had deliberately left the pot exactly above where Ditch sat, leaving it to fall on Ditch's head or not, as fate or God decreed.

I shivered. I knew now what Aunt Sophie meant when she said God had put Ditch right in the way of justice, by way of the pot.

I stood there thinking, real hard.

Then I went to a shelf and picked out two jars.

Nope, I thought, I wasn't going to tell anybody about this: not Mom, not Strut, not even Judy. After all, I didn't know that Aunt Sophie's pot had accidently or deliberately killed anybody. Besides, Aunt Sophie was worth a thousand Ditches. I vowed that next Halloween and All Souls' Day, I would make an extra basket of pansies for Ditch.

Buddy tilted his head and looked up at me. He was the only other one who knew how Ditch died. I think he knew from the day Mom had sent me to borrow the pot. But he sure wasn't going to tell anybody.

Buddy turned and bounded up the stairs, his tail wagging.

Marianne Wilski Strong is the author of several series of mystery short stories published in *Alfred Hitchcock's Mystery Magazine* and *Ellery Queen's Mystery Magazine.* She grew up in northeastern Pennsylvania and uses its coal mining background for a series of stories based on the triumphs and tragedies of that area. She used her history background for a series of stories set in ancient Greece, featuring Kleides, a sophist, as the detective figure. Her current series, using her background in American literature, features a Cape May resident who uses the gothic and mystery stories of Louisa May Alcott to solve contemporary mysteries. She is a lecturer and a writer. For more information: www.wilskistrong.com.

THE OCTOPUS GAME

BY LINDA LOMBARDI

The hall of the aquarium filled with squeals of delight as Mr. Potato Head descended into the octopus tank. I watched as Rich manipulated the toy precisely into place with a pair of long tongs while the octopus concentrated on a plastic bottle containing a piece of squid. Octopuses, in case you don't know, are very good at unscrewing jar lids, and they love to eat squid. There is no honor among different cephalopods, it seems.

Octopuses are also very good at grabbing the tongs while you're working in their exhibit—or your arm, or anything else you put in there. Hence the bottle of squid, to distract her. Rich liked to start the Mr. Potato Head game with the toy nicely presented in the foreground of the exhibit. He'd never have time to position the toy so carefully unless the octopus had something else to work on.

Everyone oohed and aahed as they watched her unscrew the lid of the jar and slip a tentacle inside. She pulled out the morsel of food, and it quickly disappeared into the opening at the center of her eight arms.

"That's where her mouth is," I said to the crowd. "It's actually a really sharp beak, so this is not an animal you want to feed by hand."

Then she started to explore the exhibit for the next diversion. Just in time, Rich had completed his staging and pulled the tongs out of the tank.

I knew that in back, Rich was now closing the tank lid carefully and latching it. Octopuses are skilled escape artists, squeezing through places so tight you'd never imagine it possible. They're very squishable and very smart. Which means they need a lot of entertainment—enrichment, we call it in the business. The more intelligent the animal, the more likely it is to get into trouble when it's bored. So you have to try to keep one step ahead. Keeping an octopus is basically like owning a monkey with eight arms.

When I thought of it that way I wondered why I'd wanted an octopus in the collection. It was definitely more work than the usual fish and frogs that were the mainstay of my section of the aquarium. I'd been an assistant curator for only a few months, and I'd decided that my major goal—to start, at least—would be not to get into trouble. If someone left the lid unlatched and the octopus ended up eating the residents of an adjacent tank, I would definitely get in hot water—a metaphor for trouble that makes more sense in an aquarium than in most places.

But then the octopus started to take Mr. Potato Head apart, and I remembered why she was here. This was without question the coolest new animal I could have come up with. Of course I thought fish were interesting—I wouldn't be here otherwise. But an eight-armed, boneless creature that can disassemble toys without being taught—come on, who wouldn't ooh and aah?

So right now, watching her take the nose off of Mr. Potato Head, hearing the public exclaim with wonder, I felt great. This acquisition was my big management success so far. I just had to hope that assigning the exhibit to Rich wouldn't turn the whole thing into my first major debacle.

I know it's hard to have sympathy when a boss worries. I know it seems like your boss has absolute power over a domain that includes forty long hours a week of your precious existence. So far, though, I hadn't found that to be the case, now that I was on the other side of the equation. On the other hand, the thing where the boss doesn't seem to have a clue? Yeah. I certainly hadn't gotten my promotion because of any particular skills. I just happened to be in the right place at the right time and appeared to be the lesser of a number of evils—those evils being my former fellow employees, who now reported to me. Bunny-hugger Janice worked with our education collection, the only place where we had furry, cuddly things and you didn't need to know how to mix salt water or restart a dying pump. Overachiever Kate's high standards made her better than everyone else, in her eyes at least. Old-timer Bob thought that if the way we did something twenty years ago was good enough then, it was good enough now. His depth of experience was great to have around; his refusal to try anything new, not so great.

And now we had Rich. I had hired Rich, and I was afraid he was my first error. He looked good on paper and had been full of enthusiasm in his interview. He had a relevant degree, an internship from a better aquarium than this one, and the appropriate nerdy passion for marine life. But none of that guarantees the right attention to detail; he was turning out to be a problem child. He was always late, left jobs half done, never left instructions for the other aquarists when he was off, and—my biggest headache—bumped up against Kate's perfectionism more than any of his colleagues.

That left me where I had started, in the middle. I wanted to do a good job, but not too good, because I also wanted to go home on time. And that's what they want in management. Someone average. Someone who'll do new things as directed, but not push for new things that the administration didn't think of first. Someone who'll get along equally well—or equally badly, it's the same thing really—with both ends of the extreme. And that's the most important part because, let's face it, managing the animals is easy compared to handling the people. Despite the job description, I didn't need a degree in marine biology nearly as much as I needed one in psychology or some kind of conflict resolution.

And speaking of which, as I walked reluctantly away from the octopus exhibit—I had way too much work to do to stand there watching any longer—I saw Kate striding down the hall toward me with that look on her face, calling out, "Sara! We need to talk."

I tried not to sigh—I knew that was probably one of my own annoying characteristics—and hurried to head her off. I didn't want to have this conversation in the public area. Before she could launch into a tirade I said, "Let's go back here," gesturing to the door to the service area behind the tanks.

Kate nodded, with only the tiniest scowl, and followed me. But she barely waited till the door closed behind us before erupting.

"I just looked at the crickets. Rich didn't clean them properly again. How many times do I have to explain to him how to do it? He shouldn't have herps in his area if he's not willing to help maintain the live food properly...."

As she ranted on, I nodded, making a sympathetic face, and let my mind wander. She always explained more than she needed to, so you only had to listen to half of what she said. Although in this case, I agreed with her. You should think of caring for your crickets like you're a farmer—you're raising food and you want it to be of high quality. And Rich was sloppy about it, like he was with everything else. But what could I do? I couldn't fire someone for not cleaning the crickets up to Kate's standards. I wasn't sure I could even put something so trivial in his performance plan. As long as he made sure they had food and water, it wasn't a matter of life or death even for the crickets.

"So what are you going to do about it?" Kate demanded.

Already six feet tall, Kate appeared to draw herself even taller, threatening. I was a little shorter than average, so she looked like an Amazon. But Kate was more than just tall. Not a single glossy blond hair was ever out of place. She never seemed to tire. After being on her feet all day she went home and played in a soccer league to relax. You wouldn't want to meet her in a dark alley, especially if she'd caught you not cleaning the crickets properly or rolling up her hoses wrong.

"I'll talk to him again," I said. Rich only took care of the crickets on Kate's days off, so it didn't have much effect in the long run, but there was no point in mentioning that. I'd found that trying to reason with her just made her angrier. She didn't want to be reassured. She wanted justice.

She made a face, of course. I clearly didn't measure up to her high standards. But I didn't expect to, so it didn't bother me.

"Okay then." I turned to go.

"Wait," she said.

I turned back, quickly planting a smile on my face. I was getting good at that.

"And Bob. Not only doesn't he roll the hoses up right—I come back from my day off and there's a huge mess in my area—but he's not following the diet changes I asked for. He's still feeding the old diets. He's not even trying to conceal it. He writes it right in the log book."

"He probably just forgets. You know he's on automatic pilot after all those years," I said before I could stop myself, momentarily forgetting that it's a waste of time trying to explain another point of view to Kate.

"That's no excuse," she said. "The rule is to follow the written diets. Mine are up to date in the records, unlike some people I could mention. It's his job."

"I'll bring it up in the weekly meeting. And we can post a reminder in the kitchen."

I felt like I was possessed, hearing the words come out of my mouth—just the sort of thing I used to hate hearing management say. But now I understood why managers said these things. When you couldn't solve the problem, you did something ineffectual but visible. That way you couldn't be accused of doing nothing. *It was right there on the whiteboard in the kitchen, see?*

"Fine." She scowled again, turned, and walked away.

As I headed back to my office, I filed the interaction away in my mind as a moderate success. The thing you have to remember is that everyone needs to feel special. Bob had to feel that his years of experience meant something, in the face of all the young whippersnappers with more education and new ways of doing things. Rich did a careful job of setting up Mr. Potato Head more nicely than anyone else would, no doubt believing it was more important than the disheveled state of his behind-the-scenes work area. And Kate, well, she had her high standards for every little thing, standards no one else could possibly live up to.

So I tried to keep conflict to a minimum by letting them all believe they were right. And believe me, there was plenty of opportunity for conflict. For one thing, people don't get into working with animals because they are good at getting along with members of their own species. And it doesn't help that we work in such tight quarters, where it's especially hard not to get on each other's nerves or step on each other's toes. From the warm, comfortable, and spacious public side of the aquarium you'd never know that behind the scenes it felt a lot like working in a submarine, and not only because of the proximity to water. Simply tripping over someone's hose for the ten millionth time could be enough to send you over the edge. But we also had to deal with it being cold all the time. The heat in back hadn't worked for a while. Because of budget cuts, it was hard to get stuff fixed that we really needed for the animals, so the humans simply put up with the cold, and everyone wore their coats. But it left people irritated. We all had different ways of handling the stress. And my way was to speak in a soothing voice, send out memos to everyone by email, and post reminders in the kitchen. It was my role in the ecosystem, and there was no point in fighting it.

I paused to commune for a moment with the hellbenders, which were out from under their rock hides for a change, but almost immediately they swam back into their little caves, leaving the exhibit apparently empty again as usual. I knew how they felt. Some days I wanted to swim under a rock and hide from everyone too. But right now I had to go write another memo.

* * * *

Most days I get to work before everyone else. It's a good time to check all the tanks and exhibits from the public side and see what needs attention without everyone thinking I'm checking up on them. Usually the issues are minor, algae on the glass or a sign peeling off. But this morning, even from the far end of the hall, I could see that something was very wrong with the octopus tank.

I broke into a trot. The octopus was my big success. And the exhibit had cost a huge amount of money. This was the last place I needed a problem.

I couldn't make sense of what I was seeing at first. My mind refused to take the patterns and resolve them into a coherent picture. It took me several moments to admit what was in front of me. Rich was floating lifelessly in the water.

Years of yelling at people not to tap on the glass failed me as I gave in to my first impulse and banged on the tank as hard as I could. Did I think maybe Rich was swimming in the fifty-degree water for fun? That he was floating there asleep and I would wake him up? I don't know. I wasn't thinking. I was panicking.

My pounding had no effect except to make the octopus stir and start to move around the tank. And immediately I realized that I'd just made matters worse. I needed to get Rich out of the tank, and the last thing I needed was competition from the octopus.

I ran around to the service-area door and fumbled with the keys. It seemed to take forever to open the lock, but finally I was inside. I climbed the ladder behind the octopus tank. The tank lid was closed, but not latched. I opened it and propped it up and then started to pull at Rich's body. He was soaking wet, wearing his coat, and bigger than me. And I couldn't get any leverage. And now the octopus had gotten interested and was trying to pull him back.

I stopped and stood there, breathing heavily. Nothing in my training had prepared me for this. You have to be able to think on your feet in an emergency if you work with animals. I'd always been good at this before. But now my brain was as sluggish as if it had been in the cold tank all night with Rich's body.

And body was what it was. I had no doubt. I was used to finding dead things in tanks occasionally, and it turned out that this wasn't that different. There was no question he was dead. I looked around, trying to calm myself by thinking logically. I was going to have to write a report, I thought, now on the verge of hysterical laughter. That was the boss's job, to write the report when something went wrong. What would I write?

Rich had been the last one on duty last night, scheduled for the late shift. I knew he usually didn't do much real work after everyone else left. He surfed the web or puttered around playing with the animals. Which was okay with me. The point of the late shift was to close up after the public left, and to have someone here if there was an animal emergency. It was more or less like being on call. I didn't demand much else.

But Rich must have been doing some actual work last night, setting up Mr. Potato Head for the octopus to play with—after all, the game was as much for her entertainment as the crowd's. Mr. Potato Head was lying on the ledge around the tank. So Rich must have climbed the steep ladder to the catwalk with both hands, Mr. Potato Head safely in his coat pocket. Then he'd have rested the toy on the ledge—it would have fallen out of his pocket otherwise—while he crawled out on the catwalk, planning to reach back with tongs to pick the toy up, then place it at the front of the tank—the very best position for visitors to see it. Other people might not have bothered to set the toy up just so, since there was no one there to watch the game, but that's Rich for you. He probably imagined the octopus liked it that way.

So what had gone wrong? He must have reached back toward Mr. Potato Head with his tongs and hit his head on one of the pipes running along the ceiling. All of us did this once in a while. No matter how often you'd climbed up on top of a particular tank, sometimes you'd make a wrong move and whack yourself. The space was just too tight to avoid it.

Usually the worst result was a headache. But Rich must have been knocked unconscious, if only for a moment. In another tank, there was a chance he might have fallen backward, floated long enough to come to, chilled but otherwise unharmed. But in this tank we had the eight-armed monkey, always looking for something to explore. She must have pulled him down like she pulled down all the objects we put in her tank.

And when he fell in he must have jarred the tank lid so it fell shut. I felt guilty for thinking this, but at least that was one bright side. Even though the lid hadn't been latched, the octopus had not gotten out. She'd had enough entertainment, I guessed, with Rich's body. I shuddered, thinking of how she must have explored all the openings she could get her tentacles into, just like she did with the different toys we gave her.

Thinking through it all logically, I was breathing more evenly now. I realized that there was nothing I could do for Rich. I climbed down the ladder and went to make the appropriate phone calls.

* * * *

They closed the aquarium for the day while the police investigated, though they seemed to believe the obvious—this was an accident. The following day we were running around like mad trying to catch up. I was doing a water change on the octopus. Something big and out of the ordinary had fallen in there. You changed the water when that happened. It was a relief to have procedure to follow. A comforting routine.

Mr. Potato Head was missing an ear. I'd noticed it when I put him away before the ambulance came to take the body, out of some odd notion that it was undignified to have the toy sitting there watching. Now I peered into the tank as I siphoned the gravel, hoping to find the missing piece. I wasn't sure I'd be able to use the toy again—it would be very different now, watching the octopus take apart something with human features. But I didn't want the ear left in the tank. I doubted she could get hurt or make trouble with it, but I didn't want to take chances. You can't trust an octopus. After siphoning the heck out of the gravel without finding the ear, I realized the piece likely was in the pocket of Rich's coat. It had probably come loose from the head while Rich climbed up the ladder.

I removed the siphon from the tank, turned on the fill valve, and rummaged in my coat pocket for my refractometer. It wasn't there, and I was too weary to look for it. I stuck my finger in the running water and put it in my mouth. It tasted normal enough. Kate usually mixed the salt water, so it was going to be right 99.9 times out of a hundred. It wasn't worth worrying about.

I sat down heavily on the catwalk and watched the water spill into the tank. I was thankful for once for the micromanagement of the curators above me. The rule that you couldn't leave the area while a tank was filling meant that I was going to get a nice long rest sitting here. Or so I thought, but then I heard the door to the service area open and slam shut.

"Have you thought about how we're going to divide up Rich's area till we get someone new?"

It was Kate, obviously. I opened my eyes. Of course I hadn't thought about it. We were all busy trying to catch up. I hadn't thought more than five minutes in advance all day.

"What would you like to do?" I said, trying to keep the weariness out of my voice. It was good to get input from the staff before making a decision. They had to feel you were listening to their concerns.

"I think I should take all of his herps. I'm not sure how well he was taking care of them. It would be good to have an expert keeping an eye out for any ill effects."

I nodded. This would be inconvenient because the handful of amphibian and reptile exhibits were scattered around his area. It would be simpler to divide everything up geographically, with each row of tanks going to a different person, instead of an exhibit here or there. But it would be even simpler not to argue with Kate.

"We can talk about it at morning meeting tomorrow," I said.

"I'm going to train Bob to clean the crickets on my days off," Kate continued. "Probably that job hasn't changed much in twenty years. I think he can handle it."

I nodded again. Let her divide up Rich's responsibilities. If she wanted to do my work for me, that was fine. Right now, she could have my job if she wanted it, I thought, my eyelids drooping again. I put the listening smile on my face and concentrated on the soothing sound of the water rushing into the tank as she began her next soliloquy.

* * * *

Rich's death was sad and horrible, but honestly, it was also a huge inconvenience. It meant a lot of extra meetings with upper management, who were demonstrating their usual hysteria in the face of every crisis. Should we have a special protocol for working the octopus, with two people needing to be present at all times, like some places did for venomous snakes? Should we shut down the exhibit and ship the animal to another facility? Should we run around shouting that the sky has fallen?

The meetings wasted a lot of time, but I knew that soon enough the administration would flutter off and take their short attention spans to the next crisis. They'd decide on some minor but visible response instead of the initial frantic and massively inconvenient proposals for major changes. Probably we'd just have to put a warning sign on the tank. For a while, we'd think of Rich every time we looked at it. But eventually, it would become background noise, like all the other labels that no one reads.

The biggest inconvenience was that I had to hire Rich's replacement. We needed a person with a little more attention to detail, so with any luck we'd get someone who didn't push all of Kate's buttons. It seemed cold to be thinking that way, because I had liked Rich despite his flaws, but I was moving on.

In the meantime, the final inconvenience was that here I was, weeks later, about to change the water in the octopus tank again. No one else wanted to work the exhibit, and I didn't want to force them.

I grabbed a coat from the hooks outside the office and carried it through the warm part of the building to the service area. When I put it on, I realized immediately that it wasn't mine. The sleeves fell to my knuckles, for one thing. I must have grabbed Kate's coat by mistake.

I let myself sigh, since there was no one nearby to be bothered by it. Even if I rolled them up, I couldn't work with those sleeves in my way, and that's assuming I had the nerve to wear Kate's jacket without asking permission. But I didn't feel like trekking all the way back to the office. I'd just put up with the cold. I took off the coat and laid it on a step stool. Then, just as I was about to climb up the ladder, Kate's voice crackled over the radio.

"I can't find my keys. Has anyone seen them?"

I waited a moment, but when no one else responded, I reluctantly unclipped my radio from my belt. "Hey, Kate, I'm sorry, I've got your coat by accident. Maybe the keys are in it. I'm behind the octopus. Let me check."

I reached down and put my hand in one of the coat's pockets and felt something. I pulled it out just as Kate walked in the door. It was Mr. Potato Head's ear.

I glanced back and forth between Kate and the ear for a moment. Suddenly a very different picture took shape in my mind. Rich is on the ladder looking into the octopus tank, and Kate storms in, screaming at him about crickets or hoses or new diets or any of the thousand other things she found to harangue him about. She climbs up after him and, either intentionally or accidentally, he hits his head. And he falls into the tank or is pushed. And she makes sure he stays there.

Then she goes back down the ladder and gets Mr. Potato Head to set up the appearance of an accident. Because placing his favorite toy in the exhibit was the obvious reason Rich would have been in a position to fall into the tank. So she climbs up the ladder with Mr. Potato Head in her pocket, and she doesn't notice his ear is missing when she sets him on the ledge of the tank. Even a person like Kate, in that situation, would be in a hurry. Even she might miss such a small detail.

And then she closes the tank lid. But she couldn't latch it, not if it was going to look like an accident. That must have driven her crazy. She'd always make such a stink when she found that someone else had left a tank cover or door unlatched. But she had no choice.

I had gone home before her that day. She worked late a lot to finish tasks up to her high standards. She could easily have stayed around till the building closed, when only the two of them were there.

I looked at her, probably stupidly gaping. Her expression dared me to say something.

There was no way to prove it. Were her fingerprints on Mr. Potato Head or the lid of the tank? Even if they were, we all had a legitimate excuse to have our fingerprints on any of the tank lids. And even if octopus enrichment wasn't usually her job, Kate could have tossed the toy in for someone who asked. Or, more in character, picked it up off the floor where some annoyingly sloppy person had let it fall.

Besides, the case was already closed. The autopsy had shown Rich hit his head, and he had drowned. There was no way to tell that he'd had help. It would be Kate's word against mine.

From the challenging look in her eyes, I knew I was right. But anyone else would think I was crazy. It was obviously a tragic accident. I wasn't going to convince the world otherwise because I'd found a plastic ear in her coat pocket.

I handed her the jacket without a word and turned to put the ear piece in the box of octopus toys.

So now you see what I mean about how the boss doesn't really have that much power. There's nothing I can do. Except that now I am extra-careful to clean Kate's cricket bin well. And I put the exact instructions in everyone's performance plan too. They don't know why I make such a big deal of it, but it's okay. I'm the boss. I don't have to explain.

Linda Lombardi is the author of two mysteries featuring small-mammal keeper Hannah Lilly, *The Sloth's Eye* and *The Lemur's Cry*. She has worked as a zookeeper and as a professor of theoretical linguistics and also writes nonfiction about pets, wildlife, and conservation. Find out more at her website www.lindalombardi.com.

THE SUPREME ART OF WAR

BY JOSH PACHTER

Sleep is not usually a problem for me. I am in fact what you'd call a sound sleeper: I could sleep through a volcanic eruption, if we had volcanos in Northern Virginia, although we don't, so it doesn't come up, but I could if we did, if I had to.

Anyway, there I was, wide awake in the middle of the night, and that was unusual, so *something* must have awakened me.

I lay there for a while, trying to figure out what it could have been, and then gave up and decided I'd better go check the house, make sure everything was as it should be.

Getting out of bed quietly is not the sharpest tool in my toolbox, and Emily stirred, groaning, as my feet hit the hardwood floor.

"Come back to bed, Eddie," she said blearily, patting the empty space beside her.

I ignored her and padded downstairs, taking care to avoid Mister, who is Emily's lazy-ass cat, a big ball of fat dipped in dirty white fur, with a nasty disposition and a set of claws and a spitting hiss…everything you know and love in a feline, right?

Mister, by the way, is a female. Don't ask me how she got saddled with the name Mister. I have no idea—she was a part of the household before Emily and I met—and, frankly, I couldn't care less. She's a cat, remember, and I am definitely no cat lover.

Emily, by the way, is my mistress. It's an old-fashioned word, I know—you tell me a better one, and I'll use it. We've been together now for six, close to seven years. You hear a lot of "they met cute" stories out there, but Emily and I did not meet cute. I don't really want to talk about it. Let me just say that I was in a bad way back then, and she totally rescued me. I owe her a lot—I'm not exaggerating when I say that I owe her my life. I would do anything for that woman, even cohabitate with a damn cat.

In the kitchen, I drank some water, which woke me up pretty thoroughly. I prowled through the living room, the dining room, the laundry room, looking for something wrong, out of place.

It was in the archway leading to the family room that I found it. *Heard* it, I guess I should say. There was a faint scraping at the window. It was almost inaudible, but I have excellent hearing, and this must have been what had awakened me.

Keeping out of sight, I slipped across the soft pile carpet. And now I could *see* it, a shadow on the glass that moved slightly with every scratch.

There was someone outside the house, trying to jiggle the window open.

I hate to admit it, but I am not a tough guy. Truth be told, I suppose I'm what you might call a little on the scrawny side, and a situation like this was completely out of my wheelhouse. I wouldn't know what to do with a gun if I *had* one, and calling the cops was out of the question. I learned *that* lesson back when I was still on the streets. But what if this jerkwad was after more than just the family silver? What if he was here to hurt Emily? What if he was here to *kill* her?

I couldn't live with myself if I let anything happen to her.

I looked around the room for something I could use as a weapon, but who was I kidding? A weapon? Me? Mister would probably have a better chance of fighting off an intruder than I would—I've had direct personal experience of those claws I mentioned earlier, and, trust me, they can inflict some damage.

No, if I was going to do anything to prevent whoever that was on the outside from coming through the window, I was going to have to figure out something other than a hardware approach.

And what—I suddenly thought—if there was more than one of them? What if it was a pair of drug-addled teenagers, or a whole gang of—you should excuse the expression—cat burglars? This was going to be challenging enough as a one-on-one encounter. If I had to take on an entire freaking *army*, then I'd better think strategically.

I've never actually read Sun Tzu—truth be told, I'm not much of a reader—but I've heard Emily talk about him and that book he wrote, *The Art of War*. That's an interesting concept, by the way, war as an art form. And one thing I remember Emily saying—on the phone, I think, one of her late-night gabfests with a girlfriend from her college days—was this: "The supreme art of war is to subdue the enemy without fighting."

Now that sounded more my speed. Subdue the enemy *without* fighting. Huh. Interesting. But what did it *mean*, exactly? And how would it work in *this* particular case?

Looking up from my hiding place, I saw that whoever it was outside the window had given up on the idea of prying it open bare-handed. He was holding some kind of implement now—a screwdriver?—and trying to draw a circle on the glass. Guy had apparently seen too many movies—or not enough of them. Did he really think he was going to punch a hole through the pane without making enough noise to wake up the household?

He or they, I mean. Whoever.

"Subdue the enemy without fighting," I reminded myself.

Well, "If it were done when 'tis done, 'twere best it were done quickly." That's another one of Emily's: Shakespeare, if memory serves. *Hamlet?* No, not *Hamlet*, that other one she likes. *Macbeth.*

So I crept closer to the window and filled my lungs with air and barked, three of my sharpest, and—what do you know?—the bad man dropped his screwdriver and scurried off out of sight.

Pretty darned proud of myself, I pushed through my special door and went out into the backyard and found the screwdriver and lifted my leg, and then I went back inside and padded up the stairs—giving that useless snoring bastard Mister a wide berth as usual—and I jumped up onto the bed and snuggled in beside my mistress and went back to sleep.

Josh Pachter's short stories have been featured in *Ellery Queen's Mystery Magazine*, *Alfred Hitchcock's Mystery Magazine*, *Black Cat Mystery Magazine*, and many other periodicals and anthologies since the late 1960s, and his translations of crime fiction by Dutch and Belgian authors appear regularly in *EQMM*. *The Tree of Life* (Wildside, 2015) collects all ten of his Mahboob Chaudri stories in a single volume; *Styx* (Simon & Schuster, 2015) is a zombie-cop novel he wrote collaboratively with Belgian author Bavo Dhooge; and *Amsterdam Noir* (Akashic Books, 2018) is a collection of dark fiction he edited with Dutch crime writer René Appel. He lives in Northern Virginia with his wife, Laurie, and their dog, Tessa. www.joshpachter.com

KILLER

BY JOANNA CAMPBELL SLAN

"You're my best friend, Jonathan." Trudy Wilton tested a small chunk of white meat for coolness, and then set it inside her Chihuahua's food dish. "We're going to get through this together."

After gobbling down the treat, the tiny fawn puppy cocked his head and stared at his mistress. Trudy wondered if he could tell how tired she was. She scooped him up and cuddled the dog. "You bring me such joy. I knew this would be tough, but..."

Trudy set the dog back onto the floor carefully, then washed her hands. "Showtime," she said to Jonathan. She picked up the tray with its steaming bowl of chicken noodle soup, glass of fresh lemonade, white damask napkin, polished silver, and plate of oyster crackers. She'd done her best to make the meal seem appetizing, but she steeled herself, knowing her mother would find fault.

"Ma's cancer has spread," Trudy said to Jonathan as he followed her out of the kitchen. "It's gone from her lungs to her bones and maybe even to her brain."

Balancing the tray, Trudy climbed the stairs and crossed the landing. Using the scuffed toe of her shoe, she opened the door to her mother's bedroom.

Ma's grizzled hair poked out from under her auburn pageboy wig. Lipstick ran above, below, and around a sullen mouth full of too-big dentures. She didn't look at all like the woman who had raised Trudy. That woman had been meticulous about her makeup and proud of her gorgeous auburn hair. The cancer had ended all of that. But it had taken away more than Ma's health. It had also destroyed any semblance of kindness. Ma had always been demanding, imperious, and self-absorbed, but now she was also downright mean. "What took you so long? I'm hungry."

"I wanted to make sure your soup was good and hot. I made lemonade the way you like it. Fresh squeezed."

"Huh," Ma grunted. A bolster propped the older woman upright so she could watch her favorite TV shows. With a wave of an age-spotted hand, she shooed her daughter away from the screen. "Move. I can't see. You're a better door than window. Barn door, that is."

Jonathan waited by the bedroom door, sniffing the air cautiously. Over the previous eight months, he'd learned to fear the wrath of the old woman, who made no secret of her dislike for the pup.

Ma adjusted her trifocals and examined the golden broth closely, twirling her spoon in the liquid. Lifting a spoonful of dripping noodles, she said, "What is this? I told you I wanted Campbell's Homestyle Soup. With the big noodles. These little ones look like worms. I can't eat worms!"

Before Trudy could respond, Ma shoved the tray so hard it went flying. The soup bowl did a complete somersault and landed upside down on the bedspread.

"Ma! You'll burn yourself!" Trudy scrambled to lift the wet covers away from her mother's body.

Wrestling with the polyester comforter, Trudy fought to keep from screaming. The bedspread would need to be washed. The lemonade had splashed all over the carpet. The crackers had scattered like confetti. More work. As if it wasn't enough to wait on her mother around the clock. Trudy never seemed able to get caught up with the messes Ma made.

Jonathan scurried over to gobble down an oyster cracker.

"Stupid dog." Ma unhooked her cane from the headboard and flailed at the dog over the side of the bed. "Get away from me."

Jonathan yipped and cowered. Trudy snatched up her pup and looked him over carefully. He didn't appear to be hurt, just scared. Without a word to her mother, Trudy carried the dog downstairs and locked him in his crate. "This isn't punishment. You'll be safe here."

She grabbed a roll of paper towels and a trash bag. Back upstairs, Trudy bundled up the bedspread, pulled a blanket over her mother, and threw herself to her knees, sopping up the mess in the carpet. She was on all fours when her mother burst into noisy sobs.

"Ma? You okay?" Trudy did her best to sound concerned, but inside she was thinking, *Now what*?

"No, I am not. Where is Roger? Why isn't he here? What did I do to deserve this? I'm so lonely." Ma's gnarled hands gripped the blanket.

The shriveled woman, decaying from the inside, broke Trudy's heart. Patting her mother's shoulder, Trudy said, "I know you miss him. But I'm here, Ma. I'm doing my best."

The old woman twisted away. "Leave me alone. I want Roger. I don't want you here. Go away!"

"I wish I could," Trudy said under her breath as she headed toward the stairs. This had all been a mistake. Giving up her job in a bookstore in Chicago, moving back home to Fenton, Missouri, and thinking she could make things right with her mother before the old woman died. Madness. Absolute madness.

The past was a spool of thread, unwound and tangled, knotted too tightly to ever be free of itself. Despite Trudy's good intentions, she would never win her mother's love. Roger had been the long-awaited fair-haired son. He'd gotten his good looks from Ma. Trudy had been a change-of-life baby, a mistake. She'd come along just in time to ruin Ma's figure and her enjoyment of her husband's rising career. Worse yet, Trudy took after her dad, struggling with her weight her whole life.

The mess in the green shag carpet could be mopped up. The disaster of moving back home would be much more difficult to fix. It wasn't like Trudy had left behind a career, but she had said good-bye to friends and co-workers when Roger asked her to help out with their mother. "I'd do it, but I can't take time from the law firm. Not now. I'm being considered for partner. Another six months, maybe a year, and I can set my own schedule."

Trudy carried another tray of food up the stairs for her mother.

As Trudy settled the tray on her mother's knees, Jonathan, still caged downstairs, began barking. Trudy figured the kids next door were home from pre-school.

"Shut up!" Ma shouted. "I hate that dog! Hate him! I never said you could bring a dog here. I don't like dogs. I like cats. You know that. Get rid of him!"

No way, Trudy thought. He's all I have. In a careful tone, she said, "Jonathan will quiet down. He's trying to protect us by being a good watchdog."

"This is still my house. Mine. I want him out. Out!"

"Guess what? *The Price is Right* is on." Trudy picked up the remote and silently thanked God that her mother was a huge Drew Carey fan.

Trudy was putting the bedspread into the dryer when she heard her mother's querulous voice. "Roger! Oh, Roger, honey. You won't believe what that awful sister of yours did to me. She served me worms. Yes, worms. And I'm hungry. I haven't had anything to eat all day."

Trudy cleared her throat and spoke into the extension. "That isn't true, Ma. Just let me speak to him—"

But Ma simply talked louder. "I'm so scared, Roger. That dog of hers gets meaner every day. He tried to bite me."

Trudy ran upstairs and pried the phone from Ma's hands. For an eighty-year-old woman who was dying of cancer, she was surprisingly strong. Especially when thwarted. Trudy took the phone with her into the hallway and closed the bedroom door. "Roger? I'm right here. Ma's fine. You know about Jonathan, my Chihuahua. He's a sweetheart."

"Hey, Sis. Yeah, he looks sweet in his pictures."

Trudy smiled. Despite their differences, she loved her brother.

"So, how goes it?" he asked.

"Tough sledding. We had a rough morning. I think I need a break. Hard to believe I've been here eight months already."

"Yeah, well, at least you're living rent free. You don't have six senior partners breathing down your neck, watching your every move."

"Listen, it ain't easy being a full-time caregiver. Trust me." In the background, Trudy heard the muffled tones of a Jimmy Buffet tune. "Roger? Since when do law firms play 'Margaritaville' in their offices?"

"There's more to being a lawyer than trying cases. You wouldn't believe the office politics. Plus, I work eighteen-hour days. Then I'm expected to make nice with clients after hours. Bringing in the business. Rainmaking. That's the name of the game."

Trudy could hear the theme song of *Wheel of Fortune* through the door behind her. Ma would be content. For now. "Where exactly are you, Roger?" Trudy said as she walked downstairs.

Jonathan was sitting quietly in his crate, cocking his head to listen as Trudy spoke to her brother. She unlocked the door of the crate and let the dog out.

"What's this about your dog trying to bite Ma? She isn't in any real danger, is she?" Roger always changed the subject when he didn't want to answer certain questions. Trudy decided to let it go for now.

"Not hardly." In fact, Jonathan was sitting patiently at Trudy's feet, a sign that he needed to go out.

A woman's voice on the other end of the phone called out, "Roger? What are you doing?"

"Got to go," Roger said quickly, then hung up.

Trudy stared at the silent receiver for a very, very long time.

* * * *

The next morning, while Trudy sipped her coffee in the living room, Jonathan ran along the back of the sofa. His tiny ears stood at attention while he looked eagerly out the front window. Two deer stared back at him as they munched on Ma's yews. The tiny puppy scolded them, trying to shoo them away with a series of urgent barks. An autumnal breeze kicked up oak leaves, lifting them like two brown kites sailing against a crystalline blue sky. Winter was coming. Trudy shivered at the thought of being snowbound with Ma. Being cooped up would drive her crazy, especially with no one but Jonathan to turn to.

Trudy had hoped to rekindle high school friendships. Maybe meet someone special. But it had been impossible with Ma being so demanding.

"Yip! Yip!"

"Are you trying to protect me from those deer?" Trudy touched Jonathan's hindquarters. He looked up at her and wagged his tail so hard his entire body shook.

"Aren't you the best watchdog ever? You are such a handsome boy." Trudy ran her palm over his rounded head and bat-wing ears. In the short time Trudy had owned him, the puppy had become the light of her life. Maybe she was destined to be single forever.

As if in response to her musings, a dark blue sedan pulled up in front of the house. Jonathan barked as a man started toward the front door. There was something familiar about him, so Trudy opened up as he rang the doorbell. Behind her, Jonathan barked a warning to the intruder.

"Paul. Is that you?" Her jaw fell open as she stared into the eyes of Paul Jankowski. A few years older than she, Paul had been a close friend of Roger's in high school. He had changed, grown into himself. Always a bit nerdy and thin, Paul now filled out his navy blue jacket and tailored gray pants nicely.

Trudy suddenly felt self-conscious about her scruffy drawstring pants and tired "Life Is Good" T-shirt. After getting her mother breakfast and helping her with a sponge bath, Trudy hadn't had the energy to shower and put on makeup. Her face colored as she thought about how unattractive she must look.

"Hey, Trudy. Your brother phoned me. Can I come in?" With one smooth move, Paul displayed a Fenton Police Department badge. Trudy noticed he wasn't wearing a wedding ring.

"Of course you can. Let me grab the dog." She swooped Jonathan into her arms.

Paul rubbed the back of his neck and adjusted his shirt collar. "Is that it? The dog? Your brother asked me to check on it. Said it might be endangering your mother."

"Paul meet Jonathan, AKA Killer. Does he look like a big threat?"

Paul laughed and offered the back of his hand for Jonathan to sniff. "Not hardly."

Trudy debated with herself. She wasn't dressed for company, yet she didn't want to turn Paul away. "Wow. It's so good to see you. Would you like to come in? Can I get you some coffee?"

"Sure. Why not. That way I can report to your brother that I did my job properly. You know how lawyers can be. Sticklers for detail."

Only after she'd closed the door and gestured toward the kitchen did Trudy grasp the full of import of Paul's words: Her brother had asked Paul to spy on her. He hadn't taken Trudy's word that Jonathan wasn't a problem. "Roger filed a report with you?"

Her emotions flitted between anger and sadness when Paul shrugged and nodded. At least he looked embarrassed about it.

After Jonathan was in his crate, she poured a mug of fresh coffee for Paul. As he reached for it, their hands touched. An electric charge zipped up her arm, nearly causing her to drop the cup of hot liquid.

Paul must have felt it, too, because his eyes locked onto hers. "It wasn't just the fact I talked to Roger." His voice was husky. "We got a call from your mother. She claims you're holding her hostage."

"W-w-what? Paul, you can't be serious."

Now Trudy felt embarrassed. His interest had nothing to do with her personally. That strange tingle she'd felt was danger, not lust. Ma's complaint was behind Paul's visit and the way he was staring at her. She was a suspect.

"Yeah, I know." He had the good grace to act sheepish. A lock of his dark, curly hair fell over one eye. "I had to at least come by and check things out."

"When did this happen? I was with her all morning. This is the first break I've had. When I left her, she was sound asleep upstairs." But the minute the words were out of her mouth, a loud *thump* came from the bottom of the stairs.

Trudy raced past Paul. Her mother sat on the bottom step, her legs akimbo. Her nightgown was hiked up around her pale thighs. "Ma! Are you okay? What are you doing? If you wanted to come downstairs, you know I would have helped you."

Paul appeared at Trudy's side. "Mrs. Wilton? I'm Paul Jankowski from the police department. I'm an old friend of Roger's. Are you all right?"

Ma nodded, then glanced at Trudy with a gleam of triumph in her eye. She thinks she's won, Trudy realized.

"You sure?" Paul asked Ma. "Okay, then, can I help you to your feet? One-two-three."

Once levered to an upright position, Ma sputtered angrily. "This woman has taken over my house. I want her out. Right now. She's holding me hostage. She and that vicious watchdog. He wants to kill me."

"Ma, that is not fair, and you know it!" Trudy said through a clenched jaw.

Had it not been so irritating, it could have been comical. The once proper mother of Roger and Trudy's childhood was a distant memory, faded like the color of Ma's skin. Their mother's wig sat on her head like an abandoned bird's nest. Her blue-veined legs stuck out from under the thin cotton nightgown like stork limbs. Her fingers clawed at the railing with yellow nails that resembled talons. Her once perfectly proportioned nose had turned into a ghastly beak.

Who or what was this snarling creature? The one Trudy had returned home to care for?

"Come on, Ma. Let me help you back to bed." Trudy slipped an arm around her mother's waist and turned her around. "You know you can't handle these stairs. All you had to do was ring the bell next to your bed. I would have come and checked on you."

"Do you need help?" Paul's voice echoed in the stairwell.

"I'm fine. We do this all the time," Trudy started to say as they neared the top, but her mother interrupted with, "See how mean she is to me? I don't want her here. And that dog? I hate him. Help me!"

Trudy got Ma tucked in and promised to bring her a cup of tea. Trotting back down the stairs, she nearly ran right into Paul as he reached out to steady her. "Appears to me that you're the one being held hostage."

His voice was so kind, his touch so gentle, that she allowed herself the luxury of leaning into him. She rested her forehead against his chest and breathed in the clean scent of his spicy cologne. Tears welled up in her eyes, and she pulled back rather than get him wet. Speaking to his tie, she said, "I can't make her happy. No matter what I do, or how hard I try, it isn't enough. And the dog. She goes on and on about the dog."

Paul stepped aside, and Trudy hurried to the stovetop where she put on the kettle, all the while feeling grateful for a chore to do. Anything to keep her from letting loose and crying the way she thought she might.

"Hey, pup. He's obviously a killer, isn't he?" Paul squatted next to the crate and let Jonathan out. The Chihuahua ran to his toy box and picked up a bone-shaped stuffed gray toy. The little dog ran in a circle with the fuzzy bone in his mouth. Paul patted the floor, and Jonathan ran over and dropped his toy at the man's feet. But when Paul went to grab it, the dog snatched it up again, chomping the toy so that it squeaked.

Paul laughed at the dog's antics. "Why did you name him Jonathan? Big name for a little dog. What's the story behind that?"

While she made Ma's tea, Trudy explained that Jonathan was an applehead Chihuahua, a perfect example of his breed and worth every cent Trudy had taken from her scant savings account. The breeder had bragged on the dog's well-rounded skull and short muzzle, but Trudy had been attracted to his fearless personality. He'd been intended for the show ring, but his teeth came in crooked, so the breeder put him up for sale.

"See?" With gentle pressure, Trudy opened the dog's mouth. "He has a bad bite. Literally. I named him after a Jonathan apple. He's all I have." She blushed with embarrassment as she poured the hot tea into a yellow mug with the iconic smiley face. She hadn't intended to sound so much like a victim. Especially in front of Paul.

"It might feel that way some days, but that's not true." Paul came over and stood uncomfortably close to Trudy.

She shrugged and lifted down the sugar bowl.

"Call me if you need a break." Paul handed over his card. "I took care of my dad before he passed. It was tough. Really tough. My cell phone number is on the back."

After he left, Trudy stuck the business card on the refrigerator with a yellow-and-green magnet that advertised Ted Drewes Frozen Custard. Just the sight of Paul's name in bold type gave Trudy's spirits a little lift. Maybe Paul was right. What she needed was a break. With a sense of renewal, Trudy text-messaged her brother:

Roger, I need a week off. At the very least, come and stay with Ma for a weekend. I'm at the end of my rope. Love, T.

* * * *

The next day at eight a.m., the home health-care nurse rang the doorbell. Mrs. Foster wore her hair in a bun so tight that it seemed to pull all the humanity from her face. Her mouth settled into a permanent pucker of distaste. Even so, Trudy welcomed the woman's visit as a chance to run some errands, including a visit to the library. Ma had given Trudy a list of her favorite authors. She only read the goriest of mysteries.

Jonathan would stay in his crate while his mistress was gone.

When Trudy returned to the house, Mrs. Foster met her at the door. "We need to chat," said the prim woman, motioning Trudy into the kitchen and pulling out a chair at the table. "I understand how challenging senior care can be. Sometimes when an elderly person gets too demanding, the caregiver can snap. Abuse is, unfortunately, more common than we like to admit."

Abuse? The world tilted. For a heartbeat, Trudy thought she might pass out. She barely managed to set down the bag of books before sinking into her chair.

"Your mother is one of my more...obstreperous patients." Mrs. Foster paused, folding her hands in front of her. "*Obstreperous* means stubbornly resistant."

"No one knows that better than me." Trudy's mouth was so dry that her lips stuck to her teeth. Was Mrs. Foster commiserating or blaming? Trudy couldn't tell.

"*I*," corrected Mrs. Foster. "Not *me*, but *I*."

"Yes." To disguise her desire to roll her eyes, Trudy turned her attention to Jonathan, sitting patiently in his crate. His tail wagged at her encouragingly. Trudy smiled at him and struggled to stay calm.

"I'm concerned about what I see. There are signs that tell me you are having a hard time coping. I've decided I need to contact your brother."

For a tick, Trudy felt relief. Maybe if Mrs. Foster explained to him how tough taking care of Ma was, Roger would listen. "Oh, he has an idea what I've been going through. Ma's been really difficult. As a matter of fact, I just told my brother yesterday that I need a break. She's too much for me to handle without a few days off now and again."

"That might be for the best. Even so, I need to contact him and file a report."

"Report?" Stars danced in the edges of Trudy's vision and she felt sick.

"On the bruises."

* * * *

After Mrs. Foster left, Trudy paced the kitchen. She sent another text to Roger. This one more urgent: *Call me ASAP!*

When the little bell rang summoning her, Trudy climbed the stairs and tended to Ma. It took every ounce of self-control, but Trudy didn't ask about the bruises. Instead, she outdid herself acting solicitous. Once the old woman fell asleep, Trudy carefully lifted the sleeve on her nightgown. Four angry purple marks dotted the woman's loose skin on the front of her upper left arm. But the marks were not perfect ovals. Instead, they were small squares. And the placement wasn't right. If Trudy had grabbed her mother, the marks would have been at the back of the arm, not the front. On closer inspection, Trudy could also see the spacing between the marks was odd and didn't match a handprint. While her mother slept, Trudy used her phone to take pictures of the bruises.

Once back downstairs, she looked over the images. She also took pictures of her own hands, carefully documenting the embarrassing fact that she'd bitten her nails to the quick, but showing how the placement of the bruises didn't make sense. Clearly, Ma had hurt herself in a bid for Roger's attention. But how had she done the injuries and what had she used? Roger would need to know all this before he heard from Mrs. Foster. Trudy sent both sets of photos to her brother and called his cell phone. It went immediately to voice mail. She texted him: *This is an emergency! Call home!*

An hour passed. Pacing the kitchen floor, Trudy debated what to do. Soon Ma would wake up from her nap. Trudy would have no chance to talk to her brother in private.

"This can't wait," Trudy told Jonathan as she dialed the law office where Roger worked. "Once he hears my side of this, he just has to stick up for me."

"Bristol, Sturbridge, and Messina," said the cultured voice of the receptionist. "How may we help you?"

"Hello, this is Trudy Wilton. I'm calling for my brother, Roger."

"Mr. Wilton is not in right now."

Panic, raw and painful, rose in Trudy's throat. "It's about our mother. It's urgent. I've called his cell phone but it goes straight to voice mail. Please help me. I really, really need to get in touch with him."

"Oh, dear! I am so sorry. The cruise ship must be out of cell tower range. They'll be docking in Jamaica tomorrow. I'm sure he'll be calling in to get his messages."

* * * *

For the rest of the afternoon, Trudy picked up Paul's business card in between chores, looked it over, and set it back down. She couldn't bring herself to call the cop. "He's Roger's friend," she muttered to Jonathan. "That's all. I can't tell him how angry I am with my brother. He was just being nice when he told me I could call. It wasn't an invitation to whine about how unfair my life is."

Jonathan didn't seem to agree. The little dog brought her his stuffed bone. He shook it vigorously at her and growled playfully when she tried to snatch it back.

"See?" Ma's voice startled Trudy. She'd managed to climb down the stairs and sneak around the corner into the kitchen. "I told you that animal is mean. You need to get rid of him. Before he hurts me. He could bite me any minute. That dog is a menace."

* * * *

When Trudy's phone rang the next day, she didn't even get the chance to spit out a greeting.

"You pinched our mother? How could you?"

"I did nothing—"

"Mrs. Foster told me everything. There are laws against what you did, Trudy. Elder abuse is a crime."

"I didn't hurt our—"

"Ma's a defenseless old lady, and you hurt her! How could you?"

"I d-d-d-didn't—" It had been like this when they were little. Roger was always able to think on his feet, while Trudy stuttered and stammered.

"Right. I saw the pictures, Trudy!"

White hot anger spilled over. "W-w-when? B-b-between drinking margaritas and—"

"I didn't expect you to understand. It's part of my job!"

"You always did get away with murder!" she screamed.

"Murder? Now you're threatening our mother? You harm one hair on her head and I'll see to it you never get a red penny of her estate!"

The estate. That was it. That was what he was after. And he'd go along with any of Ma's lies to get it. Not that there would be much in the estate. Basically, the proceeds from the house. But it would be enough to start a new life.

Roger hung up after ranting for another minute, and Trudy brewed a cup of tea. Then she sat down to think, with Jonathan settling on her lap. Okay, so her mother didn't like her. Would never like her. But with a little money, she could start over. And by God, she deserved it for all the crap she'd been putting up with. But first, she needed to prove she wasn't hurting Ma.

* * * *

That evening, while Ma was in the bathroom, Trudy dug around in her mother's bedclothes. Under the pillows, Trudy found a clothespin. According to the image on Trudy's iPhone, the clamp matched the shape of Ma's bruises perfectly.

So that was how she did it.

Ma was pinching her own skin on purpose. To get Trudy in trouble. Maybe even send her to jail. Sure, Trudy could testify that she'd found the clothespin under the pillows, but who would believe her? Trudy tucked the clothespin into the pocket of her jeans. With shaking hands, Trudy helped her mother back into bed.

Trudy tucked Ma in. She had one hand on the light switch and had opened her mouth to say "good night" when the old woman said, "You need to get rid of that dog or I'm going to get rid of you. See if I don't. This is still my house. My rules. You'll be sorry you tangled with me."

"Yes, Ma."

Once downstairs again, Trudy took Jonathan out of the crate. She sat on the sofa and hugged him. His warm tongue lapped at her cheek. She felt tired. Defeated. What was the use? It was down to her and Ma. Opponents.

Ma had Roger, Mrs. Foster, and the law on her side.

Trudy had…Jonathan.

He seemed to know what she was thinking. He put a paw on each of her shoulders and licked her face tenderly. It was almost as if he were asking, "How can I help?"

"You can't do anything, sweetie." Trudy brought him to her face to kiss his nose. "I know you'd like to be my knight in shining armor. I know you'd save me from the mean old witch. But you can't. You're just a dog. I can't give you up. I won't. No way." In an act of desperation, she went into the kitchen, grabbed Paul's card, and dialed his number.

When he answered, she burst into tears.

"I'm on my way," he said. "Hang in there."

* * * *

He arrived with a pint of Ted Drewes Frozen Custard in one hand and a bottle of Menage à Trois Midnight Dark Red Wine in the other. "Pick your poison."

Instead, she wiped her eyes and laughed. "Great. Here I am, bigger than a barn, and you're offering me more calories."

"That's baloney. You're absolutely perfect. I've always thought so."

"Really?" She couldn't believe her ears.

"Really," and his voice had turned husky again.

Without waiting for him to set down the gifts, she threw her arms around his neck. Paul rewarded her with a long, hungry kiss. That led to more of the same, until finally, he put the ice cream and the booze down on the coffee table. His hands felt cold as they crept under her blouse, but Trudy didn't care. When the banging began, she was lost in a fog of heightened senses. The noise didn't make sense. Paul moaned and pulled her closer.

A loud *clang* of metal against metal forced Trudy to tear herself away from Paul's embrace.

Trudy raced toward the noise. Jonathan sat at the bottom of the staircase. Ma stood on the top step and banged her cane against the wrought-iron bannister. "I'm going to get you! See if I don't!"

"Ma!" Trudy was exasperated. "Calm down before you fall and hurt yourself."

Paul came up behind Trudy and put his hand on her shoulder. She reached up and twined her fingers through his. She'd waited so long for a moment like this, and of course, Ma had to ruin it. What else was new?

"Yip! Yip!" Jonathan's bark broke the spell.

"I'm going to kill that dog!" Ma raised her cane over her head.

"I'll help your mother. You get the dog," Paul said.

Trudy swooped down and picked up Jonathan. From his perch in her arms, the Chihuahua bared his teeth and growled at the old woman. Trudy felt like growling too.

"That dog is a killer! I'm going to kill it before it kills me!" Ma shrieked. Then she pitched forward and tumbled down the stairs, *bump, bump, bump.* The force of her fall shook the entire house. Ma came down, head over heels, tumbling, gurgling, banging. Instinctively Trudy and Paul both jumped away from the human pinwheel of legs and arms. Ma's auburn wig skidded along the floor like a frightened guinea pig.

As the couple watched in stunned horror, Ma's body came to an abrupt stop. Her head twisted at a sharp right angle to her neck. Her unseeing eyes stared up at the ceiling.

"Oh, no," Trudy said. "No!"

Paul pressed his fingers against Ma's throat and shook his head.

"Are you okay?" he asked.

Was she? Trudy was free now, free of Ma's complaints and lies and constant nagging about Jonathan. But she also had lost her mother—the only one she'd ever have. She'd never have another chance to make things right between them. All the sadness and the pain broke free inside her, and she put Jonathan on the floor. Trudy couldn't hold back the sobs. "He'll blame me. Roger will. He'll never forgive me, and he's promised to send me to jail."

"What?" Paul wrapped his arms around Trudy as she explained about the clothespin. "Roger thinks I've been abusing her."

"Whoa," he said as he hugged her closer. "Aren't you forgetting something? I'm a police officer. I saw what happened. I'll explain it to your brother. You've got the pictures and the clothespin, right? It's going to be okay."

Jonathan whined and pawed their legs. Paul let go of Trudy and picked up the little dog. "We know who the real culprit was. Right, Killer?"

National bestselling and award-winning author **Joanna Campbell Slan** has written thirty books and twice as many short stories. *RT Reviews* has called her one of mystery's "rising stars." Joanna's nonfiction has been endorsed by Toastmasters International; her first novel was shortlisted for the Agatha Award; and her historical fiction won the Daphne du Maurier Award. She edits the Happy Homicides anthologies and coauthors the Dollhouse Décor & More series. Visit her at www.JoannaSlan.com.

CURIOSITY KILLED THE CAT LADY

BY CATHY WILEY

Detective James Whittaker had thought there was no smell worse than the stench of a dead body, especially one that had been lying in a room for days. He'd been wrong. "I'm never drinking sauvignon blanc again."

"Sauvignon blanc?" asked Arthur Freeman, Whittaker's squad mate in the Baltimore City Homicide Department.

"You've never noticed? Sauvignon blanc smells like ammonia, although some claim it smells like herbs or asparagus. But I say ammonia. Or used cat litter." He gestured at half a dozen cat boxes scattered around the apartment, boxes that obviously hadn't been cleaned in a while. Not that he was blaming the cats' owner—Mrs. Felicity Johnson—since she was lying dead on the couch.

"I'll stick with beer, thank you," Freeman said. "And I'm not letting Jada get a cat, no matter how much she begs."

"First of all, you've never been able to tell your daughter no. And second, cats aren't that bad. I get along with Donner," Whittaker said, referring to his girlfriend's cat. "Cassie cleans the litter frequently, so I don't notice a smell. But I think quantity is the issue here. Cassie's got only one cat." Whittaker turned to the medical examiner, who was standing next to Johnson's body. "Dr. Amaya, how many cats did you say Animal Control picked up?"

"The first time? Or the second?" Amaya asked, a wicked grin crossing her pretty face. "The brave agents picked up four, but once they saw the body, they scrambled out of here, missing one. Animal Control had to send out completely new agents. The new ones didn't stay long either." She looked down at the elderly woman. “I don’t know why they freaked out. What’s so bad about dead bodies?”

Whittaker shrugged. “They don’t bother me. It bothers me more how they got that way. How do you think Mrs. Johnson got to be a dead body?”

“Badly,” interjected one of the crime-scene techs, coming forward to take a few pictures.

While he was more interested in the medical examiner’s opinion, Whittaker couldn’t disagree with the tech. The poor woman was lying in a pile of vomit and unpleasant-looking liquids. Her upper body lay across the sofa, her legs askew under the coffee table. The robe she wore had ridden up, exposing bony knees and skin almost as dark as Freeman’s. Whittaker figured she weighed barely ninety pounds, if that.

“I suspect poisoning,” Dr. Amaya said. “You noticed that she voided herself before death, I’m sure. Based on the shattered pieces of porcelain littering the floor, she convulsed violently as well.”

“I deduce that the shattered porcelain came from cat figurines,” Freeman said.

Whittaker rolled his eyes. “I see that you’re putting your years of detective training to good use.” The entire apartment was full of cat figurines and other cat objects. There were cat pillows, cat toys. Paintings of cats decorated the walls. There was even an elaborate five-story cat tower in the corner. He made a note to look into buying one of those for Donner.

Dr. Amaya smiled. “I concur with your deductions, Detective Freeman. But I noticed something else more important: that glass.” She pointed to a drinking glass lying on its side on the coffee table, in close proximity to the body.

“There’s still some liquid in there,” Whittaker said, noting the yellowish color. “Lemonade?” A crime-scene tech pushed past him to tag the glass while another took photos.

“It smells more toxic than lemonade. That’s why I had Officer Collins call you again.” She nodded toward the front door, where a police officer—the first responding officer—stood, securing the apartment.

Whittaker had spoken to Officer Collins earlier that day, when the uniformed police officer had phoned in to state he had discovered a dead body while responding to a well-being check. At first,

Whittaker had assumed the death had been due to natural causes—the deceased had been eighty-seven years old, after all—but her family had insisted Mrs. Johnson was as healthy as a horse, the officer said, and she'd just gotten a clean bill of health from her doctor. So Whittaker went ahead and requested a medical examiner, just in case. It had been a good call.

Whittaker stepped back to make room for the crime-scene photographer. He was tempted to give some suggestions for photo angles, but advising only seemed to get on photographers' nerves, he'd found. Instead, Whittaker waited until the techs finished documenting the room and went into the kitchen, at which point he whipped out his iPhone and snuck in some quick photos of the body from the angles he thought particularly useful. Obviously, he couldn't use his own photos for evidence, but he'd found it helpful to take pictures for personal reference. Dr. Amaya pretended not to notice.

Freeman continued to examine the body. "Not a good way to die. Alone and all that."

"No. Not at all," Whittaker agreed.

"When I die," Freeman began, a twinkle in his brown eyes, "I want to die like my grandfather."

"I know, I know," Whittaker said. "Quietly, in your sleep, not screaming and crying like the passengers on his bus." He turned to Amaya, "*Esa broma es casi tan vieja como él es.*" Amaya blinked in surprise. People were always surprised when a white guy spoke a foreign language.

"What did you say?" Freeman asked. "You know I don't know much Spanish."

"I said that joke is almost as old as you are."

Freeman snorted. "Some day you'll respect your elders."

Shaking his head, Whittaker turned back to the medical examiner. "How long do you think Mrs. Johnson has been dead?"

"I estimate five or six days. Obviously, I'll know more after the autopsy. It's more than three, since rigor mortis has already left the body, but based on the bloating and swelling, less than a week. Added to that, per Officer Collins, the daughter said she'd talked to her mother before leaving for her vacation exactly a week ago."

"Daughter is the one who called for the well-being check?" Whittaker asked.

From his position at the door, Officer Collins nodded.

"So five or six days?" Whittaker turned back to the body again. He didn't know if it was death or old age that gave the ashy pallor to the woman's skin. And the skin was unmarred. "So why aren't there any bite marks? Cassie told me cats wait only a day or two before eating their owner."

"Your girlfriend is weird, Whittaker," Freeman said. "Be glad I know she's a mystery author or I might send the FBI to investigate her."

Amaya leaned over and lifted the deceased's arm with her gloved hands, pivoting it gently. "You're right, I hadn't noticed that. I've seen bodies with postmortem predation. Don't believe the hype that dogs will wait longer. One lady had been dead less than three hours and her Chihuahua had already taken a sample or two."

"I've never trusted Chihuahuas," one of the crime-scene techs called from the kitchen. "Found the lemonade. It definitely doesn't smell like anything I'd like to drink."

Whittaker strode into the small, galley-style kitchen. Avoiding the jungle of water bowls and automatic cat feeders, he noticed that Crime Scene had tagged the pitcher of lemonade inside the open refrigerator. Careful not to touch anything, he waved his hand over the mouth of the pitcher, wafting the odor toward his nose. "Smells like lemonade. And something much stronger."

He backed away, took a few photos of the kitchen while the techs' backs were turned, and returned to the living room where the body was being bagged.

"They missed one," called a voice from the bedroom.

Whittaker turned to see one of the techs carrying a fluffy gray cat. "Where was he hiding?" He reached out a testing hand. The cat immediately ducked underneath his palm and started purring.

"She," the tech corrected. "Under a dresser. I already called Animal Control—again—to come back. Here, you take her so she doesn't disturb my crime scene." She shoved the cat at him.

"It's my crime scene," Whittaker complained. After the tech left the room, he and the cat exchanged looks. "What am I supposed to do with you?"

"Pet her," Freeman said, stepping into the room from the balcony. "I thought you were the one who liked cats. Bring her out here. You need to see this."

As Whittaker made his way toward the balcony, he adjusted his grip on the cat—he didn't want her taking a dive—and followed Freeman into the heat of the summer afternoon. Within the door frame he halted in his tracks. "Today is a day for strong odors, I guess. Is that smell coming from the flowers?"

"Yup."

The entire balcony was covered in window boxes and hanging baskets overflowing with flowers. It stood in stark contrast to the other balconies on that side of the building, since none of Johnson's neighbors seemed to have gone in for gardening. "What kind are they?"

"Stinky ones," Freeman said. "But that's not what I wanted to show you. Look down." He gestured toward the right balcony rail. "I'll take the cat."

Whittaker carefully handed over the cat before leaning over the balcony and looking at the grass three floors below. "What, the dead spot on the lawn?"

"Right. Doesn't that seem odd? The rest of the lawn is green and lush, even between other balconies, but there's that brown patch on the ground directly below the area between this balcony and the one next to it. And the flowers up here, right along the edge of this flower pot, they're dead and brown, too. Just strikes me as odd."

Whittaker trusted Freeman's instincts. The man had been a homicide detective for years, almost as many years as Whittaker had been alive. "I'll tell Crime Scene to document it. They should get a sample of the dirt here and down on the ground. Then we'll talk to the neighbors."

They walked back inside. There was a sudden clicking, and then several subsequent pops coming from the direction of the kitchen. "What's that noise?" Whittaker asked.

"Hey, stop struggling," Freeman said to the cat, who was squirming in his arms.

Whittaker hurried into the kitchen and noticed that the automatic cat feeders had snapped open, their rectangular lids yawning wide instead of standing guard over the food contained within. The cat in Freeman's arms meowed pitifully.

A black furball streaked past to get to the food. "Missed another one!" called a tech from the living room.

* * * *

After getting all the cats removed from the apartment—another had been hiding in the space between the kitchen cabinets—Whittaker and Freeman started interviewing the neighbors.

"They shed a lot, don't they?" Freeman said as he brushed gray fur off his brown suit. "Wait, how come you don't have any on you?"

Whittaker examined his gray suit—the one Cassie always said matched his eyes—and saw no evidence of cat fur. "Mine isn't a contrasting color. They shed more when they realize you're wearing a contrasting color."

Freeman snorted. They stepped out of Johnson's apartment, number 3A. Like many apartment buildings, each floor had four apartments, two on each side of the landing. "Officer Collins said he'd tried talking to the neighbors on this level," Whittaker said. "But no one answered their door. He managed to talk to a few other residents, but he didn't get any buzz from anyone and no one seemed to have relevant information."

"Well, now that it's after five p.m., more neighbors might be back from work," Freeman observed. "Although in this neighborhood, you might have people who work nights."

Whittaker knocked on the door of Apartment 3B. "This guy shares a wall with our victim, so I wonder if he heard anything."

The door opened, only as wide as the chain would allow. "I don't want anything you're selling."

Freeman showed his badge. "Police. May we talk to you about your neighbor?"

The man closed the door before unhooking the chain and opening it wide. Now that he could see more than just a slice of the guy, Whittaker thought he bore a striking resemblance to Steve Harvey—dark skin, bald head, even the mustache.

"She called the cops on me? Hell, I know she's called the cops on the neighbors across the hall, but she's calling them on me? I never did a thing to her damn plants. She has no proof."

Whittaker stepped back to let Freeman take the lead. He hated doing so, but they had discovered that in a city full of racial tension, people were more comfortable talking to someone of their own race. He wished people would stop seeing race altogether. Still, if it meant people were more open and honest, he'd take whatever advantage he could.

"This isn't about Mrs. Johnson's plants, Mr....?" Freeman paused.

"Price. Errol Price."

"May we come in, Mr. Price?" Freeman asked.

Price looked reluctant, but he finally stepped back from the door. "I guess."

Once in, Freeman continued to ask the questions. "So, what's going on with Mrs. Johnson's plants?"

Price picked up a cigarette and a lighter from the kitchen counter. "She's got too damn many of them. Have you smelled them? She claims she planted them because she can't stand the smell of my smoke, but it's outside, isn't it? I have as much right to the outside as she does. Wanda won't let me smoke in my own house, but no one's gonna tell me I can't even smoke outdoors. And at least *I* only smoke cigarettes."

"I can see why that would make you angry. Did you have any other issues with Mrs. Johnson?"

Price glanced to the right, then focused on Freeman again. "No. Why would I? What's she been telling you?"

"She's not able to tell us anything. She's dead. Has been for a few days."

Whittaker watched closely to gauge the man's reaction. While Price's statement that he had no other issues felt like a lie, his shocked reaction to the news of his neighbor's death seemed genuine. His jaw dropped and the cigarette fell from his fingers.

"What? I—we—but." He stopped and took a deep breath. "I'm sorry to hear that. Wanda's going to be shocked. Wanda's my wife. She's been gone for a few weeks, visiting our daughter in college out west. She's a smart girl, studying finance. We'll need to tell her, too. She's known Felicity her whole life. They'll be shocked. I'm shocked. She was old, I know, but she was in good shape, one of those old broads you think will last forever. Wait a minute!" He paused, eyes narrowing. "Felicity's old, but you wouldn't be here talking to me if you thought she'd just died in her sleep. Did someone kill her?"

"Do you think someone had a reason to kill her?"

Whittaker admired Freeman's technique of never actually answering questions. He had modeled his own technique on the older man's.

"Talk to the Baileys across the hall. Hell, talk to the Jacobsens. A lot of us—a lot of them had issues with her. She was a busybody, stuck her nose in other people's business."

"Like your smoking," Freeman prompted, scribbling in his notebook.

"Like my—no, not like my smoking. That's minor." He swiped a hand over his ebony head. "Felicity liked to call the cops on the Jacobsen kid. He stayed out too long, was disrespectful to her even before she started siccing the cops on him. Then she accused the kid of taking drugs. Might be true."

"And what problem did the Baileys have with her?" Freeman asked.

"I'm not sure, actually," Price said, snagging an empty pizza box from the counter and throwing it in the trash. "I mean, Susanna—that's the woman—seemed to get along with her okay, although I think she preferred Felicity's cats. But Bobby barely talked to her."

While Freeman asked questions, Whittaker took the time to inspect the apartment. It was a mirror image of his neighbor's, minus the cat paraphernalia. It was cluttered and messy, probably due to the wife being gone. An empty wine bottle and wine glasses were on the coffee table, a few beer bottles littered the kitchen counter, and a spray bottle sat by the balcony door.

Surprisingly, Price himself didn't seem to be taking advantage of his wife's absence. He was clean-shaven, smartly dressed in blue slacks and a silk shirt, and Whittaker even detected the smell of cologne, thankfully not as strong as the balcony flowers.

"Had you noticed that Mrs. Johnson hadn't been around recently?" Freeman asked.

Price shook his head. "Not really. I wouldn't think much of it if I had. She goes off to visit her children and grandchildren for a few days at a time."

"Who takes care of the cats?" Whittaker had to ask. He couldn't imagine packing eight cats into carriers. They'd be burdensome to carry, and they'd make one heck of a racket. Donner was loud enough on his own whenever he was put in a cat carrier.

"We all have, at one time or another. She's a busybody, but we're neighbors. We take care of each other on this floor. Besides, Felicity sure can bake, and she always paid us back in cookies and pies."

"Does that mean you have a key to her apartment?" Freeman asked.

"Yeah, all of us on this floor exchanged keys, especially after my wife locked herself out of the apartment a few times. Like I said, we help each other." Price reached for a bowl on the counter, then paused. "But I didn't use the key recently. Like I said, go talk to Bobby and Susanna."

* * * *

"Well, let's talk to Bobby and Susanna," Whittaker said, raising his hand to knock on the door of 3C. It opened before he could do so.

"Hey honey, do you have dinner? Oh. Sorry. Thought you were my husband." The woman stared at them curiously. She had dreadlocks pulled back and covered with a bandana. Whittaker could never decide if he liked dreads on white women.

"Mrs. Bailey?" Whittaker asked, once more showing his badge.

"That would be my mother-in-law. Call me Susanna. What's up?" She checked behind her once, then opened the door. "Sorry about the mess in here."

"Not a problem," Freeman said.

"You've probably seen worse," Susanna said.

Whittaker *had* seen worse. To him, the apartment was more cluttered than his own, or even Cassie's, but it wasn't horrible. But it definitely smelled. Not quite as bad as Johnson's apartment, although there was the slight odor of pet urine. And on top of that a smell of…rotten eggs?

Next to him, Freeman wrinkled his nose. He'd obviously noticed it, too. "The cages?" he said, pointing toward a corner.

One seemed to contain a ferret, but Whittaker wasn't certain what the animals in the other cage were. Out of curiosity, he stepped closer.

"Oh, you like my rats?" Susanna retrieved the two animals and brought them over.

"You keep rats as pets?" Freeman asked, backing up. "Why? You can see them for free in any alley in this city."

"I saved Jenner and Sullivan from a pet store," Susanna said. "They were being sold as feeder animals, but I couldn't let such handsome rats be used as food for snakes. Aren't you a handsome little rat, Jenner?" She lifted the rat and kissed its nose.

To each their own, Whittaker thought, then tried for a casual opening. "They probably didn't get along too well with Mrs. Johnson's cats though."

As if it had heard, one of the rats squealed. "Let me put them back." Susanna deposited them back in their cage, then answered the question. "I think they would've liked each other if we had tried. Jenner and Sullivan like everybody."

Whittaker raised an eyebrow. "Is that so? How about you?"

"Of course they like me."

"No, do you like everybody?" Whittaker asked.

She shrugged and scratched at an acne scar. "I'm not sure I'd say that. Humans are hard to like sometimes. It's much easier to get along with animals. But in general, I'd say I get along with most people. And I try not to bother anyone. Except my husband, of course. That's a wife's job. In fact…" At the sound of the key in the lock, she moved to the front door and opened it. "Hi, honey." She leaned up for a kiss, standing on tiptoe since her husband was much taller, then leaned back suddenly. "You've been eating McDonald's!" she accused. "I can smell it on your breath. You know I hate it when you do that."

Bobby glanced at Whittaker and Freeman, then back at his wife. "I was hungry. Here's your dinner though. Spring rolls and tofu chow mein." He handed over the bag. "Who are these guys?"

"They're the police. They came over to—actually, you never said why you were here."

"Unfortunately, we're asking questions about your neighbor Mrs. Johnson. She passed away earlier this week."

"Oh no," Susanna said. "That's horrible. She was a good neighbor. What's going to happen to her cats?"

"That hasn't been determined yet," Whittaker said.

"When did she die?" Bobby asked. He stepped closer.

Too close, Whittaker mused. He wasn't sure he could smell McDonald's on Bobby's breath, but the man's halitosis knocked him back a few paces.

"That also hasn't been determined. When did you see her last?"

After looking at her husband, Susanna pursed her lips. "Um, I'd say it was sometime last week. It's been a while. That's not all that unusual, since she's often out of town."

"What happened the last time you saw her?"

Susanna eased into the kitchen and dropped the bag on the counter. "We talked about the neighbors. Miss Felicity was upset at the behavior of Tyler, the Jacobsens' son. Evidently he's been staying out all night. And Miss Felicity swears she saw him involved in a drug deal, too."

"Buying or selling?"

"Buying, I believe," she answered, after a quick confirming glance at Bobby. "Do you think she was *murdered*? That Tyler killed her? He's a troubled kid, but I don't think he's capable of that."

"We don't think anything right now, Mrs. Bailey. Is there anyone you think would be capable of that?"

Both Bobby and Susanna pointedly turned their heads toward the outside wall. "Errol Price could have done it," Susanna drawled. "He and Miss Felicity had a feud going over their balconies. She couldn't stand the smell of his cigarettes, so she planted all those flowers. Then he hated the flowers so much, he actually tried to kill them. Oh, he denied it, but you could see the evidence of the weed killer on the ground below. They got into a screaming match on their balconies one time. We could even hear it in here."

"Anyone else in the building have any issues with Miss Felicity?"

Bobby shook his head. "Not that we seen."

"Did you have a problem with her?" Whittaker asked, ignoring the bad grammar.

Bobby shook his head even more emphatically this time. "Nope. I didn't talk to her much, but Susanna would take care of her cats sometimes. She'd make food to thank us."

"So you have a key to her apartment?" Whittaker asked.

Both of them froze. Susanna recovered faster.

"I guess we do. It's somewhere around here. Look, can I eat? I'm starving." She picked up the bag of Chinese food for emphasis.

"Of course." Whittaker handed them his business card. "Please contact me if you think of anything else."

* * * *

Out in the hallway, Whittaker shook his head. "Why would anyone eat tofu chow mein?" He headed over to the remaining door on that floor and knocked. "Mrs. Jacobsen?" When she opened the door, he flashed his badge. "May we come in?"

She pressed a hand to her heart. "Tyler?"

"It's not about your son," Whittaker said. "It's about Mrs. Johnson."

The woman's face hardened. "What about her? Did she call you again? We're trying to do something. We haven't been able to find where he's getting the stuff. I told her that."

"It's not about Tyler, Mrs. Jacobsen. Mrs. Johnson passed away earlier this week. She was just discovered this morning."

She covered her mouth with her hand and inhaled sharply. When she lowered her hand, it was shaking. "Oh, that's horrible. I'm so sorry to hear that."

Whittaker was forever fascinated by how someone's opinion of another person altered once death was mentioned. It was like death bestowed sainthood upon a previously unlikable individual.

"Joan? Is someone at the door?" called a voice from the back hallway. "Did Tyler come home?" An older man wandered into the living room. He was probably in his late forties, but exhaustion made him look much older. "Oh. I'm sorry."

"Hello, Mr. Jacobsen. I'm Detective Whittaker. This is my partner, Detective Freeman."

Joan grabbed her husband's arm. "It's not about Tyler, Dave. It's about Felicity. She's dead."

Unlike his wife, Dave didn't show shock or sadness. He barely reacted at all. "That's too bad."

"Had you seen her lately?" Whittaker asked.

"Not since she called the cops on our boy. That was what, last week?" He turned to his wife for confirmation. "They almost arrested him, you know that? Don't you all have better things to do than to harass a confused teenager?"

"Where is your son now?" Whittaker asked, following a hunch.

He shrugged. "Gone. He's probably afraid to come home, afraid you people will come and—"

"Be quiet for a minute," Joan scolded her husband, then turned to Whittaker. "What happened to Felicity?"

Dave interrupted. "She was old, Joan. What do you think happened to her?"

"Be quiet," she said again, gripping his arm. "The cops wouldn't be talking to us if she died just because she was old."

"We're not sure at this point how she died," Whittaker said. "But we're interviewing her neighbors, trying to piece together a picture of her last moments."

"That's bullshit police talk. You think we killed her." Dave wrenched his arm away. "They think we did it, Joan. Why the hell would we kill her? Because she caught our kid doing drugs? It's just pot. Harmless. That's not the worst thing happening in these apartments. Maybe you should talk to the Baileys. Or talk to Errol. Felicity had info on him, too. You know, when the cat's away."

"We've spoken to them previously. We're not accusing anyone of anything."

"Settle down, Dave," Joan said. "Why don't we go sit in the living room?"

The furniture was old but well kept. That description could apply to the Jacobsens as well, Whittaker thought as he sat down. It was exhaustion that made them look old. Still, they were presentable with nice enough, if not expensive, clothes.

"I feel so bad," Joan said. "I should have checked on her! Susanna had even commented on how she hadn't seen Felicity for a while. We have a key to the apartment," she offered. "I could have looked in at any time."

Dave flinched at that. "We aren't the only ones to have her key."

"No. She gave a key to everyone who helped with her cats. And she's managed to recruit lots of us to do that. Here let me get it." Joan stood up and headed toward a key rack by the door. "Wait, what…"

Whittaker stood up. "What's wrong?"

Joan turned around, her face paler, as she stared at her husband. "The key is missing." Her eyes welled with tears. "Tyler's missing. The key is missing. What's going on?"

Whittaker asked them more questions about their son's potential whereabouts, but they continued to insist that they didn't know. After a while, he didn't have the heart to continue questioning. They really did look exhausted. "Thank you very much for your time. We appreciate your help. If you'd like to report your son as missing, I can help you with that process."

Joan shook her head emphatically. "No. He's done this before. He'll come home."

Whittaker stood and headed for the door, passing a photograph in a silver frame propped up on the hall table. "Is this Tyler?" he asked, lifting the frame.

Dave nodded, a look of half pride, half dismay on his face.

Whittaker studied the photo. The boy was handsome, with dark hair like his mother. But the pock marks on his face indicated either a bad case of acne, or that the drugs the kid was taking were far from harmless. "Good-looking kid." He set the photo down and headed for the door. Freeman remained behind. Whittaker watched his partner slip something into Joan's hand.

"What did you give them?" he asked Freeman once they were back in the privacy of the hallway.

"Gave them a card for a drug treatment program in the city that worked for my cousin's kid. Maybe it'll help. If he comes home."

"That's a big if," Whittaker said. "Especially if he's the one who poisoned the old lady. The timing's about right."

"Could be," Freeman said. "For the mother's sake, I hope not. She was kind."

"Father was a hothead."

"He was worried, Whittaker. Worried about his son. Worried *for* his son. I think they feared he *had* done something to the old lady. And terrified that's why we were there. I think that's what really set the father off."

Outside the building, Whittaker wandered over to the dead grass below Johnson's balcony. He stared at it for a moment, then whipped out his smartphone and swiped it on.

"What are you looking up now?" Freeman asked, rolling his eyes.

"Symptoms of weed-killer poisoning. Following a hunch." He read quietly for a few moments. "Vomiting, diarrhea, convulsions. Coma that can lead to death, especially if you're a little old lady living by yourself. Well, other than eight cats. Why don't we try and speed up the testing of that lemonade? And we should probably get that spray bottle of Roundup that was in Price's apartment."

"You think Price poisoned the old lady?" Freeman asked.

"I think he had a motive, and it had nothing to do with the flowers. I suspect the old lady had figured out that Errol was cheating on his wife."

"Ah, you noticed the extra wine glass, too."

"That and Dave's strong hint about 'when the cat's away.' But I don't know, he's not the only one with a motive. Or means and opportunity, considering they all had access to her apartment. And Tyler has some bad scabs on his face. I'm guessing he's taking more than just marijuana."

"Yeah, that was my take as well." Freeman sighed. "That's why I gave them the card. I've seen lots of meth addicts with those scab marks. I don't get why people take that stuff. Messes you up. Still, you think he took the key and killed the old lady?"

Whittaker shrugged as they walked toward the car. "Maybe. Again, I think they all had motives of one sort or another. Not sure what she had on the Baileys, but she seemed to be nosy enough. Maybe she caught them doing something wrong."

"Keeping rats in your apartment is wrong."

Whittaker laughed as he opened the door to the car and slid in to the driver's seat.

"But you may be right," Freeman continued as Whittaker pulled into traffic. "I was thinking—"

Whittaker's phone rang, and he answered using his car's Bluetooth connection. "Hello, Cassie," he said. "Watch what you're saying, because Freeman can hear every word."

"You busy?" his girlfriend asked.

"We are, unfortunately. What's up?"

"I was going to invite you for dinner tonight since you had the early shift. But I assume this means you're on a case." She sounded more curious than annoyed.

"I am." He smiled when he heard Donner meowing in the background. "Involving someone with eight cats."

"Eight! That's a lot of cats. I can barely keep up with one. He's demanding food again. No, Donner." Cassie's voice faded as she spoke to the cat. "You still have a whole two hours before your magical food dish provides you with dinner."

Whittaker chuckled again. He had bought the "magical food dish." Since Cassie often got distracted by her writing, an automatic food dispenser was a great gift for her...and the cat. It was the first gift he had bought her, before they had even started dating. He then paused as a thought occurred to him. "Say, Cassie, for how long can you set the timer on your automatic dispenser?"

"On the one you bought me, I can program it to dispense for however long I'd like. You sprang for a top-of-the-line model. Remember? I've got it set to dispense every five hours until it runs out of food, which could last for over a week since I've got the high-capacity tank."

"How about the cheap plastic-looking ones that simply pop open?"

"The ones with the spring timer that flips the lid up? I had one of those, but Donner figured out how to use his teeth to advance the timer."

Normally, he'd be amused at Donner's skill at acquiring food, but he had a more pressing need. "So how long can you program those for?"

"The one I had was only for eight hours at a time, but..." She paused a moment; he heard typing. That was one thing he loved about her. He never told her much about his cases, but she was often able to connect the dots herself. "The longest time I can find online is forty-eight hours in advance. What brand would you, perchance, be curious about?"

Whittaker pulled into an empty parking space and took out his phone. He scrolled through his pictures, then zoomed in on one from the kitchen. "The Auto-Meow-Tic 2000."

After a short burst of typing, Cassie answered. "That one, you can only set twenty-four hours in advance."

The wheels in Whittaker's head spun. "Thanks, Cassie. Talk to you later." He smacked the steering wheel. "She was dead for more than twenty-four hours."

"By far," said Freeman. "And her ghost didn't fill up those food dispensers."

Whittaker put the car in gear and made a U-turn back to the apartment complex. "I think it's time for us to have another talk with the animal-loving Susanna Bailey. This time we're bringing her and her husband to our house. Reserve us an interview room."

Freeman made the necessary phone calls.

"What was their motive?" Whittaker asked. "You think Johnson found out something about them?"

"Well, they are definitely doing drugs," Freeman said as he closed his flip phone. Whittaker had been trying for years to get the old man to upgrade.

"What? Oh, the scars on her face. Bobby's bad breath."

"That and the smell," Freeman added. "I kept thinking I smelled meth."

"How did you smell anything but rat and ferret?"

"One of the cases I caught while you were on your cruise was a murder/suicide in a meth lab," Freeman said. "Smells like a combination of rotten eggs and cat urine. Plenty of that going around today. At first, I wondered if it was just residual from Johnson's apartment. Then I thought, nah, maybe those rats. It's been a rough day with smells. I didn't quite trust my nose. But looking back, I'm thinking it was meth."

"You think they're manufacturing?" Whittaker asked.

"Not manufacturing, no. That smell would have been even more obvious. And in that small space, it would have been toxic to anyone who stepped into the apartment. It would leach through walls. But they're using. Might explain why she thinks owning rats is a good idea."

* * * *

Back at the station, Whittaker finished up the paperwork at his desk while waiting for Freeman to get off the phone. It had been, by far, one of the easiest confessions he'd ever gotten out of someone. Whittaker hadn't even been 100 percent certain the Baileys had committed the murder; hell, there hadn't even been time to get results back from the medical examiner or crime lab proving that a murder had been committed. Whittaker simply claimed there was forensic evidence that the couple had killed Johnson. First Susanna and then Bobby had confessed to everything wrong they had ever done in their lives.

Freeman hung up the phone. "It's taking you longer to finish that paperwork than it did to get them to confess to the murder. What idiots."

"Agreed. Using your own products. Always a bad idea."

"Yeah, but a lot of dealers do. I have pity for addicts, as you know, but not for dealers, especially when they get young teenagers like Tyler hooked. He came home, by the way. His mother just called." He shook his head. "I simply can't stand how little drug dealers value life. Killing an old lady 'cause she witnessed them committing a crime…" His voice trailed off.

It had been simple, really. The detectives separated the husband and wife, told them that their fingerprints had been found on the lemonade pitcher and on the weed killer bottle, and they immediately folded.

They told him how Felicity Johnson had threatened to call the cops after seeing Tyler purchase drugs from them. How she had suspected it for a while, but now had proof. She'd even taken pictures. So Susanna snuck into Errol's apartment while he was at work and borrowed his weed killer. Then Bobby went into Johnson's place when she was out shopping for cat food and poisoned her lemonade.

Then they waited. When Johnson failed to emerge from her apartment the following day, Susanna went over to check that the deed was done. It was, but her animal-loving bleeding heart couldn't let the cats go hungry, so she fed them. And kept feeding them every day as she waited for someone to miss the old lady and figure out that Johnson was dead. She even tried to convince Joan to go and check on her.

"And Narcotics is excited to nab their supplier as well," Freeman said. "I can't believe the Baileys were willing to blow the whistle on their source. It won't cut them any slack on the homicide charge."

"Were you just on the phone with Narcotics?" Whittaker asked. He was surprised when Freeman looked embarrassed at the question.

"No. That was, well, um… Animal Control." Freeman rearranged some papers on his desk.

"Animal Control?"

"Turns out the Johnson family doesn't want to adopt all those cats." Freeman scowled as Whittaker started laughing. "Look, I liked the gray one, okay? And Jada's been asking and everything. Jordan even thought it was a good idea."

Whittaker grinned. "Just make sure you don't end up with all eight."

Cathy Wiley is happiest when plotting stories in her head or on the computer, or when she's delving into research. In 2015, she was nominated for a Derringer Award for her short story "Dead Men Tell No Tales," which appeared in *Chesapeake Crimes: Homicidal Holidays*. She lives outside of Baltimore, Maryland, with one spoiled cat and an equally spoiled husband. Visit her website at www.cathywileyauthor.com.

SUNSET BEAUREGARD

BY KAREN CANTWELL

July 3, 1936

Like a gorilla, Johnny Roland ruled the jungle known as Hollywood. He didn't ask permission to enter the crime scene on 21 Summit Drive; instead, he carried his reputation like a badge, daring the blue suits to refute his authority. He had arrived before the investigation began. He always did. That was his job. When the studio needed a problem fixed, they sent Johnny to do the dirty work.

Folding a stick of Clark's Teaberry into his mouth, Johnny regarded the body on the floor. Beau Kellum's half naked corpse lay sprawled facedown. From the angle, Kellum might have been headed to the front door when the killer plugged him. Johnny chewed. Careful of his wing tips, he tangoed around two different pools of blood, surveying. Finally, he acknowledged Detective Roy Jackson, who stood near the dead man's feet. "Thanks for the call."

"Like I had a choice." Jackson's reply was bored.

"How's the wife?"

"You're an ass."

"And the girlfriend?"

"Don't push me, Roland."

Johnny Roland picked a piece of lint from his sleeve. "What, a friend can't kid around?"

"I need better friends."

"Apparently so did Kellum. I always said he'd piss off the wrong guy one day. Who found him?"

"Maid. One of my guys has her upstairs, trying to calm her down."

"Bad way to start a day." Johnny scanned the room. "Murder weapon?"

"Haven't found it yet."

Johnny slipped Jackson two C-notes. "Where's McCord?"

Jackson took the bribe and gestured toward the back of the Beverly Hills mansion. "Kitchen. The idiot crawled through a window. Caught him going through Kellum's desk in the library. Get him out of here so I can start doing my job, would ya?"

Johnny'd been in Beau Kellum's place on countless occasions—usually to bring him home after a drunken bar fight. So yeah, he knew where the kitchen was. Halfway there, he paused and turned. "Where's the dog?" he asked Jackson.

The detective scowled. "What dog?"

Johnny shook his head and continued on, wondering how crimes ever got solved in this town. Evidence that Beau Kellum owned a dog hung like a neon sign by the front door: a six-foot leash. They'd need to find that animal because, frankly, Beau Kellum's dog, Sunset Beauregard, was easily as famous as the film star himself.

In the dimly lit kitchen, Johnny had to resist smacking Dix McCord when he found the slight man hunched on a wooden stool, his blond hair uncharacteristically mussed. "I thought I told you to watch yourself."

"I didn't do it, Johnny, I swear. He was dead when I got here."

"I don't care if you did or you didn't." Johnny eyed something stuffed under Dix's shirt. "Is that what you came for?"

Dix nodded.

"Let me see."

"Please, Johnny."

"Now."

Dix obeyed, giving up a handful of photographs.

Johnny flipped through them, unfazed by the images. "Kellum take these?"

"Yeah."

"Are there others?"

"I don't think so."

He slapped a hand against Dix's shoulder. "Stand up. Time to go then. I didn't buy us time for yakking." Johnny had no intention of walking Dix out the front door. Studio execs were grooming the pretty boy to hit the headlines as a dreamy leading man, not a murder suspect. Johnny pushed him toward the back door. "Where'd the dog go?"

Dix shuffled, tucking the secret stash back under his shirt. "Don't know, Johnny."

Two steps from the back door, Johnny spied a familiar pearl earring on the floor. He picked it up and slipped it into his breast pocket.

* * * *

Like an enchanted cobra, a trail of smoke slithered skyward from the tip of a lit cigarette. The lipstick-stained cigarette rested in a metal ashtray on the Andersons' kitchen table. Dressed for a day at the diner taking orders and schlepping food, Mary Anderson unfolded the morning paper. She read the headline and fell into her chair. "Georgie," she said, grabbing her heart. "Beau Kellum is dead."

Mary's husband, George, fiddled with a hinge on the kitchen cupboard. His massive hand twisted a screwdriver. "Don't know 'im."

"Beau Kellum, the actor. He was in *The Devil Heart*, *Poor Pauline*, and oh, what was that one about the ranch hand?" Her gaze wandered around the boxy kitchen, but the name didn't come to her. She returned her attention to the story. "Says here he was murdered in his own house. Shot in the back."

Working the screwdriver, George grunted. "Almost got this fixed."

"I wonder if it was a mob hit." Having grown up in South Boston, Mary always thought of the mob when she heard about a murder. It's why they had left—to steal her Georgie away from the gangster-run boxing world.

"He probably just pissed off the wrong guy."

Mary set the paper down and took a long drag from her cigarette. Smoke swelled from her mouth and nose when she spoke again. "The article don't say nothin' about Sunset Beauregard. I wonder what happened to him. I sure hope he's okay."

George stopped what he was doing to look at Mary. "Who's Sunset Beauregard?"

"His dog. Gorgeous Irish setter. His lucky charm he used to say."

"Guess he ain't lucky no more."

* * * *

Johnny Roland sat opposite the pert-nosed platinum-blond Ida Flory. Even without makeup or lighting, the actress managed to vibrate with the regal sensuality of a proud tiger. People knew Ida Flory first for her films and second for her rocky romance with Beau Kellum. Burning tobacco crackled as she sucked elegantly on a long black-and-ivory cigarette holder. In her other hand she swirled a scotch neat. Her foot twitched rhythmically.

"I swear I didn't do it, Johnny." She purposely blew smoke in his direction.

Johnny's nose itched. "I don't care if you did or you didn't."

"I was at his place yesterday. They'll find my fingerprints all over the house." Ida's voice was smooth, her diction polished from years of training.

"I saw the blood. It was fresh. Didn't happen during the day. Where were you last night? Late last night."

"Home alone. Drank too much and passed out. Is that a crime? What happens when they find my fingerprints?"

"Finish your drink and simmer down. What do you think I'm here for? You think I like hiding in hotel rooms with egomaniacal actresses?" He peeled the wrapper off a stick of gum. "Frankly, fingerprints are the least of your problems, beautiful. A neighbor of Kellum's told police about that fight you had yesterday before you went home and drank yourself silly. Says you screamed rather loudly that you'd kill him if you caught him cheating again. So now I have to find you an alibi."

"How is it neighbors hear me yelling in the middle of the day, but not gunshots in the middle of the night? Tell me that."

"They heard all right. Thought they were firecrackers. Kids had been setting them off for nights."

Ida drained the glass in a single gulp and raised it in the air. "Get me another."

A less confident man would have bristled, but not Johnny Roland. When a dame needed a scotch, he poured her a scotch. He didn't get paid the good money to be annoyed by screen stars. He got paid to keep them in the right headlines and out of the wrong ones.

"Beau was in deep with a man named Panzini. You know him?"

Johnny knew that name all right. But he didn't let Ida know that she'd just blindsided him with the news that Kellum had been gambling again. He kept his cool and handed her the glass. "I know Panzini."

"So maybe it was the mob, right?"

"Maybe."

She cocked her famously seductive eyebrow, as if a director had just yelled *action*. "Johnny?"

"Yeah?"

"Where is Sunny?"

"You're babbling."

"The dog, Johnny. Sunset Beauregard. Where is the dog?"

"I know what you meant." Johnny shrugged. "No one knows."

* * * *

Aching with melancholy, Mary shuffled into the kitchen where the smell of bacon improved her mood a little. George stood over the cast-iron pan easing two eggs over as they sizzled in bacon grease. She hugged his brawny bicep. "You're makin' breakfast? I must be the luckiest woman in the world, Georgie."

"You sound sad, Mar. Everything okay?"

Her throat hurt from stifling a cry. "Got my lady's day." She patted his chest to stop him from repeating the story about Aunt Ruby and how it took her six years to get pregnant. He meant well, but the story didn't ease her pain. She ogled the mountain of bacon he'd fried up. "That's an awful lot, dontcha think?"

"We need to eat, right?"

"You must be exhausted. I hate you workin' nights."

"I sleep when I'm ready."

Mary found the morning paper on the table. Georgie really did treat her like a queen some days. Not all, but some. "Edith says there's a security job opening up at the studio, honey. Daytime. Good hours, good money. Will ya try for it?"

"I don't know."

"Why not?"

"What if they ask to meet me? I don't talk so good, ya know."

"It's a security job, you big lug, not vice president." Grateful for the freshly made pot of coffee, she poured a cup, stirred in some sugar, lit a cigarette, sat, and unfolded the paper.

"Oh no," she said. "They're questioning Ida Flory in Beau Kellum's murder. I love her!"

George slid a fried egg onto the plate near Mary. "Who's that?"

"Ida Flory—Beau's girlfriend. She was in *The High Hat* and *The Dark Tunnel*. She's got the kinda nose I wish I had."

"You got the perfect nose, Mar."

"They been back and forth with goin' out then breakin' up, then back goin' out again. Lots of fightin', so I guess it kinda makes sense." She scanned the article to the end, sighing as she set the paper aside to take a stab at the egg. "Nothin' about Sunset Beauregard. I hope he's okay."

"You like dogs, sugarplum?"

"Yeah, I like dogs. We should get one someday."

* * * *

Johnny washed his hands in the pristine basin. One of the enviable perks of his job was a bungalow on the studio lot, complete with washroom and a cleaning lady to disinfect it three times daily. He detested dirt and germs and anything remotely related, including cigarette ash and butts. Everyone on the lot knew the law: no snipes in Johnny Roland's bungalow. Not even near it. Word was if Johnny found someone's stamped-out butt on the ground within forty feet, he'd have them shot. Johnny smiled at the rumor. Fired, maybe, but he'd certainly never have a guy killed for a stray butt. He liked that people believed it though. The power that came from such a fear made his job easier.

He patted his hands dry with the crisp white towel, then rolled his sleeves back down. He refastened twenty-four-carat gold cuff links on the way back to his imposing mahogany desk. Situated on a love seat that faced Johnny's desk was Grover Shaw, the man who had much to lose if Ida Flory's reputation was tarnished. He had his future pinned on Ida's potential box-office draw. So far, she'd made him ten times more than he'd lost at the track. Audiences loved her, women wanted to be her, and Hollywood's prime gossip columnist gushed over her like a teenager with a mad crush.

Shaw tried to play it calm, but Johnny saw the beads of perspiration. When Johnny sat and gazed calmly out the window, Shaw dropped his composure. He took to the edge of the love seat, nervous as a cat. "What's the plan?"

Johnny laughed. He spun the chair back around to face Shaw. "You're asking that now? Seriously, Shaw. You're a putz."

"Putz? You're calling me a putz? That's my word."

"I know. And you deserve to wear it."

The phone on Johnny's desk rang. He answered. "Thank you, Edith, put him through." Johnny waited for the transfer while observing another bead of sweat trickle down Shaw's fat cheek. "Detective Roy Jackson, sir," he said eventually, "tell me a story. You find that weapon yet?"

Johnny listened to the detective without reacting. He didn't raise a brow or twitch a finger. With each passing second, he sensed Shaw's growing anxiety. "Right," Johnny finally spoke into the phone again. "Now that we have that settled, Jackson, I think you should know that Beau Kellum had been sleeping with the actress Annie Diggs. A reputable source tells me Miss Diggs was upset with Kellum when he wouldn't call things off with Ida Flory."

Johnny laughed at Detective Jackson's response. "Yeah, I happen to know a lot of things. For instance, how's that habit of yours?"

Johnny hung up and folded his hands on the desk. "Ida's alibi checked out," he told Shaw. "She was with two friends the night of the murder. They just finished giving their accounts."

"Ida told me she was alone that night."

"When she talked to you, she was alone that night. Turns out she remembered later that she was with friends in Santa Monica. What exactly do you think I do all day, Shaw?"

"Just keep my name out of it, Roland."

"I always do."

"So you're framing Annie Diggs."

"You told me yourself you wanted Annie Diggs off the contract. Personally, I think she still has a few good years left, but if you think she's too old, who am I to argue? I'm just making sure the studio stays solvent. The more money you make, the more I make. Simple math."

"Speaking of money, that pansy Dix McCord is costing me lots of it, showing up late to the set every day."

"You know I hate that word, Shaw."

"Money?"

"You're a funny guy now. Not sure you pulled it off. I'm not laughing."

The studio exec stood. "See to it that McCord falls in line."

Grover Shaw's shoe caught the edge of an area rug on his way to the door, making his exit more comical than a Laurel and Hardy short. At the door, he turned to Roland once more. "Everyone is wondering about Sunset Beauregard. Any news?"

"Not yet."

"Do something about that. The fans love that dog."

* * * *

Mary Anderson sat at the table, anxious to read the latest on the Beau Kellum murder. She'd had a dream that the authorities had hauled poor Ida Flory off in handcuffs as she cried out her innocence to a crowd of adoring fans. Then, as is the way of dreams, Ida transformed into the stunning Irish setter Sunset Beauregard and her cries turned into muffled, distant dog barks. Mary knew it was silly to care so much about the stars as if she knew them. But she did daydream sometimes that her friend Edith would help get her a studio job, and then she'd meet big stars like Ida Flory, and they would find her funny and lovable and invite her and Georgie to fantastic parties.

As a cigarette burned in the ashtray, Mary was opening her morning paper when she heard the back screen door slam shut. George lumbered in to wash his hands.

"There you are," Mary said. "What were ya doin'?"

"Fixin' that line in the backyard like you asked."

"Thanks, honey. I was afraid the clothes would just fall right to the ground and I'd have to wash 'em all over again."

"It's good now." He dried his hands. "What's the news today?"

She opened the paper and read the headline. "Ida Flory ain't a suspect in Beau's murder no more. Two witnesses say she was with them the night he was killed. I didn't think it was her. She seems like a really nice lady. Classy, with morals, ya know."

"Beau's the guy with the dog?"

"Yeah. And Ida Flory was his girlfriend. She was a suspect, but now they're questionin' Annie Diggs." Mary shook her head. "I used to love her in all those funny movies. Holy cow. Says here that Annie and Beau were having an affair. She's married, for cripes sake. And look here, George." She smoothed the paper and folded it just right so George could see. "That's him. That's Sunset Beauregard—Sunny for short. He's a show dog. Ain't he a beaut?"

George squinted at the paper. "Five thousand dollar reward for a dog? Are they crazy?"

* * * *

Annie Diggs stormed into Johnny Roland's bungalow. On camera, Annie had the perfect comic timing necessary to earn the best laughs. Off camera, she'd earned a reputation for being hot-headed and difficult to control. "What're you doin' to me, Johnny?"

Dix McCord slunk in behind his wife, crumpling into the love seat. He removed his fedora, placing it beside him.

Sliding an open newspaper to one side, Johnny fell just short of smiling at Annie. He relished her bouts of fury, but now was not the time to provoke one. "You're welcome."

"Welcome? What the hell for? I barely knew Beau Kellum. Now my friends are admitting I slept with him? You of all people know that's not true."

"Speaking of your husband," which Johnny knew Annie was not, "Dix, make room for your wife so she can take a load off. How about a whiskey?" Johnny got up to pour the lady a drink.

Dix moved the hat to his lap, making space for Annie. "None for me," he said.

"I wasn't asking you," Johnny snapped. "Annie, sit. Relax. What's your poison?"

Not one to take orders from any man, the comedienne held her pose. "I quit drinking. Muddies the mind, cripples the work."

Who was she kidding? She'd been drinking plenty just a couple of nights earlier. Johnny rested on the edge of his desk. "You're too smart for this studio, Annie, and you know it."

"Grover wants me out, doesn't he? He wants a reason to kill my contract. Is this his doing?"

"He wants you out, but it isn't his doing, it's mine."

"Why?"

"Julius Blaine wants you, and you don't have to sign a contract."

"You're playing studios against each other? You're dirtier than I thought. I knew you didn't have a heart, but I figured you were loyal, at least."

Dix chuckled and shook his head. "The cameras aren't rolling, sweetheart. You can drop the loyalty-to-the-studio act."

Annie fired one back at Dix. "Okay, stud, how about I drop the passion-for-my-husband act?"

Johnny interrupted the tender display of marital bliss. "You don't think I'm being loyal right now, Annie?"

She crossed her arms. "What if I don't want to go to Blaine Studios? Word is they're in trouble because Julius is distracted by that pervert politician son of his."

"All the more reason Julius needs you."

"You always say your job is to keep us out of the wrong headlines and in the right ones. So why tell the world I could be a killer?"

"A bad headline isn't always the wrong headline for the right person, baby."

Dix rolled the hat back onto his head and snorted. "Good line. Maybe you should take up screenwriting."

Johnny didn't bother to respond.

"I need to be at makeup in five minutes," Dix said, backing off. "Can I go?"

Annie laughed. "Be sure they cover up that lingering hickey, dear. Your boyfriend gave you a good one."

Standing, Dix played along. "See you at home, honey?"

"Can't wait, sugar pie."

Annie didn't follow her husband out the door. Instead, she joined Johnny on the edge of the desk. "I never should have agreed to marry him. Hasn't helped my career one iota. Can I divorce him now?"

"Wait until this Kellum story fades."

"Dix was screwing Kellum."

"Kellum thrived on adulation. He screwed anyone who fed his appetite for more."

"I want the truth: are you sacrificing me to save Dix?"

"No."

Annie's shoulders relaxed. She caressed Johnny's hand. "Come by for a drink tonight?"

"Thought you don't partake anymore."

"Maybe I changed my mind."

He considered the usual evolution of that drink. One drink would lead to another and then another. And they'd all bite with the rancid flavor of menace. "I'm not thinking that far ahead right now."

Wincing at the brush-off, she withdrew her hand. "You sure this plan is going to work?"

"Maintain your innocence and in due time, you can have your pick of projects with Julius."

"You promise?"

"I never promise anything, Annie. You know my rule. Now go throw one of your famous tantrums and make it good."

Annie Diggs flew out of the bungalow in a flawlessly staged rage.

Johnny smirked.

In short order though, his mouth formed a hard line. He tapped on the dog's picture staring up at him from the newspaper. Sunset Beauregard. Where was that damn animal? Feeling the need to clear his head of this Kellum business, Johnny decided to take a little drive. He stuffed a wad of gum into his mouth, took his hat, and closed the door behind him.

* * * *

Mary woke up the next morning with the usual childless ache in her heart. But wallowing wasn't Mary's way. When she forced herself to roll out of bed, she found George sitting in the bedside chair. The chair was small and George was large.

"George? Is something wrong?"

"I gotta come clean, Mar."

"My God, honey. What is it? Is it bad?"

"I ain't proud, that's for sure."

George studied his hands. He balled them into fists and then relaxed them. He repeated this action over and over, the confession stuck.

"Georgie!" She shook his shoulder. "Just spit it out fast like it ain't no big deal. Like you're tellin' me the time or somethin', okay?"

He pulled in a long breath. On exhale, the words tumbled. "I been workin' for a gangster nights, not jockeyin' mops like I told ya, and I'm sorry I lied, but I was there the night that Beau fella was shot, and I got the dog, Mar. I got the dog."

Mary's head reeled from the wallop of shock. Sure, she'd had her suspicions that George wasn't cleaning offices at night. His hours were too irregular, and he'd been sketchy on the location when she asked. But she never imagined he'd taken up with gangsters again. He hated that way of life more than she did. But this news about Beau Kellum—that was a bombshell. "You was in the house? How?"

"The guy was already dead when we got there, I swear. But did ya hear me? I got the dog."

"What did you do to the dog?"

"I didn't do nothin' to him. I brung him home."

Then Mary heard an animal snort under the bedroom door and nails scratching the wood floor.

"He's here," George said. "Been keepin' him in the shed. You wanna see him? He's real sweet."

* * * *

Waves crashed against the pilings of the Santa Monica pier as Johnny Roland challenged the sea with a cold, brutal stare. Detective Roy Jackson stood beside Johnny, mirroring his stance—elbows on the pier railing, gaze set on the horizon.

"How did this happen?" Johnny asked the cop.

"This guy, Jones—he can't be bought. Has principles or something."

"You're off the case?"

"Nah, just partnered with Jones. I can't get him off the scent. He plans to question your Annie Diggs, but he's bringing in Ida Flory again."

"She's got the alibi."

Jackson shrugged. "You're preaching to the wrong congregation. That's not all. Dix McCord is on his list."

"Christ."

"He's like a bloodhound this guy—he found more prints. Seven distinct fingerprints. It was like Grand fudgin' Central, that house."

Johnny broke his stare to raise an eyebrow at Jackson. "Fudgin'?"

"The wife's on me to watch my mouth around the kids. Set a good example, that kinda shit."

Johnny huffed. He set his gaze back to the waves. "Oh yeah, you're a good example."

"You're an ass. What do you know about the fingerprints, Roland?"

"What do you know about the dog?" Johnny countered.

"Looks like he escaped out the back door. Possibly with a male, size-twelve shoe."

"Maybe someone snuffed the dog."

"Maybe. Maybe not. If Jones finds the dog alive, he's planning to hire an animal psychologist. Figures the dog is a witness."

"Sounds like this Jones guy is in need of some analysis himself."

"You didn't answer me about the prints."

"This Jones, does he have a wife? Girlfriend? Boyfriend?"

"Not that I'm aware."

Johnny pushed away from the railing. "Get me his address." He wasn't about to let a cop with a conscience get in his way. He straightened one shirt cuff, then the other, and strode back down the long pier toward land.

* * * *

Mary held George's sweaty hand. He was more nervous than she was, and she felt ready to faint dead away. Together they trailed behind her best friend, Edith. Edith had been acting strangely the last couple of days, but Mary didn't know where else to turn. When she had confided in Edith their situation with Sunset Beauregard, the color had drained from Edith's face, but right away, she'd known what to do.

Now they walked across the studio lot, following Edith, who was taking them to meet her boss, Mr. Roland. Mary tingled from nerves and excitement. She hadn't spotted anyone famous like Clark Gable or Greta Garbo, but she was almost positive she'd caught a glimpse of that dreamy new actor, Dix McCord. All the ladies just loved him.

"Hey, Edith," Mary asked, "I see you're wearin' your earrings again."

Her friend touched her ears, then waved it off like it was no big deal. "Oh yeah, found 'em in some silly place."

From the day Edith's new beau gave her the pearl earrings, Mary hadn't known her to ever take them off long, much less lose track of them.

Edith stopped at a small building with big windows and a fancy wooden door. She knocked only once before opening the door. "Mr. Roland, they're here. My friend and her husband. Like I told ya."

George and Mary crossed over the Oriental rugs that covered polished wooden floors. Mary had never seen such fancy furnishings. Mr. Roland sat behind a desk that looked big enough for three men. He had perfect black hair and a heavy brow. He wore a ring on his right pinky finger. And he might be a tall man, but Mary figured she wasn't going to find out for sure since he hadn't bothered to stand upon their arrival.

Edith closed and locked the door. She ushered Mary and George to the love seat. Edith remained standing.

"You okay, Edith?" Mr. Roland asked her friend.

Mary thought his question was odd. She craned her neck to see Edith's reaction.

"I'm good," Edith replied with a small nod. Then added, as if an afterthought, "sir."

"And you're sure about this?"

"I am. They's good people. I'd trust 'em with my life."

"They *are*, Edith. They *are*," he corrected.

"Right. I'm working on that."

Mary heard the effort in Edith's voice as she stressed to enunciate work*ing*. Keenly aware that the air was charged, Mary knew now that Edith had been holding something back. She wasn't sure what, but it was something all right. She began to worry for her friend.

Mr. Roland gave Mary his attention. "You're Mary Anderson?"

"Yes, sir," she answered, feeling like a witness on trial.

"Call me Johnny."

Mary wasn't sure she could do that comfortably, but she'd try. "Okay."

"You're George?" Johnny Roland asked her husband.

George stared at the floor. "Yes, sir, Johnny."

"You were at the house the night Beau Kellum was killed?"

"Yes, sir, Johnny."

"Just Johnny, George. No sir. We're all friends here."

George lifted his gaze, looking Johnny in the eye.

"Did you see the body?" Johnny asked George.

"No, sir. I mean, Johnny."

"Were you in the house at all?"

"No, sir, I mean, Johnny."

"Didn't I just say we were friends, George?"

"Yes."

"Do friends lie to one another?"

"If they do, they shouldn't," George answered.

"That's right, George. So now that we're friends, tell me where you were in that house, because I know you were there."

"A hallway at the back of the place. There was a couple a lights on the wall. That's as far as I got. I was wit' a guy, and we were just supposed to scare this Kellum fella, ya know. Not hurt 'im or nothin'. Just make him think we would if he didn't pay up."

"Who was this other guy?"

George paused before answering. "Just a guy. Don't know his name."

"He saw the body?"

"Yeah."

"You and this other guy—you were working for Bruno Panzini?"

"Aw, Mr. Johnny, ya gotta understand. I can't say."

Mary was relieved when Mr. Roland didn't press George to admit the gangster's name.

"And the dog—why did you steal the dog?"

"I wasn't meanin' to take him. He wouldn't let me leave. He's what stopped me in the hallway, whinin' and nudgin' at me. I couldn't leave him there like that. He was just beggin' me to get him out."

"So you want the reward money."

"Johnny," Edith said, jumping into the conversation. "I mean Mr. Roland, that's not what I—"

Johnny waved a hand at Edith. "Let them talk, Edith."

Like a light switched on, Mary knew what was bothering her about Edith. She never admitted the man she'd been seeing was an actor, but Mary always suspected as much by the secrecy. Edith's mystery flame had to be Beau Kellum. He was exactly her type.

Mary pressed forward, responding to Johnny's assumption. "We don't want the money." Her voice had gone hoarse. She cleared her throat. "We want Sunset Beauregard."

"That's a lot of money you're giving up just to own a dog."

Mary fidgeted on the love seat, her head throbbing from the tension. "Also, we were hopin' you could see that Georgie gets that security guard job here at the studio. If he has a good, steady job, I can quit work and we can start a family."

"A dog and a job. That's all you want from me?"

Mary nodded.

The powerful man stared at her and then at George. He leaned slowly over his desk. "It isn't as simple as that, you understand. Right, Mary?"

"I figured as much."

"Here I am sitting five feet away from the two of you, and the stench of cigarette smoke is enough to make my stomach churn. You'll both have to quit. Sunset Beauregard deserves a clean house. Can you agree to that?"

Edith often remarked to Mary on Johnny's queer disdain for cigarettes, but Mary had never expected this comical demand as a condition of keeping Sunset Beauregard. She was too terrified of the man to laugh, however. She exchanged confused looks with George. "Uh, I guess we could do that," she answered. "George, you okay with that?"

George shrugged. "Sure." But then his face caved in a little. "Is drinkin' all right? Mar and I like a beer some nights."

For the first time since they'd arrived, Johnny Roland stood. Mary realized he resembled an ape with that heavy forehead and wide shoulders. But now, his fierce brow softened, and she thought he almost smiled.

"You can have your beers, George," Johnny said. He pushed his chair back and adjusted the lapels of his jacket. "But there are a few other stipulations as well."

* * * *

Johnny Roland sent the awkward couple on their way with instructions to wait for Edith's visit that night. She'd arrive with a contract, which they were to sign and follow to the letter.

Before closing the door behind her, Edith whispered to him, "Thank you again, Johnny. I just don't know how I can ever repay you for all you done."

"You can start by reading that grammar book I gave you."

"You make jokes, but you saved my life, and I *won't* ever forget that as long as I live."

When the door closed behind them, Johnny opened every window in the place. Despite their odor, he couldn't help but like the Andersons. Edith had apprised him of their wishes to keep the dog before the meeting. Knowing the studio wanted Sunset back in the spotlight, she proposed a clever arrangement that, frankly, he should have concocted himself. The scheme would keep Sunset Beauregard and the Andersons together as well as pay out a much-needed publicity jackpot for the studio and Ida Flory. Everyone would win.

Johnny was atomizing the air with citrus oil when Grover Shaw shoved the bungalow's front door open without knocking.

This annoyed Johnny, but showing annoyance was weak. He'd be done in this city if he became weak. Instead he studied the studio exec's bald head. It was as red as a party balloon. Johnny pointed to his wet bar. "Have a drink before you pop a cork, Shaw."

Shaw made a beeline, poured a whiskey, and tossed it back in a single, frantic motion. He slammed the empty highball back down and wiped his mouth. "I thought you'd fixed things."

"You're confusing life with those moving pictures of yours, Shaw. Things aren't black and white. You need to learn patience and have a little faith."

"I need assurances, Roland. Ida tells me they grilled her and Dix McCord down at the precinct like there's evidence against them. I may not care for Dix personally, but he's a studio asset. And if I lose Ida, I don't know what I'll do."

"What if I told you we found Sunset Beauregard?"

"Yesterday that would have been great news. Today, that doesn't cure this ulcer growing in my gut."

"Find Ida and tell her that she's about to be the proud owner of a beloved Irish setter that, by the grace of God, has been found healthy and unharmed. Edith is working the media angle now. She'll have the dog in Ida's possession in time for appropriate photo opportunities."

"What about the police?"

Johnny wanted to wallop the fat bastard. "I might tell them you killed Kellum so I can get some peace around here."

Grover Shaw did a poor job of feigning indignation when he slammed the door behind him. Of course, the problem cop had to be dealt with. Johnny had nothing on him. Things would have to get messy. Johnny closed and locked the windows, washed his hands, donned his hat, and then took a short drive to a dark restaurant where he knew he'd find mob capo Bruno Panzini holding court at his usual table in the corner.

When he left the restaurant a half hour later, he'd been assured the scrupulous do-gooder, Detective Jones, wouldn't be healthy enough to ask questions much longer.

On the sidewalk, with cars buzzing past, Johnny shielded his eyes from the sun and calculated his next move. He needed one more story now. One so big that it would bury this Kellum problem once and for all. The bright infamy of a Hollywood scandal was always easily dimmed when a new scandal emerged. Without knowing it, Annie Diggs had planted the seed of that new scandal in Johnny's mind. *What if I don't want to go to Blaine Studios?* she had said. *Word is they're in trouble because Julius is distracted by that pervert politician son of his.*

Johnny knew all about Senator Marshall Blaine's vices. He got in his car and drove a few blocks to the Fairmont Hotel, where he parked across the street. He slid down in his seat and pulled his hat over his eyes. Twenty minutes later, a Rolls pulled up to the lobby door of the Fairmont. The doorman wrenched the back door open, and two young girls emerged. They were dressed and made up to look older than their probable thirteen or fourteen years, but Johnny knew better.

The girls scampered into the hotel, ushered by a man Johnny knew as Julius Blaine's right-hand man. Sadly, those girls weren't going in for ice cream sodas. Soon, Marshall Blaine would slip into the hotel through the back entrance. Blaine was a state senator with his sights set on the White House. It was common knowledge around town that Blaine liked them young, and he liked them off Daddy's studio lot. Unfortunately for Blaine, he also liked them at the same time every week. The man revolted Johnny. He had no problem using the pay phone on the corner to call the police. He called Edith too. Politicians could be tricky about burying their crimes, but Edith knew reporters with agendas.

Johnny didn't wait for the squad cars. Instead, he drove west toward the sea, toward home.

Inside his Malibu retreat, with walls washed pink by the setting sun, Johnny found a gorgeous blond draped over his brown leather sofa. Sick and tired of spoiled studio brats, Johnny threw his hat onto a chair. He turned his back to the unwanted guest and poured a tall scotch.

"Pour me one too?" the blond asked.

Johnny stared at his glass. "Go home."

"But the sunset. It's so beautiful. Let's watch it together."

"Don't make me throw you out."

"Please, Johnny. I think I'm falling in love with you."

Snapping, Johnny growled and hurled the glass across the room. As the glass shattered, he spun and charged pretty-boy Dix McCord, seizing him by the shirt collar. Johnny pulled him close. "Are you falling in love with me like you fell in love with Beau Kellum? Is that how you show men you love them—with bullets?"

Rendered helpless, Dix moaned. "I told you I didn't—"

"I know you did. You weren't alone in the house with Kellum."

"Who saw?"

Johnny would take Edith's identity to the grave. "She didn't see anything. She heard plenty."

"I thought you didn't care if I did it."

Johnny Roland didn't have a snappy comeback. Dread washed over him like a brutal storm. Maybe he did care. But in the jungle, when you care, you're done for.

Tears streamed down Dix McCord's cheeks. "He was awful to me, Johnny. So awful. I gave him everything, and he gave me nothing back."

Johnny released him back into the couch. "Kellum loved no one but himself. That's not a reason to shoot him in the back."

"He was blackmailing me. Your lady witness must've missed that part."

"The pictures."

Dix nodded. He wept, his head buried in his hands now. "I never wanted to shoot him. Just scare him into giving me the photos. But then he was so smug and said he was going to go outside and shout to the whole world what I was. He wasn't afraid of me at all. And then, I don't know what happened, but I just fired. I fired and I ran."

So that was the real story. Kellum needed money to pay off Panzini, so he was bleeding Dix dry.

When Johnny had confronted Edith with the lost earring the day after the murder, she spilled her own story about that night. She'd gone to Kellum's to break it off, but he wooed her upstairs to his bedroom again, like he always did. She wasn't proud of it. They'd only made it to the top of the stairs when Dix stormed into the house shouting, raging. The screaming incited Sunset Beauregard to bark incessantly. When Kellum left her to deal with Dix, she closed the bedroom door. From upstairs, over the din of Sunny's barking, Edith made out what sounded like a lovers' quarrel, the revelation of which shocked her to the core. Terrified when the shots were fired, she hid in the closet in case Dix came after her. Eventually, she crept downstairs and found Kellum dead in the middle of the floor. She panicked. She didn't want to be a suspect or a witness, so she fled. Sunset followed her as she ran to escape out the back door. That's where she assumed she lost the earring, hugging the agitated dog before she pushed him away to leave.

"Where's the gun?" Johnny asked Dix.

"Drove it to the canyon. Buried it. When I got back, I realized I'd bolted without the damn pictures."

Johnny poured two drinks. He handed one to Dix. "Going back for the photographs wasn't the stupidest thing you did. Not coming to me when Kellum started blackmailing you—that was your mistake."

"I was trying to watch myself—like you told me to."

Johnny was tired. He didn't want to talk anymore. "You can stay here tonight, but you're sleeping on the couch. Tomorrow you'll go the studio, make a movie, and pretend like none of this ever happened. I'm going outside to be alone and clear my head. You understand?"

Dix wiped his eyes. "Yes, Johnny."

On his balcony overlooking the sea, Johnny closed his eyes and let the sound of the waves calm him.

* * * *

Mary and George Anderson walked hand in hand on their new ranch in the Valley. Sunset Beauregard raced in front of them, his shiny red coat a metaphor for their shiny new life. Of course, they didn't call him Sunny anymore. He was Bo Bo now, and he answered to his new name with enthusiasm.

Five days a week, George drove his new Chrysler Imperial into town, worked eight hours as a front gate security guard, then drove home to be with his Mary and Bo Bo. Sunset Beauregard, it turned out, had been their lucky charm.

Mary never stopped reading the headlines. The day after she and George met with Edith's boss, the entire front page was dedicated to the arrest of state Senator Marshall Blaine. He'd been caught with two underage starlets from his father's studio. "Poor girls," she told George, as she popped a cherry gumdrop into her mouth to ward off a cigarette craving. A small story three pages in mentioned that Ida Flory, Annie Diggs, and her husband, actor Dix McCord, had all been questioned in Beau Kellum's murder, but no charges were filed.

The next day, state Senator Blaine was still front-page fodder. Scanning for news of the Beau Kellum investigation or anything about Sunset Beauregard, Mary found a three-paragraph column about the apparent accidental death of LA police detective Fred Jones. His car had careened off the road in the canyons, bursting into flames. His partner, Roy Jackson, was quoted in the paper. "He was a good cop," Jackson said. "One of LA's finest."

On the morning of the day when they were to pick up the keys for the ranch, Mary marveled at the front page photo. "Look, George, he looks just like Bo Bo." She showed the paper to George, who laughed at the headline. "Sunset Beauregard Found, Ida Flory Gives Him Happy Home." In the photograph, a smiling Ida Flory, revealing the right amount of leg, held onto a leash. At the end, posed and panting, was an Irish setter that the world now believed was the missing Sunset Beauregard. Mary could see the difference in their eyes, but mostly, the likeness was remarkable.

Their first morning in the ranch house, Mary read that Annie Diggs, still a person of interest in Beau Kellum's murder, had been released from her contract with her current studio and was being wooed by Julius Blaine. Julius wanted Annie's brand of comedy at his studio. The reporter speculated that Blaine *needed* Annie Diggs in order to shift focus away from his son's scandal and legal troubles. And another article talked about Ida Flory starring with Dix McCord in an epic biblical saga.

Two years later, Mary, five-months pregnant, stroked Bo Bo's head as she flipped through the morning paper. George worked a screwdriver at a sticky hinge on one of the kitchen cupboards. "Look here," she said. "An article about unsolved murders in Hollywood. They got a bit here about Beau Kellum."

"Yeah?"

"Yeah. Says the detective on the case never found any credible leads. He figures they may never know who killed Beau Kellum."

"Maybe that's as it should be, huh, Mar?"

Of course, Mary knew who had killed Beau Kellum. A couple of months after the murder, Edith told Mary everything.

Beau Kellum played majestic heroes on the big screen, but in his own life, he played people for chumps. He was the lowly sort who gave pretty pearl earrings to pretend he was sorry for the heartache he caused. Her friend deserved way better than the selfish, puffed-up Beau Kellums of the world. Edith deserved a man who gave her love and respect. Thankfully, she had that now.

"You're right, Georgie, that's as it should be." Mary folded the paper. "Hey, Edith says she and Johnny can make it for dinner this weekend. Should I cook a chicken or pot roast?"

Karen Cantwell enjoys writing both short stories and novels. Her stories have appeared in *Chesapeake Crimes: They Had it Comin'*, *Chesapeake Crimes: This Job is Murder*, and *Noir at the Salad Bar: Culinary Tales with a Bite*. On the novel front, Karen loves to make people laugh with her Barbara Marr Murder Mystery series and Sophie Rhodes Ghostly Romance series. You can learn more about Karen and her works at www.KarenCantwell.com.

ABOUT THE EDITORIAL PANEL AND COORDINATING EDITORS

Donna Andrews was born in Yorktown, Virginia, and now lives in Reston, Virginia. *Gone Gull* (Minotaur, August 2017) and *How the Finch Stole Christmas* (Minotaur, October 2017) are the twenty-first and twenty-second books in her Agatha, Anthony, and Lefty award-winning Meg Langslow series, to be followed by *Toucan Keep a Secret* in 2018. *Fur, Feathers, and Felonies* is her eighth outing as one of the editors of the Chesapeake Crimes anthology series. She is an active member of Sisters in Crime and Mystery Writers of America, and she served as MWA's executive vice president during the past three years. She blogs with the Femmes Fatales at femmesfatales.typepad.com. For more information: www.donnaandrews.com.

Brendan DuBois is an award-winning author of twenty novels and more than 150 short stories. He's currently working on a series of works with bestselling novelist James Patterson. His short fiction has appeared in *Playboy*, *Analog*, *Asimov's Science Fiction Magazine*, *Ellery Queen's Mystery Magazine*, *Alfred Hitchcock's Mystery Magazine*, and numerous anthologies, including *Best American Mystery Stories of the Century*, published in 2000, as well as *Best American Noir of the Century*. His stories have thrice won him the Shamus Award from Private Eye Writers of America, and have earned him three Edgar Award nominations from Mystery Writers of America. He is also a *Jeopardy!* game show champion. Visit his website: www.BrendanDuBois.com.

Barb Goffman's bio appears with her story.

Lapsed librarian and former mystery bookseller **Mary Jane Maffini** is the author of the Camilla MacPhee, the Fiona Silk, and the Charlotte Adams mysteries and two dozen mystery shorts. As Victoria Abbott, Mary Jane collaborated on five book-collector mysteries with her daughter, Victoria. Mary Jane holds three Arthur Ellis awards and an Agatha for short stories. *The Busy Woman's Guide to Murder* won the Romantic Times award for Best Amateur Sleuth in 2012 and Victoria Abbott snagged the 2016 Bony Blithe Award. Mary Jane lives in Manotick, Ontario, Canada, with two princessy miniature dachshunds and a husband who looks over his shoulder a lot. www.maryjanemaffini.com

Leigh Perry writes the Family Skeleton mysteries featuring adjunct English professor Georgia Thackery and her best friend, an ambulatory skeleton named Sid. *The Skeleton Paints a Picture* is the fourth and most recent. As Toni L.P. Kelner, she's the coeditor of paranormal fiction anthologies with Charlaine Harris; the author of eleven mystery novels; and an Agatha Award winner and multiple award nominee for short fiction. No matter what you call her, she lives north of Boston with her husband, two daughters, one guinea pig, and an ever-increasing number of books. www.leighperryauthor.com

Marcia Talley is the author of *Mile High Murder* and fifteen previous novels featuring Maryland sleuth Hannah Ives. A winner of the Malice Domestic Grant and an Agatha Award nominee for Best First Novel, Marcia won an Agatha and an Anthony Award for her short story "Too Many Cooks" and an Agatha Award for her short story "Driven to Distraction." She is the editor of two mystery collaborations, and her short stories have appeared in more than a dozen collections. She divides her time between Annapolis, Maryland, and a quaint Loyalist-style cottage in Hope Town, Bahamas. www.marciatalley.com